perfect fifths

perfect fifths

a novel

MEGAN McCAFFERTY

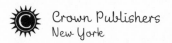

Crown Publishers
New York

This is a work of fiction. Names, characters, places, and incidents either are the product of the author's imagination or are used fictitiously. Any resemblance to actual persons, living or dead, events, or locales is entirely coincidental.

Published in the United States by Crown Publishers, an imprint of the Crown Publishing Group, a division of Random House, Inc., New York.
www.crownpublishing.com

CROWN and the Crown colophon are registered trademarks of Random House, Inc.

Library of Congress Cataloging-in-Publication Data

McCafferty, Megan.
  Perfect fifths / Megan McCafferty.—1st ed.
    p. cm.
1. Darling, Jessica (Fictitious character)—Fiction. 2. Young women—Fiction.
  I. Title.
  PS3613.C34P47 2009
  813'.6—dc22   2008050525

ISBN 978-0-307-34652-0

Printed in the United States of America

10 9 8 7 6 5 4 3 2 1

First Edition

For all the readers who have cared enough
to find out what happens next

In our artificial civilization many young people at twenty-five are still on the threshold of activity. As one looks back then, over eight or nine years, one sees a panorama of seemingly formidable length. So many crises, so many startling surprises, so many vivid joys and harrowing humiliations and disappointments, that one feels startlingly old; one wonders if one will ever feel so old again.

—*Youth and Life*, Randolph S. Bourne (1886–1918)

Even now, when I have come so far, I wonder where you are . . .

—"Even Now," Barry Manilow (1943–)

part one: before

one

When Jessica Darling blindly collides into Marcus Flutie on this crisp, unclouded January morning, she can't remember the last time she had imagined where she would be—and who he would be—at the moment of their inevitable collision.

For him, however, it's a very different story.

two

Regrets. Jessica has so many regrets. She should have stopped pouring after that first glass of wine last night. Shouldn't have watched the ceiling swirl for hours. Should have resorted to a narcotic sleep aid sooner. Shouldn't have hit the snooze button one, two, three times before rocketing (*"I'm late!"*) out of bed this morning. Should have skipped the shower, not breakfast. Shouldn't have turned down her dad's offer to drive her to the airport instead of proving her mother right about the unpunctual local car service. Should have chosen the security screening line to the right, not the left, not the one that put her directly behind the starving and savage middle-aged trafficker of more than three ounces of the liquid weight-loss supplement with the funny name, a name Jessica keeps repeating in her head in rhythm with her sneakered feet sprinting across Concourse C.

Hoodia. Hoodia. Hoodia.

So many split decisions and judgment calls and incorrect estimations have led to this. To being late. She's late late late late for Gate C-88. She likes the rhyme, especially when timed with the beat of her feet, and chooses this staccato incantation over the silly-sounding appetite suppressant.

I'm late late late late for Gate C-88.

She recalls how she used to silently mouth spur-of-the-moment mantras back in her competitive high school running days. Hand-slapping rhymes from her youth: *Miss Mary Mack Mack Mack . . . All dressed in black, black, black.* Boy-band lyrics she would never say out loud: *You might hate me but it ain't no lie . . . Baby, bye, bye, bye.* Even her own name: *Jessica Darling . . . Darling . . . Darling . . . Jessica Darling . . . Darling . . . Darling.* These invocations lacked deep meaning—even the song of herself—and were meant only to distract her from how much she hated having to pretend she cared about the outcome of the race.

Today she cares. And no matter how fast she sprints through this airport, there are too many people standing still. Standing in her way. Or stretched across the floor in carefree repose, smudgy fingertips plucking chips and curls and twists out of the bags of overpriced snacks in their laps. Seemingly in no hurry to get anywhere, which is funny if you think about it (but Jessica doesn't have time to think about it), because this is the place where passengers pass time until they can be jet-propelled across states and nations, oceans and continents, at six hundred miles per hour. Why are they standing still, standing in the way of where she needs to be? Surrounded on all sides by the drone of wheeled luggage buzzing across the concourse, she speeds up, slows down, stutter-steps, and shimmies her way through the hive. Onward, onward, onward. She was wide-awake, wild-eyed with worry, for most of the night, and this adrenalized marathon sprint is already taking its toll. She can feel fatigue settling into her muscles, her bones, her brain, her spirit. But no. *No!* She can't slow down now. She can't miss this flight. *I can't miss this flight.* The concourse splits down the middle, and she must quickly consider yet another option. Should she hop on the human conveyor belt or just keep running?

There is pure goodness awaiting her in the Virgin Islands. Her best friends are all together to "celebrate the rarest love between two people, the flawed yet fearless union that everyone hopes to find but almost always turns out to be illusive if not elusive." (Quotation marks needed because it comes directly from the speech Jessica has prepared for the occasion.) Jessica knows her friends will forgive her if she misses this flight—as they have forgiven so many of her unintentional slights and oversights—but she won't forgive herself.

I can't miss this flight, she silently says once more before choosing to trust her own two feet over technology, the last in a series of synchronistic decisions that contribute to everything that happens afterward.

three

"This is a final boarding call for passenger Jessica Darling."

After Marcus hears it the first time, he makes sure to listen extra carefully the second time, just to confirm it *is* her name being called over the public address system and not a phantom echo in his mind.

"This is a final boarding call for Clear Sky Flight 1884 with nonstop service to St. Thomas, U.S. Virgin Islands. Final boarding call for passenger Jessica Darling."

Jessica Darling. It's been years since he's heard her full name spoken out loud. Not that Jessica Darling hasn't been analyzed, assailed, or alluded to in conversations with family, friends, and near strangers from their shared past. As a subject of discussion, Jessica Darling has been elevated by—not reduced to—pronoun status. Have you seen *her*? What's *she* up to these days? Whenever anyone asks these questions, there's never any doubt as to whom the "her" or "she" refers. But those questions haven't been asked lately, not since Marcus has—by all actions and outward appearances—finally gotten over her.

Even after hearing her name once, now twice, Marcus still needs a confirmation from somewhere outside his imagination. He seizes his friend Natty by the lapels and asks.

"Dude, no," Natty insists. "I didn't hear her name. And neither did you." Natty's sharp tone can't burst the pop-eyed, expectant expression on Marcus's face. "And even if you *did* hear her name, there's no way it's her. Now let go of me, because I gotta take a piss."

Natty strands Marcus between the entrance to the men's restroom

and the fiberglass Betty Boop sculpture boop-boop-be-beckoning customers into the faux-retro Garden State Diner for a greasy preflight
meal. Marcus feels overexposed, overstimulated, as if his whole body is
on extrasensory alert. Marcus's nerves rattle and clang like the dirty sil-
verware carelessly thrown into plastic takeaway tubs by the too-busy
busboys. He tries to calm himself with a series of deep inhalations and
exhalations, but breathing cheeseburger smog only makes him more
queasy and ill at ease. The alarms going off in his nervous system evoke
the erratic animal behavior that precedes natural disasters: a mass exo-
dus of elephants seeking higher ground, dogs wailing under door frames,
rabbits clawing at cages, snakes shaken from hibernation slithering
through the snow. His instincts, too, urge him to flee. He half jogs away
from the diner and heads for the blue-screened monitors announcing
arrivals and departures.

As Marcus searches for Clear Sky Flight 1884 on the departures
board, he makes an effort to accept Natty's logic. After all, didn't his
Jessica Darling often joke about being confused with a porn star also
named Jessica Darling? Perhaps it's the X-rated Jessica Darling being
called over the public address system, or maybe even a third unknown
Jessica Darling who shares nothing but a name with the other two.
A newborn Jessica Darling. A granny Jessica Darling. An African-
American, Asian, Hispanic, Pacific Islander, or Other Jessica Darling.
It must be one of these alternative Jessica Darlings flying out to St.
Thomas on Clear Sky Flight 1884, not his Jessica Darling, not the one
he proposed to over three years ago, not the one he hasn't seen, spoken
to, or otherwise communicated with since he quietly accepted that her
answer was no.

He's found it: Gate C-88. Clear Sky Flight 1884 to St. Thomas is
departing from Gate C-88.

What harm could there be in wandering over to Gate C-88 to see
for himself which incarnation of Jessica Darling is being called out loud?
None at all, save for the minor embarrassment of being suckered into a
one in six billion long shot. But what if it turns out that the familiar
name does belong to her familiar face? Marcus is incapable of calculating
the risks of such an improbable outcome. Still, he knows himself well

enough to understand how the powers of his masochistic imagination would make the coward's alternative—never knowing, always wondering *was it her? was it her? was it her?*—a far greater punishment than any awkward small talk.

He looks away from the monitors because the orange font/blue screen makes his pupils vibrate. On the wall directly in front of him is a changing digital screen advertisement for the Shops at Newark Liberty International Airport. Before he even realizes he's doing it, Marcus impassively watches the images shift.

The picture: A gold-foil box of gourmet chocolates.

The words: MISSING HER.

The picture: A string of black South Sea pearls.

The words: MISSING HER LIKE CRAZY.

Marcus, wowed by the lack of subtlety, looks away and laughs at himself.

No. He can't give in to narcissistic folly and read this sign as a Sign. It's taken him three years to finally pull himself together, and he refuses to come undone by commonplace coincidence. In fact, he's just about convinced himself that Natty is right, that there's no way it was his Jessica Darling being summoned over the Clear Sky PA system, that there's no need to head to Gate C-88 to verify this impossibility for himself because it is not, it cannot be, her, not his Jessica Darling (why does his skin still prickle with premonitory anticipation?), when his Jessica Darling slams right into him and bounces onto the floor.

four

A body in motion. A body at rest. Forces coming together—CRASH!—in an instant. Energy spent, energy exchanged, and energy conserved. Jutting elbows, bared teeth. Elastic arms, slack mouths. To every action there is an equal but opposite reaction. This woman and this man, a living demonstration of Newton's Third Law.

five

Jessica curses herself as she scrambles across the marble tiles. Clad in head-to-toe black, she resembles a desperate beetle stuck on its back, arms and legs flailing for her flung-to-the-ground carry-on bag. She finds it, scrapes herself off the floor, and decides that a curt give-and-take of apologies is the path of least resistance, the quickest way to get past this stranger, this nuisance, this object of interference with feet stuffed into scuffed Vans. There are already too many eyes on them, watching, wondering what will happen next. A combative confrontation will only attract more rubberneckers, and she doesn't want anyone else slowing her down.

Marcus waits until she stands up before he takes a chance. "Jessica?"

It's the voice that reaches her first, not the correct first name uttered by the voice. Her head bolts up, and when her eyes corroborate with her ears, her breath catches and her hands fly up to her face. She breathes in and out through her palms, once, twice, before taking them away. Miraculously, he's still there. She is perfectly still for the first time since vaulting out of bed this morning.

"Marcus!"

He nods to confirm what should be obvious but is still too unbelievable.

"Marcus," she repeats, softer.

He nods again.

"I . . ." she begins. "I'm . . ."

They are standing inches apart, not touching. Jessica clutches her ergonomic teardrop-shaped carry-on bag to her chest, sensing that the moment to embrace has passed. A spontaneous show of emotion now would be too conspicuous, too much, too late.

"Late!" Jessica blurts. "I'm too late."

Hundreds of passengers swirl around and away from them, like so many snowflakes in a blizzard.

"Oh," Marcus says. He's contemplating whether he could get away with playfully swatting her arm in what he hopes is a neutral zone, between her shoulder and elbow. Behind her flashes the sign. The gold-foil box of gourmet chocolates. MISSING HER. The string of black South Sea pearls. MISSING HER LIKE CRAZY. The sign. The Sign. He wants to make contact when he makes his confession, that he'd heard her name, and how he had hoped for the illogical, the impossible, to be true: that it was really her. And *today* of all days. He's about to touch her, then deliver the befitting wishes, when she casts a nervous sidelong glance at his turned-out palm, the part of him that dares to come too close. He drops the offending hand and stuffs it deep into the front pocket of his corduroys, knowing there's no time for such intimacies.

He says nothing.

"We should—" Jessica starts. She's rocking from side to side now, an anxious, joyless dance. "You should—" The pronoun change doesn't go unnoticed by either of them. "E-mail. Or, I don't know. Text. Something . . ."

"Something," he says simply.

Marcus musters the courage to look Jessica right in the face. She still wears her hair like an afterthought, pulled back with a few quick twists of a rubber band. If she removed the elastic and shook it out, he would breathe in the fruity scent of shampoo, certain that the chestnut tresses resting against her neck are still damp from her morning shower. He finds some comfort in this knowledge, as well as in the overall familiarity of her features, which haven't changed that much since he last saw her. But he must admit to himself—only to himself, never to her, even if she'd had the time or the temerity to ask—that her casual loveliness is more than a little washed-out. Her eyes are tired, tinged pink, and buffered by puffy purple undereye circles. Her lips are crackled dry, her nostrils chapped and flaking around the corners, perhaps from too many rubs with a paper towel, a wool coat sleeve, or some other rough tissue substitute. He hopes that her careworn appearance is an aberration, that her immune system is down but she's not. He wants her to be sick *or* tired, but not sick *and* tired, or just plain sad.

"I'd catch up if . . ." Her cheeks glow an embarrassed red, and her pale complexion is better for it.

"If you had time," Marcus finishes for her, trying to determine from her voice whether she's suffering from a cold or something worse.

"If—" she starts again, but doesn't finish.

She can't look up at him. If she looks up at him, she will see him. And if she sees him, she'll be compelled to ask questions she doesn't have time for. Instead, she concentrates on her own familiar Converses, but even that fails to bring her relief. That they both still wear their same favorite brands of sneakers after all these years is only a minor revelation, and yet even this tiny glimpse of his world going on without her—and hers without him—is almost too much for Jessica to bear. What else hasn't changed? Does he still meditate for hours on the floor of his closet? Jessica braces herself with a deep breath. Would he still smell like smoldering leaves if she leaned in close enough? Does he still compose elliptical, poetic songs on his acoustic guitar?

Derelict lyrics force themselves to the front of her consciousness, a ballad softly sung when they were still teenagers, the only one Marcus ever wrote or sang for her:

I confess, yes, our fall was all my fault
If you kissed my eyes, your lips would taste salt . . .

Her watery eyes stay fixed on the unraveled seams splitting his mossy V-neck a quarter inch lower than the designer's intentions. This is an expensive-looking sweater—two-ply cashmere, she guesses—and she doubts Marcus could afford to buy it for himself. She assumes it was a gift from someone who is very familiar with his face, one who knew how this gray-green shade would shake loose those evasive hues from his multifaceted brown eyes. Definitely a gift. He doesn't even have the cash to care for this item properly with regular dry-cleaning. She imagines him blithely tossing the sweater into one of his college's communal washing machines, along with his T-shirts, jeans, and underwear, the tender cashmere threads coming more and more undone.

"Go," he urges gently, pointing toward Gate C-88. "Don't miss your flight."

She pulls a wad of scrunched-up paper towel out of the front pocket of her hoodie, rubs her nose, and jerks her head in agreement. They offer hasty good-byes but no hugs, not even a handshake, before she takes off for the gate.

"I'm sorry I ran you over," Jessica calls out, barely casting a glance back as she hurtles herself forward.

I should be, too, thinks Marcus. *But I'm not.*

And then she's gone again.

SIX

Jessica can't catch her breath, but she won't stop running. Panting, she picks up the pace.

A new mantra: *That didn't happen.* She runs faster than ever, even with her palms burrowing into her eye sockets to push away tears, memories, perhaps both. *That didn't happen.* Part of her wants to remove her hands, look back, and contradict her desperate denials. *That didn't happen.* She wants to look behind her and take him in, Marcus Flutie, looking every inch the rumpled grad student in his choice of clothing (the sweater, the thin-wale corduroys), hairstyle (the finger-picked brush cut), and eyewear. (*Glasses?* She does a mental double take. *He was wearing glasses, wasn't he? When did Marcus start wearing glasses?*) Only he's not in graduate school, he's still a superannuated undergraduate, a twenty-six-year-old senior. (*Is he graduating this semester? On time? Only four years late?*)

Time. Late. There's no time to contemplate any of these questions because she is still late late late late for Gate C-88. (*They weren't annoying emo glasses, were they?*) She steels herself against the temptation to look back for any reason. An apology, maybe. Or a simple explanation. (*No, they were just regular wire-rimmed glasses, I think.*) Her face burns still hotter; she's mortified by how she must have looked to him in both appearance and in action. (*Oh fuck.*) What was he doing just standing there like that in the middle of the airport? Meditating? Seeking inner peace with no regard to his fellow travelers? Marcus Flutie standing still amid the chaos on the concourse was an accident waiting to happen. And it did. It finally did.

Jessica wonders who will be the first to find out about their momentous collision, and when. Such a reunion has been a forgone conclusion among Jessica's best friends since the breakup. They would not only expect a second-by-second reenactment but are exponentially invested to demand one. And on any other day Jessica would have complied. She would have told them everything, starting with how calmly Marcus reacted to being run over by his ex-girlfriend in the middle of Newark Liberty International Airport, as if he'd been expecting it, not in the same "someday" way that Jessica and her friends had expected it to happen, but almost as if he had chosen to wait in that exact spot on the straightaway under the arrivals and departures boards outside the men's restroom because he knew she was on her way.

But not today. No. Even before the crash, she'd already had her reasons for not making today about her. And because it is definitely not about Marcus Flutie, either, she forces him out of her mind. She keeps moving. She must keep moving if there's any hope of her making this flight. (*I can't miss this flight.*) Bridget and Percy didn't question Jessica's need to make a pit stop in Pineville before traveling to the Virgin Islands, which only makes her feel worse about having bailed on the bridal shower and the bachelorette party. She has little hope of arriving in time for tonight's rehearsal dinner even if the flight (*I won't miss this flight*) hasn't already taken off without her. But Jessica must be there for tomorrow's wedding, because she is the ministress of ceremonies, after all.

That didn't happen.

Oh, yes, it did.

Her thoughts ineluctably return to Marcus and the last time they were in the same room together: He was hunched over, bent at the waist on the edge of his bed, slowly turning two unopened notebooks over and over in his hands. Four sides. Turn, turn, turn, turning. Pages, pages, pages, binding. He had just listened to Jessica explain that those two black-and-white-speckled composition notebooks contained all the reasons why she couldn't be with him anymore. His callused palms shushed across the pages, pages, pages, binding—the only sound.

He read them and, a week later, returned them. "They belong to you," he said in a letter written on the second notebook's final pages. Marcus had vowed to honor Jessica's request to let her go, and let her be, and he had shocked her by actually making good on that promise. Some might puzzle for years trying to remember the final word exchanged with an ex-lover. But no such ruminations have been necessary for Jessica, because the last word from Marcus was definitively written in ink as the closing to that final communiqué:

WHATEVER

WHATEVER, as he explained in that letter, was the double-meaning irony that wrapped around his bicep in the form of a poorly executed Chinese-character tattoo, one that Marcus had wanted to spell FOREVER but that had gotten lost in translation. Since the return of those note-books, since WHATEVER, Jessica hasn't heard another word from him.

She has, however, heard the gossip.

He got into Princeton's most prestigious secret society.

He failed out.

He won a Rhodes.

He lost his mind.

The most obstreperous rumors were inspired and spread by the usual suspects, Pineville High alumni such as Sara D'Abruzzi-Glazer and Scotty Glazer, whose social orbit barely extended beyond their home-town since the birth of their third kid in as many years. And Manda Powers, who (the last Jessica had heard) was couch-surfing around the world all by herself and had an uncanny knack for bumping backpacks with adventurous nomads who claimed to have met someone who met someone who met someone from her suburban New Jersey hometown, someone whose name is—*What was it? Oh, right!*—Marcus Flutie.

He's fucking an eighteen-year-old freshgirl.

He's fucking a forty-eight-year-old professor.

He's not fucking anyone.

He's engaged.

He's gay.

13

The more legitimate updates were always provided by well-intentioned friends and family members who mistakenly believed that Jessica wanted to know what Marcus Flutie was up to. Like Paul Parlipi-ano, who e-mailed to express his surprise to find himself hammering alongside Marcus on a neighborhood rebuilding project in the Lower Ninth Ward. Or Cinthia Wallace, who swore she saw him in the audience during the opening-night performance of the off-off-Broadway musical satire of *Bubblegum Bimbos and Assembly-Line Meatballers*. Or Jessica's niece, Marin, who, apropos of nothing other than the fact that she was a child and still begrudged the missed opportunity to be a flower girl, occasionally asked, "Do you think Marcus has proposed to someone else by now?" Or Marin's mother, Jessica's own sister, Bethany, who didn't have the naïveté of youth to account for answering "Oh, I hope not," followed by "But could you blame him if he has?"

He started drinking again.

He quit speaking again.

He started drugging again.

He quit cold turkey again.

Then there are those who indirectly court conjecture, like Bridget, who sent links to Found.com asking, "Could this be a page from Marcus's journals that were stolen out of your car?" (To which Jessica always answered no.) Or Percy, responding to the schlub whose NBA half-court halftime marriage proposal was turned down on live TV, asked, "Jessica, you tell me, how's a man supposed to recover from a rejection like that?" before being shoved into silence by Bridget. Or Len Levy, another one of Jessica's lovers (a number best described as threeish, or three and two halves, the halves referring to two separate one-time-only nonpenetrative lapses in judgment involving two separate men and therefore not equaling a whole lover), who turned everything he thinks he knows about Jessica and Marcus into a song titled "My Song Will Never Mean as Much (As the One He Once Sang for You)." Despite college radio play and its current status as the eighty-seventh-most-downloaded single on iTunes, this other song turned out to be a self-fulfilling prophecy. Because it is indeed Marcus's song (*You, yes, you linger inside my heart / The same you who stopped us before we could start . . .*) that plays in Jessica's head right now.

He looks totally different.

He looks happy.

He looks tortured.

He looks exactly the same.

He looks as hot as he ever did.

Oh, no, he looks hotter than ever.

It is with a palpable measure of disquietude that Jessica acknowledges that her dumbfounding full-body bender with Marcus has only served to confirm the last and most superficial of these hypotheticals.

Was he coming or going? Jessica can't stop herself from wondering. If she had asked that single simple question, Marcus would have provided an answer. And this information—any information—would have piqued her curiosity and required her to ask more questions that she didn't—*doesn't*—have time to ask.

Jessica rushes up to Gate C-88. A lone Clear Sky representative named Sylvia is stationed alongside the velvet rope separating the terminal tunnel from the plane on the tarmac.

"I made it!" Jessica exclaims.

Sylvia pinches a heavy-lip-lined smirk. The jetway door, as Jessica can't help but notice, is closed.

seven

The baby-faced college senior bounds out of the bathroom less than two minutes after he went in.

"Ready?" asks Natty.

Natty has been Marcus's improbable best friend since they were randomly assigned as roommates during their first year at Princeton University. Despite their difference in ages (five years), roots (Jersey Shore suburbia versus Alabama antebellum), and modus operandi (get serious versus get seriously laid) they have lived with—or near—each other ever since. Natty knows Marcus in a way that is possible only when one is forced to share roughly 125 square feet of living space. Natty doesn't like the implications of his friend's stricken expression, one that puts an unusual strain on the peaceful facade for which Marcus has become known.

"Dude?" When his friend doesn't answer, Natty sucker-punches him in the sternum just hard enough to get his attention. "It wasn't *her* being called over the PA system, okay? It was someone else. So stop—"

"It *was* her," Marcus interrupts, soothing circles into his chest with his fingertips, still not taking his attention off Gate C-88.

Natty laughs too loudly, too eagerly, in the vain attempt to get Marcus to see his own ridiculousness. "Do you *seriously* believe The Queen?"

The Queen. Marcus paid service to The Queen while in New Orleans for what Natty likes to call a "humanitarian vacation"; it evokes a certain Jolie-Pittesque selflessness that makes girls want to have sex with him. And it isn't untrue—Marcus persuaded Natty to spend the useless reading period before final exams working to rebuild homes in the still-devastated parts of the city. Even though they put in long days of hammering, sawing, and standing around waiting for someone to tell them what to do, Marcus and Natty still had more than enough free time to devote their evenings and early mornings to living up to the city's unofficial motto—*laissez les bon temps rouler.*

After a few years of volunteering in the city made famous for its sordid decadence, Marcus is no longer content to sit elbow-to-elbow with tourists in the French Quarter, the kind who consider it a hoot to order an arm's-length cocktail called the Hurricane Katrina (citrus vodka, blue curaçao, spiced rum, Plymouth Gin, tequila, and apple vinegar, garnished with lime) dreamed up by the more mercenary—or wickedly funny, depending on your point of view—bartenders in town. And he never matched Natty's enthusiasm for slipping dollar bills to the titty-tassel-twirling pros at the sex palace promising more "N'awlins Bounce to the Ounce" (which, in turn, prompted their carnal rivals across the street to promote "MORE N'awlins Booty Meat by the Pound"). Even the novelty of the jazz clubs had worn off when Marcus noticed that he was nodding along with the lazy behind-the-beat rhythms of the city's take on the blues, just like everyone else in the crowd. To him, it felt less like collective pleasure than passive conformity.

Marcus wanted to feel something real. He wanted to be taxi-driven away from the city's most famous streets, through the swampy morass of the outlining parishes, to the temple of a voodoo priestess known only as The Queen. As Marcus had been told by those who know, The Queen was blessed (or cursed) with unrivaled gifts in the necromantic arts, as well as widely considered to be the best of all such practitioners of black magic in a city that boasted more licensed shamans than schoolteachers. He was told that The Queen wasn't much of a show-woman, having dispensed with the ornamental masks, orgiastic dances, and other tropes of the trade that were attractive to tourists. She didn't even advertise her talents, relying solely on word-of-mouth recommendation. Her demeanor was brisk and no-nonsense, so much so that she never let customers inside her home, and she always made it very clear that she wanted nothing other than to get them off her porch as soon as possible. A true artist, The Queen refused to take money from just anyone, only from those who were approved by the Loa, or spirits who watch over earth. Her services—divination, mostly, with some faith healing and spell-casting on the side when the spirits moved her—could not be validated by any on- or offline guidebook. But if the Loa vouched for Marcus, The Queen would give him the most profound spiritual reading he would ever receive . . . *just by holding his hands.*

It was this last bit that really sucked Marcus in. It was preposterous. He was in on her shtick, and he knew that this out-of-the-way place was as much of a tourist trap as any jazz bar or strip club in the French Quarter, just one that required slightly more effort than a less adventurous visitor would give. In fact, for that reason alone, his feeble quest for authenticity was a cliché far worse than the French Quarter frat boys, because at least the brothers of Sigma Chi weren't puking in the alleys under the pretense of *keepin' it real.* And yet for someone who had spent countless hours seeking enlightenment through silent meditation, even a false promise of instantaneous truth was too much for Marcus to resist.

It should be noted that he had been drinking the night of his visit to The Queen. After years of post-teen-in-rehab teetotaling, he had reacquainted himself with alcohol in his freshman year of college at the age of twenty-three. He didn't indulge very often, and he never set out to get drunk, but his years of abstinence had affected his body's ability to metabolize booze, making him a lightweight, a cheap date. The disorienting buzz Marcus felt after one or two beers was similar to that which would be expected from someone a foot shorter, fifty pounds lighter, and female.

So it was in such a delicately soused state that Marcus paid audience to The Queen. Even in retrospect, he couldn't decide whether a response to the alcohol or a genuine spiritual crisis had brought him to this neighborhood of off-the-map shotgun shacks, some of which appeared to have been semi-condemned since the first bitch—Hurricane Betsy—hit in 1965. But once he found himself in front of The Queen's one-story home, painted a magisterial purple worthy of her reputation, he was glad he had listened to the NOLA local who had tipped him off earlier that afternoon over the spray of dust exploding from the circular saw. Natty was not impressed, however, and chose to stay inside the idling cab so the driver wouldn't take off without them.

"We ah gone dah hee-yah," Natty twanged. His accent always came back whenever he drank too much or spent time below the Mason-Dixon Line. On this evening, both qualifications had been met.

"We are not going to die here," Marcus assured him as he gingerly made his way up the battered stairs leading to a lopsided doorstep. He was about to ring the bell when he heard the metal-on-metal slide of multiple locks. The inside door swung open, first releasing the sweet pungency of dried sassafras and cigar smoke, then revealing a Creole woman in a faded polka-dot housecoat who didn't look a day over 150 years old.

"Doggone it," The Queen grumbled. " 'Nother one."

"I'm sorry to bother you," Marcus said, barely overcoming his urge to bow at her feet.

"Fa sho," she replied. "'S'what y'all say."

She contemplated Marcus through the sliced-up screen door, apparently waiting for word from the Loa as to whether he passed muster. He stood in silence, watching hummingbirdlike moths hurling themselves into the irresistible lamplight, flinching whenever one met its end with a metallic *ding!*

"Yeah, you right," agreed The Queen, though it wasn't clear if she was speaking to Marcus or the all-knowing undead. She pointed to a long slit in the screen and said, "Give it here, dawlin'."

Dutifully, Marcus pushed through five twenties, as he had been instructed before he came.

She counted the bills, then slipped them into the front pocket of her housecoat. The fabric was so faded that Marcus could still see the face of wild-haired Andrew Jackson on the outermost bill. Then The Queen gestured for Marcus to slip his hands through the same open space in the torn screen. She closed her eyes as she took his hands in hers, hands that felt not unlike Jessica's grandmother's hands, or those of any of the other elderly patients he used to take care of when he did community service at Silver Meadows Assisted Living Facility—fragile, like decaying paper or the wings of those suicidal moths. And it struck him as odd at the time that he should think of Gladdie, someone he hadn't thought of in years. He remembered the last time he had visited Jessica's grandmother before she died—she had beaten him at hearts, her favorite card game, by shooting the moon—and then, of course, he thought of Gladdie's wake, when he had boldly followed a grieving Jessica into the bathroom, locked the door behind them, and kissed her— hungrily, sloppily—for the very first time—

The Queen suddenly let go. No more than ten seconds had passed.

"Y'all gone get run ovah," she said.

"Run over?" asked Marcus, making sure he had heard her correctly. "By a car?"

"Noooooo." She cackled. "Mo' trouble den dat."

"A bus?"

"Her," she said with emphasis, the power of the pronoun in full effect.

Marcus's mouth dropped open. The Queen's front door slammed shut.

"Git off mah poach," she shouted from inside. "I'm fixin' to watch 'Merican Ah-dol."

Natty taunted Marcus for the rest of the trip. "A hundred dollars wasted! That's ten Hurricane Katrinas! Or one *hay-yell* of a lap dance!"

Now, back in the airport, Natty still spits with laughter. "Dude, *seriously*. You believe The Queen?"

"I didn't," Marcus says, angling his head to the side and down so he can look Natty in the eye. "Not until Jessica Darling ran over me while you were in there taking a piss."

Natty still assumes this must be the setup for a practical joke, though he's hard-pressed to come up with a reason why Marcus would joke about this, about *her*, of all subjects. "Oh, come on. You expect me to believe that? Try harder . . ."

"She was standing right there, where you are right now," says Marcus, first pointing at the floor under Natty's flip-flops before lifting his finger to gesture across the concourse. "She's over there, in black."

Natty looks to Gate C-88. There is a female who, from behind, at a distance of about a hundred yards, vaguely fits the physical description of the girl he met once over three years ago. "Are you sure it's her?"

"I talked to her, Natty," Marcus replies. "We *talked*."

Just then the girl in question twitches a glance over her shoulder, and Natty must concede: Yes, it's definitely her.

"Oh, fuck," Natty groans.

"Indeed."

"So," Natty says. "What did she have to say for herself?"

An apprehensive smile brings relief to his afflicted face. Marcus removes his thin wire-rimmed glasses, cautiously rubs the lenses with an untucked shirttail, then puts them back on again. He surrenders a sad laugh. Then, finally, answers.

"Not enough."

eight

"I made it!" Jessica repeats triumphantly, thrusting her boarding pass at Sylvia. "The plane is still here!"

Sylvia barely glances at the document. "Yes, ma'am," she says. "But we have completed the final boarding of this aircraft. The jetway door is closed."

Jessica doesn't know what's more troubling: that the jetway door is closed? Or that she looks old enough to qualify for "ma'am" status? Either way, she has to stay on Sylvia's good side if she has any hope of getting on the plane and staying out of the airport detention center for problem passengers.

"But the plane is right there," Jessica says, desperation creeping into her voice despite her best efforts to keep calm. "And I've got my boarding pass."

Sylvia is no-nonsense. When she shakes her head, her sprayed blond flip moves as a single unit; not one of the hundreds of thousands of individual hairs has the audacity to stray. "We have completed the final boarding of this aircraft. The jetway door is closed." Her tone is like an automated recording, unchanged from the first time she said it.

"But I'm just one person—"

In that moment of weakness and doubt, Jessica half swivels her head. It's an almost unconscious impulse, too quick to register anything or anyone behind her.

"Once the jetway door is closed, it stays closed." Sylvia claps her hands together to illustrate her point. Her nails sparkle with the same opalescence as her lips, both painted an infantilizing pink that coordinates with her powder-blue Clear Sky uniform only in the sense that they are hues best left to gender-specific bibs and diaper bags. "It would be against TSA regulations to allow any passenger to board this aircraft," she briskly insists, her smile tightening with every word. "We always advise our passengers to provide adequate time to—"

"I _did_ provide adequate time! I was held up at security by a stark-raving madwoman trying to smuggle . . ."

Sylvia's smile is frozen and synthetic, like a plastic-flavored Popsicle; she is clearly bracing herself for the tirade of passenger complaints against the incompetent Transportation Security Administration, the inconvenient Newark Liberty International Airport, the inhospitality of Clear Sky airlines, the indignities of air travel in general, none of which she can solve herself. But Jessica stops midsentence, distracted by a blurry movement in her peripheral vision. It's the plane, of course, taxiing away from the gate and toward the runway. It's her flight, Clear Sky Flight 1884 with nonstop service to St. Thomas, the one she can't miss. And it's leaving without her.

Was Marcus coming or going? she wonders again. And this time, when she turns her head, it's deliberate. She looks long enough to confirm—*he's gone*—that she's missed her opportunity to get the answer.

Jessica's cell phone comes to life inside her bag, and she jumps—jumps!—as if she just discovered a venomous snake rattling around in there. She gets ahold of the vibrating device, then fumbles with the buttons for a few surprised moments before confirming that it isn't a phone call from Pineville but a short video from the Virgin Islands.

"Woo-hoo!" shouts Bridget, hair whipping up and airborne like patriotic yellow ribbons as she leaps in front of an impossibly blue sea. "Woo-hoo! We're getting married tomorrow!"

The tiny screen goes blurry as Percy turns the lens on himself. "I'm marrying a freak," he says. "A beautiful freak." His grin takes up the whole screen.

The action returns to Bridget, now turning floppy cartwheels across the sand. "This is paradise! Just wait until you get here! You won't believe it!"

Percy swivels to catch Hope photographing Bridget with a very large and expensive-looking camera. Hope realizes she's being filmed, goes cartoonishly cross-eyed, then shouts something that can't be heard over the rumbling wind and the waves. Then, without an official sign-off, the screen goes blank.

Jessica covers her face with her hands, breathes in and out. Sylvia, who has been waiting professionally if not patiently all this time, clears her throat.

"So," Jessica says, revealing what she hopes resembles the face of composure. "What do I do now?"

nine

Marcus is peeking out from behind a cylindrical floor-to-ceiling metal column roughly seventy-five yards away from Gate C-88.

A hand yanks at his shirttail. "Let's go."

Marcus shoves it away. "I'm just waiting to see what happens to her."

"Ten more seconds, and you've crossed the line between bittersweet reunion and restraining order."

Marcus watches Jessica's plane pull away.

"And I'm crouched behind you because . . . ?" Natty asks.

"Because she might recognize you."

"I doubt it," Natty snorts, standing up to his full height, which, in truth, isn't that high off the ground. "She only met me that one time. Remember? Right before she rejected you. Remember that? Remember when you thought you wanted to get married at twenty-fucking-three? Remember when you proposed and she said no? Remember how our room reeked like sweaty balls because you were too depressed to pick up a bar of goddamn soap and get in the shower . . . ?"

"Yeah, Natty," Marcus says. "I remember."

"Good times."

Marcus watches as Jessica palm-heel massages her eye sockets, ignoring the Clear Sky Airlines rep drawing an air map with her fingers. When she's finished, Jessica takes a whole-body breath, one visible from seventy-five yards away, and sets out in their direction.

"Duck!" Marcus whisper-yells.

Natty instinctively dips behind Marcus and feels like a sycophantic jackass for doing so. Yet in deference to his friend, Natty waits until Jessica passes before commencing with the brotherly emasculation. "Have you lost your *balls?*"

"Calm down, Tater Tot," Marcus commands sotto voce.

Natty will not calm down. He is outraged by this turn of events. "What are you? Twenty-six going on twelve? Wanna write her a note asking her to check the box if she still likes you? I'll pass it to her during recess!" Natty is just getting started. "This is not acceptable. Not at all. Not from the same guy who rode his anthropology professor so hard *she lost tenure.*"

Marcus ignores this last comment especially, then waits until Jessica turns a corner before addressing his friend. "I liked you better before you got rid of your accent." Natty's parents had paid a vocal instructor two hundred dollars an hour to "deregionalize" their son's speech so he'd be taken more seriously in the realm of international business. "When you were all 'aw shucks' and scared of me."

"Ah hah-vaynt lahst mah raid-nake ak-say-ent," says Natty in a deep-fried squirrelly drawl. "Ah jus choos naht t' yooose eee-it." He double-time scurries to keep up with Marcus, whose stride is twice the length of his own. "And I was never scared of you," continues Natty, returning to his foreign tongue, the neutral dialect known as Standard American with a strong hint of college-male braggadocio and puerility. "I was scared of the smell. Of. . . . your . . . balls."

"Now who's the one acting twelve, Junior High?" Marcus asks, pausing to look around the bend before turning the same corner. He catches sight of Jessica's back just before she enters the glass doors of the Clear Sky customer service center. He can relax now, seeing that there are at least twenty people on line in front of her. She'll be there for a while.

Natty steps right in front of him, but it's a symbolic gesture of protest at best. With a twelve-inch height advantage over his friend, Marcus's view of Jessica is still unobstructed. This is not lost on Natty, a tenacious flea who leaps into the air to block the sight line between him and her. Marcus sidesteps left, Natty bounces right. Marcus sidesteps right, Natty bounces left.

"That's right, Professor," Natty taunts. "I can do this shiz all damn day." To onlookers, it looks like an outmatched game of one-on-one, only without a ball or a hoop. Had Marcus not so carefully hidden himself around the corner and out of her view, Natty's gamesmanship surely would have attracted Jessica's attention, too.

Marcus gives up. Stops. "Are you really a Rhodes Scholar?"

"Never forget," Natty says, puffing up his birdcage chest, "that the primary export of Nathaniel Addison is *awesome*."

"I pity the British," Marcus says before returning his attention to the Clear Sky Airlines customer service center. Jessica is no longer the last person on line—there's a woman behind her—but no one has moved forward.

"I'm trying to help you here," Natty says. "I was there when this girl fucked you up. I was there when you only got out of bed for class. I was the one who was nearly suffocated by the stank of your unwashed balls—"

"You take far too much pleasure in talking about my balls," Marcus counters.

A bald (him) blue-haired (her) couple in their Boca Raton best has just hobbled up to the departures board. They harrumph over the use of such coarse language.

"I can't help it," Natty says to them with a mischievous grin. "I just love every inch of this man, especially his balls."

The geriatrics scurry away as quickly as they possibly can, outraged at the crudity of youth.

"Testicles!" Natty shouts after them. "If you prefer the proper termimology!"

"Are you done talking about my balls, Brokeback?" Marcus asks.

Natty frowns, a gesture that takes a lot of effort from his freckled, preternaturally sunshiny face. "I wasn't kidding, dude. I've got a whole heart full of nonsexual man love for you," he says. "Which is why I am asking you to leave this airport with me right now. Take the train back to Princeton. We'll head to Ivy Inn, toast a few rounds to our final semester, chat up some new lady friends, and forget that you ever saw the bitch—"

Marcus lunges. "Don't *ever* call her that!" Natty is pinned against the wall by the menace in Marcus's voice, the fury in his stare. Both men are staggered by Marcus's feral instinct to protect and defend the only woman who doesn't want his protection or defense.

"S-s-orry," Natty stammers, still taken aback by this never-before-seen burst of violence from Marcus, a bona fide pacifist with whom he has never, not once, had a serious argument.

Marcus relaxes his stance, closes his eyes, shakes his head ruefully. "My response had more to do with what's fucked up about *me* than anything that's fucked up about *her*."

Natty parses that bit of inarticulation, amazed by his friend's swift degeneration at the mere mention of *her*. "It's just, well, I was *there*. I saw how long it took you to recover."

"That's just it, Natty." Marcus opens his eyes. "I'm not sure I ever did."

Natty holds up his palms in surrender because there is no suitable response to this confession. Whether innate or the result of so many hours practicing meditation, Marcus's single-mindedness is unrivaled and legendary, even on a campus with more than its share of freakish overachieving geniuses. When Marcus turns his annihilative attention to something—or someone—there is nothing else. He will not shift his focus until he has won the impossible bet, been awarded the impossible fellowship, bedded the impossible woman. Natty has no idea what Marcus ultimately seeks from Jessica Darling. He knows only that he doesn't want to stick around long enough to see his infallible friend be defeated by her again.

"Dude," Natty says, shouldering his bag and turning toward the signs pointing in the direction of the AirTrain exit. "You need a roundhouse kick to the brain."

"You wish you could kick that high, Booster Seat."

Natty is marginally cheered by Marcus's put-down. "Oh, fuck you, Professor."

They stand face-to-face for a moment before Natty silently extends his fist. Marcus grabs him by the hand and pulls Natty to his chest for a backslapping bro hug.

"Yeah," Marcus replies. "I love you, too."

ten

Jessica is thinking about the wedding. Bridget and Percy liked how the numbers looked: 01/20/2010. All those zeroes, ones, and twos, nearly palindromic, only with a 20/20 in the center, "like perfect vision," Percy said. Choosing to get married on this strange date—a *Wednesday?*, double-checked by all the invited guests after consulting their calendars—wasn't just a fit of numerical whimsy. The date was a significant part of their romantic history.

"It's the eighth anniversary of our first kiss," Percy explained when Jessica inquired about the date.

"His girlie knack for remembering such details," replied Bridget in a playful tone, "is why I finally gave in and agreed to this whole wedding thing."

Jessica tries to remember the particulars of that conversation. Had she gone uptown to visit Bridget and Percy's West Harlem loft? Or had they made it out to her place in Brooklyn? Had they met somewhere in the middle, Hell's Kitchen, maybe, for beers and burritos? She's unable to piece together the details; she can remember only the words. All her memories are fuzzed over today, symptomatic of the disembodied disassociation of frequent air travel, but also the murky consequences of her mind's slog through logical and illogical, fact versus fiction, what just happened, what's happening now, and what could possibly happen next.

Jessica works harder at pinning down this memory of Bridget and Percy's engagement as she stands on line at the Clear Sky customer service center. This is not a happy place. If you're there, you're supposed to be in the air, but for some reason—be it a chaotic weather pattern, a missed connection, or some security line clusterfuckery involving a cactus plant derivative—you are not. The CSCSC is about as utilitarian and unadorned as a space can be. It has no inspirational artwork or vases of silk flowers on display, no smooth jazz or soothing aromatherapeutic scents piped in through the walls. Jessica appreciates and even respects that the CSCSC does not attempt to convince its customers that it is anything other than what it is: an unhappy place.

Thinking about Bridget and Percy as she stands on line is preferable to obsessing over the strange particulars of the line itself. Specifically, that she appears to be only one of two people who were *not* on the flight to Las Vegas canceled due to "unforeseeable mechanical complications," and that the majority of these distressed passengers desperate to get the

27

next flight out to Las Vegas are traveling together as a group consisting of the most devoted members of a fan club for a performer Jessica cannot think about if she's going to make it through the day.

"Holding!" brays the woman behind Jessica to no one in particular and everyone in general. Never has a person so meticulously ("Holding...") chronicled ("On hold...") the ("Still on hold...") drama ("Still holding...") of ("Can ya believe I'm still on hold?") being ("I can't believe I'm still on hold...") on ("Finally! A live person! What? You have to put me back on hold?") hold. Jessica finally gives in to her curiosity and turns around to find a woman a few inches shorter than she is, but much wider, with a formidable bosom. Definitely middle-aged, if not chronologically, then sartorially, in her wrinkle-resistant zebra-trimmed-in-giraffe-print travel separates. But at least this woman in her grown-up Garanimals isn't a member of the fan club. Her existence is Jessica's only link to reality in an otherwise surreal situation, another witness that all this is, in fact, actually happening.

That is, unless Jessica is making her up, too.

"I'm holding," Garanimals explains, gesturing with her cell phone.

"I had no idea," Jessica deadpans before facing forward again.

Garanimals pokes her in the shoulder blade. "You got a better shot of solving your problem on the phone."

"Really?"

"The phone number's on your boarding pass." Garanimals holds up a finger, listens for a moment. "Ooh! I think I've got somebody," she says before frowning. "Nope. Still holding." A sigh. "I have a friend who works for the airline. She says the phone is the faster, better way to go. Though she's not such a good friend that she can get me the hell out of coach. The only Coach that makes me happy is a five-hundred-dollar purse, ya know what I'm saying?"

Jessica smiles weakly. "Then why do you bother with the line?"

Garanimals tips her head back and cackles, revealing silver fillings in her back molars. "I'm not taking any chances. 'Cause the one time I missed my connection and I didn't get on this line, I was told that I could only solve my customer service problem if I got on this line. Catch-22, ya know what I'm saying?"

"Oh," Jessica replies, unzipping the bag that holds her phone.

The fan club president and VP (designated as such by their person-alized baseball caps) are arguing with the Clear Sky customer service representatives at the desk. "This is not our problem! This is your prob-lem! And it's gonna be an ever-bigger problem for you if you can't get all twenty of us there before the curtain goes up tonight!"

Meanwhile, the eighteen members without titles have cell phones pressed to their ears, hoping to talk to someone, *anyone*, who can get them on the next flight to Vegas. Few speak; most commiserate with huffs and upthrown hands as they endure the interminable hold that has been put on them by the Clear Sky automated customer service system. They are stuck in both virtual and real-life standstills.

Jessica fumbles around inside her bag, thinking, as she always does when she's looking for something inside this bag—usually her cell phone, a stick of gum, or a pen—that there are too many pockets within pockets. Multiple options has always been a problem for Jessica, in lug-gage and in life. She imagines that this pockets-within-pockets design is meant to make things more convenient for the traveler, as it's possible to designate a specific pocket for each and every item one could possibly need on the go. But Jessica has never had the inclination to devise such an organizational system, though it would hardly take that much time to assign the slanty side pocket on the left FOR GUM ONLY, or those skinny tubular pockets FOR PENS ONLY, especially in the case of the latter, when it's obvious that those pockets are indeed meant FOR PENS ONLY because nothing else would fit inside them. But no, she's never bothered to put anything in a specific place, choosing instead to stuff items in the bag at random, which always results in moments like this, when she is pulling out an unusable tampon half emancipated from its protective paper wrapper, a bottle of generic medicinal-smelling hand sanitizer, a fossilized trick-or-treat-size Baby Ruth bar . . . everything but the cell phone she's looking for. She usually curses the pockets, but today she's grateful for them, if only because contemplating the pockets helped waste brain time that might have been devoted to other subjects.

"Where is my ph—?"

The phone. Bridget and Percy had told her about the wedding over the phone. They had grabbed the phone out of each other's hands to relay the story of how he had convinced her to make good on their engagement and get married already.

"I want a wedding," Percy said.

"He's the bride in this scenario," Bridget added.

"I want a public ceremony, a celebration of how much I love her . . ."

"I was, like, why do we need a piece of paper?"

"I told her that we didn't need it. I just wanted it . . ."

"I needed Percy to point out to me that my fears weren't really about us but about my parents . . ."

"Their divorce really messed her up . . ."

"It did, it really did . . ."

"She was afraid that getting married would somehow complicate things, make things worse . . ."

"I was afraid of history repeating itself. I mean, my parents must have liked each other at some point, though it never seemed to be while they were actually married to each other . . ."

"We are not our parents . . ."

"We're just us . . ."

Jessica was happily mum during their back-and-forth banter, speaking up ("What?!") only when they asked her to be the ministress of ceremonies.

"Um, I'm a nonbeliever," Jessica reminded them.

"We know!" they chorused.

"You can get ordained over the Internet," Bridget explained.

"By the Universal Ministry of Secular Humanity," Percy added.

Jessica found it interesting that Bridget and Percy had assumed she was referring to her lack of faith in God, when she just as easily could have been referring to her lack of faith in the institution of marriage. Of the two, Jessica actually considered the latter a greater obstacle to overcome for the purposes of performing a marriage ceremony. She kept this opinion to herself, however, knowing that if any couple's union was worth forsaking her anti-matrimonial stance, it was Bridget and Percy's.

"Is the Universal Ministry of Secular Humanity anything like Pastafarianism?" Jessica asked.

Bridget and Percy had anticipated Jessica's every argument and verbally climbed all over each other in presenting their counterarguments.

"We actually looked into getting you ordained by the Church of the Flying Spaghetti Monster . . ."

"But it seems that you can only be ordained by a real church, not a heretical parody of a church . . ."

"The Universal Ministry of Secular Humanity, however, is the best alternative because it makes a big deal out of being nondenominational and supportive of all religious practice—including the right not to practice . . ."

"Its emphasis is on *this* life and simply doing what's right . . ."

"And once you get ordained, you can perform weddings throughout the United States, including the Virgin Islands, which is where we want to get it done . . ."

"Why go through all this trouble?" Jessica asked, flattered by how much effort they had already put in.

"We want you!"

"After all," Percy added, "you were the first to know."

"How old were we?" Bridget asked.

"You were a junior. I was a sophomore. Sixteen? Seventeen?" Percy said.

"Omigod! How can it be possible that we've been together that long? That's crazy!"

"Crazy . . ."

Where was Jessica during this conversation? Cross-legged on a quilted, garishly floral-patterned bedspread sprinkled with crumbs that had escaped the exorbitantly priced bag of chips from the hospitality bar. She had tuned out of the conversation briefly to calculate the cost of those crumbs, then soon realized that an accurate estimate would require math skills she hasn't used since filling in the last bubble on the SAT with her number two pencil. The bag of chips, the bedspread, the beige walls, the framed reproductions of unmemorable landscapes. A hotel room, obviously. But where?

She reviews all the cities she traveled to in the last two years: Los Angeles. Minneapolis. Phoenix. Seattle. Atlanta. She rarely has time to spend in the cities themselves, just enough to land at the airport, get the rental car, and drive to the suburban residence hotel closest to the next high school on her itinerary, to the next group of girls—some boys but mostly girls—who signed up for the ten-week Do Better High School Storytellers project. That's what they call themselves: *girls*. Not girlz, or grrls, which are misguided marketing terms, and certainly not young adults, young women, or young ladies, as they are usually called by parents, teachers, coaches, counselors, and others of their clueless ilk. Jessica is paid to encourage the Girls—who have attained capital-G status in her mind—to speak up, speak out.

Jessica has heard dozens of stories, and they come to her now—still on line at the Clear Sky customer service center—in bits and pieces. A story about a designated driver, the only sober one at the party, who slipped, fell flat on her face, and cracked her front tooth trying to steal her wasted boyfriend's keys. A story about a fourth-grader shaving off her eyebrows after the class bully compared them to squirrel tails. A story about watching a father throw a favorite porcelain doll on the floor just to prove that it wouldn't break, but it broke. A story about eating frog legs at an elegant five-star restaurant in Paris and insulting the chef with a request for ketchup. A story about discovering Ayn Rand and railing against the "second-handers." A story about passing a joint to a secret crush and getting higher from being one degree of separation from his lips than from the marijuana itself. A story about former best friends who looked the other way in the hallway. A story about a spitball landing in a laughing mouth. A story about how a star mathematician's skills were wasted on anorexic word problems like "How many hours on the treadmill does it take to subtract an apple, a slice of cheese, and four almonds?" A story about going on a roller coaster for the first time, vomiting, and going for a second round. A story about a boy who loved a girl, fucked her, and never texted again. A story about running into a tetherball pole.

The stories teach them valuable life lessons. That good things happen to bad people. That it's possible to make a bad situation even worse if you don't think it through. That parents are clueless except when they're not. That it's good to try new things even when a new thing is kind of disgusting, because new experiences make you a well-rounded person. That art can be transcendent. That lust is all-powerful, that drugs are fun, and that not everyone who does them is a loser. That losing people is part of life. That where comedy goes, tragedy isn't far behind. That everyone has issues with their bodies, but some take it too far, almost to death. That fear can be exhilarating. That boys are assholes. That it's important to look forward and never look back . . .

Dozens of stories, dozens of lessons learned. One unfortunate consequence of hearing so many stories is that Jessica often remembers vivid details from the story itself but not the Girl who told it. When Jessica tries to visualize the Girls, she sees slideshow images from opposing ends of the aesthetic spectrum. On one side, the Ugly Girls with precocious dowager's humps and threadbare hair, orthodontic protuberances and archipelagic acne. On the other, the Beautiful Girls with endless legs and well-filled bras, bedroom eyes and sensuous pouts. It's unfair to think of the Girls in these extremes when the vast majority—including Jessica herself in high school—fall somewhere in between.

The Girls always remember her, however, which has lead to several semi-awkward ambushes at the supermarket, the mall, the four-hundred-meter outdoor track, when the grateful, gushing teenager rushes to thank Jessica for encouraging her to find her unique voice and use it to tell a story as no one else can, and Jessica, the beloved mentor, must cheerlead her way through catchy but vague platitudes of self-confidence, creativity, and encouragement because she has no clue which Girl she is talking to.

Most days Jessica loves her work because it doesn't feel like work. But she has come to hate being away from home. For the first few assignments, air travel was still a novelty to her. She found joy in the unexpected—and in the beginning, it was *all* unexpected. Catching herself laughing at the corny but inoffensive family comedy on the free movie menu in Santa Clarita, California. Awakening to the verbena-scented hotel shower gel in Bloomington, Minnesota. Humming, then mumbling, then full-out belting along with the cheerfully bullying theme song (*Get up, get up! The day is waiting! Wake up, wake up! No hes-i-tat-ing! Out of bed, you sleepyhead! Get up! Get up! Get uuuuuuuuuuup!*) for the local morning show in Chandler, Arizona. Blushing every time the flirtatious attendant at the Chevron station in Mukilteo, Washington, joked about

New Jersey drivers unable to pump their own gas. Cheering at the sight of Baby Ruths and Coca-Cola in the hospitality bar in Roswell, Georgia, and feeling a sense of kinship and solidarity with the person in charge of stocking the mini-fridge for selecting these items over inferior Snickers and Pepsi. Silly thrills were enough to help her overlook the unpleasant realities of never staying in these cities for longer than three months. Until the silly thrills weren't enough anymore.

Because after two years of constant travel, she's tired. She's tired of three-ounce containers, for example, and selfish passengers who choose to overlook the rule and inconvenience everyone else trying to get through security. She's tired of having to fly to and from New York on the weekends to see family and friends. She's tired of hotels trying to pass off their miniature French-milled bath bars and mini-miniature French-milled facial care bars as two different products for her skin's varying needs, when under minimal scrutiny, it's clear that they are the same exact soap in two different sizes. She's tired of forgetting to pack dental floss, socks, a lint brush. Or condoms, which is proving to be more important for the Girls than it is for her because over the past two years, Jessica has provided more prophylactic devices for her teenage mentees (ten) than she has used for herself (one). She's tired of single-cup coffee-makers and scary nondairy creamers that flake like dandruff into the bitter blackness and contain ingredients like sodium aluminosilicate that she suspects might be the root of the short-term neurological impairment that restricts her airport reading to the exclamations (BAD BRIT! LOCO LILO!) accompanying tabloid paparazzi shots. She's tired of using her suitcase as a makeshift dining table, tired of using plastic knives to pop open individual packets of cream cheese to smear on the doughy, flavorless bread products that other states try to pass off as bagels, tired of dropping half of her breakfast on her knee, tired of unsuccessful attempts to paper-towel-and-spit-clean the gluey smudge off her jeans, and tired of having no choice but to wear those jeans all day, all throughout boarding, taking off, accelerating, cruising, decelerating, landing, deplaning, claiming baggage, renting a car, driving, checking in, and unpacking, at which point she's so damn tired that she gives up on getting re-dressed, strips down to her underwear, yanks open the overtucked sheets, climbs in, and calls it a night. Tired of feeling like a close but imperfect counterfeit self.

Jessica feels another shoulder poke. It's Garanimals again. "It only works if you actually press the numbers," the woman jokes.

"Right." Jessica looks down at the phone resting in her hand. "Thanks." She flips open the cell and is about to start dialing when it lights up. She had unintentionally taken it off vibrate after fumbling for the video from the Virgin Islands. Now the phone plays its customized ring tone, a song that hit number one on the adult contemporary charts in 1978 and has been vilified or deified ever since.

You know I can't smile without you . . .

Twenty heads turning. Twenty voices overlapping. Twenty middle-aged women wearing "Music and Passion" T-shirts, "COPA" baseball caps, and ticket frame necklaces commemorating the most memorable of all the many thousands of standing ovations for the Showman of Our Time. Twenty members of the Tristate Chapter of the Barry Manilow International Fan Club.

"A fellow Fanilow!"

"Look how young she is! A mini Maniloony!"

"Headed to Vegas?"

"The Final Farewell tour . . ."

"Stop saying that. I can't handle it!"

"I really, *really* can't believe it's his *final* Final Farewell show and we're gonna miss it . . ."

"Shaddap! I'm having a mental breakdown over here!"

"He'll be back. He *always* comes back . . ."

Jessica thinks of the Girl who genius-rigged her phone to play Barry Manilow for every incoming call or message, the sixteen-year-old sopho-more (now eighteen-year-old senior) she visited in Pineville last night, and for whom she rearranged her travel plans. Jessica works hard to remember this Girl as she always knew her—in graphic-print thermals and baggy jeans, dark hair hidden under an assortment of scarves, headbands, and caps until she finally, *finally* got through the awkward and never-ending growing-out phase—and not as she left her last night. Jessica fought against this most recent memory to see the Girl who claimed that she was so fiercely against cosmetic enhancements that she refused to get any piercings, not even in her ears, but later confessed to Jessica that the real reason she rejected body mods was because the sight of needles made her pass out. The Girl who described herself as possessing a "postmodern sensibility trapped in a prepubescent body," whose first story for the Do Better High School Storytellers project was about (in the sixteen-year-old's own words):

> . . . the out-of-the-womb chasm separating her from her parents. When Mr. and Mrs. Dae chose to name their colicky then melancholicky daughter Sunny after the opening words to the Sesame Street theme song, they guaranteed there would be no crossing the gulf between parent and progeny. The cheerful opening notes of that song were permanently embedded like DNA, an earworm that burrowed so deep that no matter how many hours she spent with her headphones on, nothing—not even the Sex Pistols—could blast it out . . . Later, Pineville Elementary School's earliest adopters to irony would rechristen her Sunny Delight, after the refreshing fruit-flavored, heavily fortified beverage that smells like orange juice made with one part frozen concentrate, two parts ammonia—an olfactory revelation that actually made Sunny appreciate the moniker for the first time as being unintentionally suited to her disposition . . .

Sunny Dae would find Jessica's situation downright uproarious. Jessica could see Sunny tucking in her arms, legs, and head, shrinking herself into a seed pod as she always did when life's hilarity was too much to handle, before—BAM!—bursting wide-open like a trigger-sprung blossom when she couldn't contain her laughter any longer.

"Who else?" Jessica imagined Sunny asking. "Who else but Jessica Darling would find herself on a line full of middle-aged Barry Manilow fans?"

Jessica grimace-grins at the twenty members of the BMIFC whose spirits have been lifted by the revelation that there is another one of their own in their midst. She presses TALK on her phone.

"Hey, Hope," she says, having no idea what she will say next to her best friend.

eleven

Marcus needs a plan. He can spy on Jessica Darling from behind this bank of pay phones for only so long. Eventually, she will make her way to the front of the line, then off the line, then out of the Clear Sky customer service center altogether. And he must have a strategy for what he'll do when that occurs.

He already has part of the plan in order. That's the part where he follows her wherever she goes next and tries to engage her in a second conversation. It's the rest that needs work. The way he sees it, he has two options: (1) lie or (2) tell the truth.

He could stage another accident. *Wow! Here we are again! You were craving a Nathan's Famous pretzel dog, too? Wow. Uncanny. Your next flight leaves in six hours? Wow. Mine leaves right after that . . . Uncanny . . .*

Marcus lowers his head in shame, burying his face in the fake potted ferns atop the phone bank. Dust flies off the silk leaves, tickles his nose, and triggers a convulsive series of sneezes. *"AW-CHOO-WAH!"*

Marcus has barely recovered when he's overtaken by a second spasm. *"AW-CHOO-WAH!"*

And another. *"AW-CHOO-WAH!"*

He's being blessed by strangers on all sides as he stands with his head tipped back, eyes shut, mouth agape, hand waving in a *come on, come on* gesture as he waits to be overtaken by the next nasal paroxysm.

"AW-CHOO-WAH! AW-CHOO-WAH!"

He hesitates before opening his eyes, now teary with histamines. But his nose is still tingling, *There's still one more in there,* he's thinking, when it comes.

"AW-CHOO-WAH!"

The blessings continue, but he is cursed. He surrendered all worries

to this unrestrained reflex, and now that the sneezing fit is over, his worries have returned. While he rebukes the urban legend equating sneezes
and orgasms, they did serve as a momentary mind eraser, making Marcus
consider whether he should escape reality by snorting dust mites the way
drug addicts Hoover opiates.

His senses fully restored, Marcus reconsiders his options. An
orchestrated run-in? Never! How could he have considered such a preposterous lie even for a moment? And not only because he has a long-
standing policy against mendacity. Jessica would instantly see through
the loserish ruse and abandon what remaining respect she may or may
not have for him. And as he catches another glimpse of Jessica through
the layers of frayed silk leaves—she's talking on her cell phone now—
he can't help but take her side. However, the truth wouldn't fare much
better, now, would it? *Hey, Jessica. I have no reason to still be in this airport, and I've been stalking you for the last hour* . . . Too much, too soon,
too *creepy*.

There is a minor commotion at the Clear Sky customer service center. It's difficult for Marcus to see or hear from this distance, but it
appears and sounds as if the women in front of Jessica have linked arms
and are sway-bouncing side to side and . . . *singing*? He tilts his ear in
the direction of the noise and can barely make out the *aaaaaahs*,
oooooows, and *oooooohs*, something vaguely musical . . .

"Tissue?" flirts a voice behind him.

Marcus turns to address the woman possessing this studied, seductive voice. She's attractive in a way that most men would find attractive,
but Marcus isn't most men. According to the name tag pinned to her
shrunken black suit jacket, her name is Jonelle. Marcus free-associates
professions for Jonelle: She's a clinical therapist. A perfume spritzer. A
masseuse. He instantly regrets falling into the trap of snap judgments
and tries to make up for it with a smile. He also takes a tissue, out of
courtesy, but he doesn't use it.

"You seem lost," Jonelle says.

He knows Natty would lose his mind if he were here right now, as
he always does whenever Marcus gets approached by an attractive

woman. He would be particularly amused by Jonelle's reversal of the standard hot-girl gambit.

"You can't go out in public without some hot girl asking you for the time, or directions, or what's good on the menu," Natty once pointed out.

"So?"

"Hot girls are always coming up with excuses just to strike up a conversation with you," Natty said. "It's just like the awkward dialogue before the fuck scenes in porn."

Marcus shrugged off his friend's observation not because it was untrue but because the truth was an embarrassment. He has been chatted up by attractive women since the onset of puberty, even more so now that he has stumbled into his current state of dead-sexy dishevelment, which earned him the nickname "The Slutty Professor" by the smitten first-year females who pass by him on campus. He isn't *really* a professor, of course, but because he's nearly a decade older than the youngest students, he might as well be. (Had most of their affair not taken place during the summer, when few students were on campus, the moniker might have shifted to describe the infamous anthropology professor. But Marcus doesn't like to think about how close it came to that.)

Before he even started orientation at Princeton, Jessica warned Marcus about the nicknames. She knew they were inevitable for someone destined to become such an obtrusive, potentially empyreal presence on campus, and she even used them as evidence as to why she couldn't possibly be the girlfriend—or fiancée—of a twenty-three-year-old college freshman. But Jessica failed to predict just how many women would be compelled to call him by a code name. For a tight-knit study group whose members daydream about him every Monday and Wednesday between 1:30 and 2:50 P.M. during REL 382 Death and the Afterlife in East Asian Cultures, he's "The Wounded Buddha." A chattering clique from one of Princeton's oldest and most pretentious secret societies refers to him as "The Mark," which is not a misspelled foreshortening of his name but a synonym for "target" because there is big money to be won by the lucky Ivy girl who lands him in bed. Marcus wouldn't know about any of this if it weren't for Natty, who benefits greatly from his friend's refusal to sleep with anyone whose birth doesn't predate the 1990s, and whose ever-present proximity to Marcus makes him the first and most logical choice for girls who want to save face ("Who does Marcus think he is? He's not *that* hot!") with a fallback fuck.

If not for Natty, these girls would barely register with Marcus. He's too preoccupied by the ones in his past with whom he shared a genuine— if brief and debauched—connection. Forty-something girls, or so he has been told. He must rely on secondhand information because his teen years were dominated by drugged-and-alcoholic fugue-state fuckery. Forty-something is a number that he honestly cannot confirm but has never tried to deny. He suspects the real number is maybe half that tally, if only because he cannot live with the idea of so many girls (now women) once fucked and forever forgotten. That he made it through this satyric phase unscathed isn't as miraculous as it seems. Marcus always used protection, but not because he was so concerned about his own reproductive health or that of his partner. No, he always wore a rubber because an older friend (possibly Hope's own brother, Heath) told him it would make him last longer, and Marcus certainly didn't want to be known as a two-pump chump. It was this own egotistic preoccupation with his budding reputation as a sex machine that, ironically, prevented his contracting what Natty calls "cock rot," not to mention the proliferation of illegitimate Fluties toddling around South Central New Jersey.

"I can help you," Jonelle promises.

The watch Marcus is wearing—the one he's worn and scarcely noticed all day—starts to weigh heavy on his wrist.

twelve

"Hey, Jess," Hope chimes. "Happy—"

"Thanks," Jessica interrupts. "But it's already too late. It's not so happy."

"Well," Hope says, her voice taken down a notch, "we miss you here."

"I miss you, too."

Jessica misses Hope more than a roommate logically should. But for the last two years, Jessica has spent far more time on the road than in their subterranean apartment in Brooklyn. This is the same long, thin, dark space that once served as the former bowling alley of the Swedish American Men's Athletic Club, where Jessica and Hope split two bedrooms four ways with their high school classmate Manda Powers and her genderqueer boifriend, Shea. They were all supposed to lose this apartment once the family on the lease returned from a yearlong sabbatical in Europe, but that one year has turned into four. Manda and Shea moved out after that first year, leaving a spare bedroom for either Jessica or Hope to grab. The two of them flipped a coin. Jessica lost. She agreed to move into the former playground of fetish and flesh only after hiring a professional cleaning service to perform a wall-to-wall, floor-to-ceiling sexorcism.

Jessica didn't admit it to Hope, but there was another reason she wasn't so eager to dismantle the bunk beds and move out of the tiny bedroom nicknamed the Cupcake, after the cloying color scheme selected by the tween twins who were its previous tenants. Chloe and Claire were in high school now—just like the Girls, just like Sunny—and would definitely balk at bunk beds if their two mommies ever did choose to return to Brooklyn. The twins had outgrown the decor, so it stood to reason that Jessica should, too.

Jessica dragged her belongings down the hall, bought a queen-size bed frame and a button-tufted headboard. This is a luxurious bed. There is nothing stopping her from sleeping vertically, horizontally, or diagonally across this vast expanse of mattress. There is no one. And yet to this very day, whenever she thinks about those cramped, uncomfortable bunk beds and all those months of twilight giggles and moonlight sighs—Hope above, Jessica below, and yes, Marcus occasionally astride—she fears she might never feel that close to anyone ever again.

Hope would want to know about her run-in with Marcus, but there is no casual way to broach the subject. No breezy "oh by the way" segue. Not today.

"How is she?" Hope asks. "How are you?"

"She's the same," Jessica replies. "I'm . . ." Her voice drops out suddenly. Whether Jessica is overcome with emotion or undermined by a bad connection, Hope doesn't ask the second question again.

"I'm sorry," Hope says. She never met Sunny but has come to feel like she knows her through stories. Sunny has often said the same thing about Hope.

"Yeah, well," Jessica says, "me, too." *I should just say it now,* she thinks. *Hey, Hope! Guess who I just ran into? Literally! Marcus Flutie!*

"I just wanted to see how you were doing." Hope pauses before cautiously adding, "And to find out what time you think you'll get here." Hope flew to St. Thomas yesterday, took the ferry, and met Bridget and Percy and a well-edited group of family members and close friends on the smaller, less touristy island of St. John. Jessica originally booked herself on the same flight, same ferry, before she got the news that forced the detour in Pineville.

"I've been better." *I'm in shock. I just ran into Marcus Flutie.* "I missed my flight."

"Oh," Hope groans before revising her tone. "Oh!"

"I shouldn't have gone back to Pineville yesterday. I should have just flown down for the wedding, like I originally planned, *then* back to New Jersey to see Sunny before flying to Chicago . . ." *But if I hadn't changed my plans, I wouldn't have run into Marcus Flutie.*

"No, you did the right thing," Hope insists. "Bridget and Percy understand. With them, it's not about the ceremony, it's about everything that comes after."

"Yeah, I know," Jessica replies. "But I'm kind of a major part of the ceremony."

"If it makes you feel any better, they've found a backup minister, you know, just in case."

This does not make Jessica feel any better. Of course Bridget and Percy found another minister, you know, just in case. It was the practical thing to do, but the news overwhelms Jessica nevertheless. Hearing that they have prepared themselves for the probability of another no-show forces Jessica to pinch back the swelling storm of emotion gathering between her eyes.

This is too much, she thinks. *This is all too fucking much.*

"He's a pro, the local go-to guy for secular celebrations," Hope is saying, totally unaware of Jessica's meltdown. "We crashed one of his services today so we could check him out. He's not so bad, though he acts as if he's the first minister to ever come up with the whole spiel about how wedding rings are circles, and circles symbolize eternity, and that this ceremony symbolizes the bride and groom's eternal love."

Hope has heard just about every version and variation of the modern wedding ceremony. Before she made a name and a living with her portraits and original paintings, Hope had attended approximately two hundred weddings in her two years of employment with Capture the Moment. This photography firm specialized in documenting wow-factor weddings involving acrobats, belly dancers, drag queens, drum cores, magicians, fireworks, Klezmer bands, celebrity look-alikes (fat Elvis, Marilyn Monroe, and *Thriller*-era Michael Jackson are very popular), Disney On Ice (the princesses, mostly) on a portable dance rink, and a combination of the Viennese table and Japanese Nyotaimori known as the Naked Human Dessert Tray. Such tacky pageantry was enough to turn even a swoony romantic like Hope into a valentine-stomping hater.

But it was the trend toward paparazzi-style wedding photography— wherein Hope was paid to stalk the future Mr. and Mrs. D'Abruzzi-Glazer in the weeks leading up to their wedding as if they were Hollywood A-listers whose every gesture was worthy of a million flash-bulbs—that epitomized the loss of moral values in favor of production values and gave Hope the final incentive she needed to quit the business once and for all. Bridget and Percy never would have asked her to make a reluctant return to the genre. Hope surprised them by offering up her services for free.

"I need to document two people who care more about the marriage than the wedding," Hope said a few months ago, when she first told Jessica about her role in Bridget and Percy's celebration. "It will give me, um, hope." She half laughed, the way she always did when she caught herself optimistically evoking her own name. "I have to remember to make the photos about Bridget and Percy and not give in to the temptation to make it a crass composition of contrasts. His dark skin, her white skin. Dark suit, white dress. Dark sky, white sand. The stuff of dorm room posters the world over." She sighed in admiration. "Jeez oh man, those two are so gorgeous. Who could pass up the opportunity to photograph them? I don't know how they manage to do anything else, quite frankly. If I looked like either one of them, I would just spend every minute of every day capturing my own gorgeousness as a form of performance art."

"You *could* do that," Jessica said from another bedspread. Another assortment of minibar snacks. Another hotel room somewhere. Another phone call.

"And Cinthia's gallerina friends would pay any price!"

Hope made this joke because she could. Her career took off when a piece from her (Re)Collection series (*Birthday Girl, 1973*) was featured in a *Wallpaper* magazine spread devoted to the former wig factory on the East River that was gutted, renovated, and decorated at the behest of Cinthia Wallace, the twenty-five-year-old party girl turned philanthropist/patron of the arts with her finger on the arrhythmic pulse of anything worth knowing anywhere. Hope had no qualms with whatever impact Cinthia's money and connections had on her own success as an artist. Even if it were true that the only people commissioning portraits were Z-list artfuckers who had too much money to spend—which wasn't the case at all—Hope honestly doesn't care. Not if they allowed her to make a decent living doing what she loves.

Similarly, without Cinthia's vision and investments, the Do Better High School Storytellers project wouldn't exist. The Girls—and Jessica— would be a lot worse off. Unlike her blithe-spirited friend, however, Jessica felt guilty about having her life's work both founded and funded by Cinthia's charity. What Hope viewed as friends helping other friends, Jessica considered a form of freeloading. Jessica knows she's being unnecessarily neurotic when she worries about what a dead-end in-debt position she'd be in right now if it weren't for Cinthia's big faith in her little idea. Her only comfort for this onus of unworthiness is the hope that one day she'll be in a position to return the favor for someone *she* believes in.

"And if you stack the rings on top of each other," Hope is saying on the other end of the phone, presumably paraphrasing the backup minister, "the circles come together to make a figure eight, which is the symbol for infinity, and . . ."

Jessica knows she should be on the phone with the Clear Sky automated customer service system right now and not on the phone with Hope. And even if it were okay for her to be on the phone with Hope right now, she shouldn't be having a leisurely, inconsequential discussion but a hysterical heart-to-heart rant about how *she just ran over Marcus Flutie*. Jessica knows this. Yet she's desperate for a diversion, and there's no one more qualified than Hope to provide it.

"Hey, Hope," she breaks in. "Tell me a strange-but-true story right now. One I haven't heard before."

Hope is used to this random request. "A strange-but-true story you haven't heard before. Okaaaaay." Jessica can picture Hope scrunching her sunrise-orange curls with her fingertips, a primitive way of stimulating her brain. "How about this? A twenty-five-year-old woman with gaidrophobia—"

"You're *still* afraid of donkeys?" Jessica blurts, remembering her best friend's most irrational—and therefore comical—fear.

"You would be, too, if you nearly got trampled to death at the Ocean County fair when you were three years old," Hope retorts, dead serious. "And I'll have you know, Jessica, that more people die every year from donkey kicks than in airplane crashes."

"As encouraging as it is to hear that while I'm in an airport waiting to get on an airplane, I'm pretty certain that's an urban legend. I mean, what's your resource for death-by-donkey statistics?"

"May I continue?" Hope asks.

"Yes."

"So a twenty-five-year-old woman with gaidrophobia, who has spent her whole life avoiding county fairs, petting zoos, farms—"

"Pin-the-tail games, the whole *Shrek* franchise, and the Democratic National Convention," Jessica adds, trying her best to play along.

". . . is invited to a destination wedding on St. John, the smallest and most unspoiled of the U.S. Virgin Islands. St. John may not have its own airport, but it does boast an abundance of plant and animal life, including a *thriving wild donkey population!*"

"Oh, no," Jessica says.

"Oh yeah. And I'm freaking out, Jess, just like the Pickle Girl on *Maury Povich*. Wild donkeys are to St. John what pigeons are to the city, only they have a tendency to mount each other during beachfront wedding ceremonies. There are packs of fornicating donkeys *all over this island.*"

Jessica has to cover her open ear to block out the ruckus being made by the Tristate Chapter of the Barry Manilow International Fan Club. They have made a collective decision to shut off their cell phones and are now loudly debating their options for recompense.

"The locals say that wild donkeys are highly perceptive creatures, very in tune with other animals' emotions. So they, like any human wedding guest, get so caught up in the display of love between bride and groom that they are driven by instinct to mate right there on the sand."

The volume has suddenly dropped in the BMIFC's discussion. They turn in Jessica's direction, give her a big thumbs-up and exaggerated winks.

"At first Percy and Bridget were all for it, like, *Let them do their thing, make it a wedding that no one will ever forget,*" Hope continues. "Until they actually *saw* a pack of wild donkeys going at it as the backdrop to some other couple's wedding. I mean, have you ever seen two wild donkeys going at it? The male donkey is swinging one heckuva meatbat. It's very disturbing even for someone without my, you know, *problem.*"

It begins hushed and hesitant.

You . . . know . . . I . . .

Then gets louder, more confident.

Can't smile without you . . .

"The only way to stop two wild donkeys from humping—" Hope breaks off. "Am I hearing things, or are there people singing in the background?"

"I'm on line behind twenty disgruntled members of the Tristate Chapter of the Barry Manilow International Fan Club," Jessica replies matter-of-factly. "And they have apparently decided to stage a sing-in."

"Are you making this up?" Hope asks.

Jessica holds her phone out toward the voices, which spurs the protestors to sing even louder and more off-key. CAN'T SMILE WITHOUT YOU. CAN'T SMILE WITHOUT YOU.

Jessica says, "Now hold out *your* phone so I can hear the sound of wild donkeys humping."

"No way! I'm safe in my room right now. I'm not going out there to court the attention of lusty donkeys."

"How can I know your story is both strange and true?"

"You'll just have to trust me."

I do, thinks Jessica. *More than anyone.* "I better go," she says instead. "I'm having trouble hearing you, and my phone is on borrowed time because I think I packed my charger in my checked luggage."

"So what should I tell Bridget and Percy?" Hope asks.

Jessica can tell from Hope's serious shift in tone that she was specifically instructed by Bridget and Percy to find out if they need to book the local guy. "Honestly?"

"Honestly."

"Tell them I'll do everything in my power to get out of here today," Jessica says with resignation. "But in all likelihood, I won't get down there until tomorrow afternoon."

Jessica doesn't elaborate on the consequences of an afternoon arrival. Hope understands.

"You'll be here soon enough," Hope replies with forced cheer. "And I've somehow managed to take many donkey-free pictures, so you'll feel like you didn't miss anything. You'll feel like you were here the whole time."

But I'm not, thinks Jessica as she shuts off her cell. *I'm not.*

The phone is barely back in the bag before Jessica is debriefing herself on why she never got around to mentioning Marcus. Perhaps she's worried that this accidental omission will turn into a conspicuous one—the kind that has caused problems in the past. But she quickly dismisses the notion as absurd. There was never the right moment to bring it up. And besides, it was a run-in, not a reunion. "Accident" is a more accurate description, and it was over almost as soon as it started. What happened with Marcus amounted to a few minutes so fleeting and insignificant that Jessica may fail to find a good reason to tell anyone about it at all.

Jessica's stomach growls, and it's almost loud enough to be heard over the BMIFC's second protest song.

But it's daybreak! If you wanna believe!

Jessica is famished. She didn't have time for breakfast, or rather, she chose a shower over breakfast, and now she's starving. Before dashing out the door, her mother insisted that Jessica take along a travel mug full of coffee and a waxy paper bag promoting Papa D's donuts, the chain now fully owned and operated by her sister's ex-husband.

"Take it," her mother insisted. "You may not be hungry now, but you'll thank me later."

Jessica scowled at the bag.

"You told me you'd be in the Virgin Islands," Mrs. Darling said. "If I had known you were coming home, I could have shopped accordingly."

"But from Papa D's donuts, Mom? *Really?*"

"Those donuts still pay for Marin's private school education, Jessica."

Jessica now growled and scowled. She didn't have a problem with the donut, per se; she didn't want to take it as a matter of principle. G-Money had bought out his business partner a year or two before and now was reaping the profits from dozens of drive-through locations all over the country, proving his theory that portable angioplastic treats were a recession-proof commodity. Apparently, in times of crisis, Americans cling not to guns and religion, but coffee and crullers. Therefore, to support Papa D's donuts was to support G-Money. And though G-Money and Bethany had, by all accounts (both figurative and literal— as there were several million dollars in assets to divvy up), divorced amicably two years ago, and had both quickly and happily reattached themselves to new romantic partners, Jessica wasn't so eager to forgive and forget as everyone else—including the betrayed. Bethany's apparent ambivalence about her ex-husband's affairs ("Once the divorce papers were signed, it was all water under the bridge," she said. "More like sewage," Jessica muttered) and her insistence on shielding seven-year-old Marin from any of her Daddy's wrongdoing ("He's a jerk, but he's still her father!") sometimes made it difficult for Jessica to talk to her sister about anything deeper than the latest tabloid captions. (BAD BRIT! LOCO LILO!)

While Jessica obviously hasn't been married and freely claims ignorance on the complexities of that subject, she does understand the motivation to cheat, having once been a cheater herself. She cheated on Marcus as a sophomore in college. She cheated with someone she didn't care about. She cheated knowing that Marcus would be devastated by the betrayal. She loved Marcus, knew he loved her back, and yet she cheated anyway.

One might think that her own experiences would make her more sympathetic toward Bethany's straying husband, since she had failed to make good on her own monogamous promises. But the truth is, every cheater is a saboteur. Cheaters make the choice to violate trust, break vows, renege on promises in full view of the messy consequences. Jessica suspects that G-Money's reason for cheating on Bethany was similar to her own reason for cheating on Marcus: It requires less effort to fuck up a relationship than to make it work. At twenty years old, this behavior is condemnable yet indicative of the inexperience of youth. Fifteen years later, it's just goddamn pathetic. Bethany and Marin deserved better, and they got better. And if G-Money was so unhappy in the marriage, so did he.

Jessica couldn't explain this to her mother, especially not in the last seconds before heading out the door for the airport. Mrs. Darling, as always, was fully turned out at eight A.M., her professionally unlined face all the more awakened by the invigorating presence of her daughter back, albeit briefly, in the fold. She welcomed this opportunity to be helpful, to serve a purpose in her younger child's independent life, even if the attempt was unwanted and wrongheaded. Jessica could see how eager, almost desperate, her mother was to provide her with this coffee and donut. To reject the offering would be to reject her. Haunted by the memory of Mrs. Dae's shattered face the night before, Jessica accepted both the coffee and the donut bag with a smile and a simple thank-you. Seeing her mother's expansive, overreciprocated smile made Jessica want to pay reparations for every smirk, snort, and eye roll she'd ever casually and cruelly delivered.

Jessica downed the coffee and jettisoned the mug, accidentally leaving it on the floor of the Town Car in the chaos of arrival. The donut—spurned by the only vegan livery driver in New Jersey—is still in its unopened bag, tucked deep within one of the hidden pockets of Jessica's carry-on, completely forgotten until right now. Jessica reaches in and rummages around until she feels something soft and crinkly. She unfolds the donut bag, peers inside, and recognizes one of the shop's best sellers, a pink-frosted, rainbow-sprinkled vanilla cream puff once called the McGreevey during a brief and ill-conceived marketing campaign in which all Papa D's products were named after famous New Jerseyans. This donut, more like a cupcake than anything anyone should ever eat for breakfast, was her mother's way of making the morning more festive, distinct from the other 364 days of the year.

The McGreevey is something she wouldn't normally eat in her real life, as opposed to her *airport* life, which, if Jessica thinks about it, is slowly but surely taking over the former. Despite her frequent flying, Jessica is merely a competent traveler. She hasn't spent enough time in the air to become a sky warrior, one of the savvy business-class masses who manage to fit an impressive array of gourmet foodstuffs in their carry-on luggage. As such, Jessica continually finds herself in one airport newsstand or another, her common sense and taste buds dulled by jet lag, swiping her debit card to buy bags of crunchy, starchy, salty, sugary crap that she wouldn't consume anywhere else in the world, as if the airport's artificial atmosphere makes her crave only the fakest approximations of food. How many times has she found herself slumped on a bench at the departures gate, licking high-fructose residue from her fingers and thinking, *Why the* hell *did I just eat that?*

This donut will be good for a brief rush of sweet elation, quickly followed by the inevitable crash, withdrawal, and lingering sugar hangover, but she doesn't care. Hell no, not today. Her teeth sink into the dense cake, and the sensation brings such indulgent relief that she scarcely notices when a glob of vanilla cream filling oozes from the opposite side and splats onto her foot.

thirteen

"Let me help you," cajoles Jonelle, blinking up at Marcus through three coats of mascara.

This woman peddles an ersatz eroticism that Marcus does not buy in to. Men are anthropologically programmed to want women with violin curves and poreless skin, saucer eyes and plump lips, but this one looks like what happens when a seventh-grade girl creates a I WANNA LOOK LIKE THIS composite of celebrity body parts and facial features that reflects an immature idea of perfection. On their own, the features are alluring. But when the disparate parts are all awkwardly glued together through cosmetic surgery, it comes across as a collagelike caricature of sexiness that makes Marcus feel bad for Jonelle.

A *Frankenskank*, thinks Marcus. *That's what Jessica would call her.*

He winces, regretting the expression as soon as it comes to him as being unfair to Jonelle and Jessica. *Especially* Jessica. He hates when he does this, when he puts hypothetical words in her mouth, imagining how she might react to different moments in his life without her. It has been many months since Marcus has spoken her name aloud, but that hasn't stopped the conversations inside his mind. Like when he sees a film he knows she would appreciate (*Before Sunset*), reads a book that could speak to her like it has spoken to him (*Youth and Life*), or hears a song that should be on her iPod (anything by the Mighties—that is, before the group's lead singer/songwriter made himself the "my," Marcus the "he," and Jessica the "you" in their viral sensation, "My Song Will Never Mean as Much [As the One He Once Sang for You].") Marcus sees, hears, reads, and thinks of Jessica, inventing her side of the dialogue in the absence of the real thing. Far less inspired and more shameful are the artless, mundane moments like this, when it's almost as if his subconscious is reaching for excuses to remember Jessica for no legitimate reason other than that he can't stop himself from doing so. And what a word to put in her mouth—Frankenskank! It's hardly charitable of him to think of Jessica as being as snarky and judgmental as ever. And if she is? So be it. He always loved her because of, not in spite of, her flaws. Her biggest flaw, in his mind, was her inability to believe that was true.

Marcus delivers a wan smile.

"I can help you," Jonelle promises.

Marcus focuses on a tiny heart-shaped gold charm trapped between her mountainous breasts like an unlucky climber abandoned in a crevasse. He identifies with the poor guy. "I doubt it," he replies.

"I really want to help," she insists huskily.

Marcus takes off his glasses and looks at her through fuzzier, more forgiving 20/60 vision. He wonders if this change in perspective makes it easier to see what she looked like before she felt like she had to do this to herself in order to be loved. Make no mistake, no matter what explanations or excuses or equivocations she's given—from "It's my body and I can do whatever I damn well please" to "Everyone gets a little work done these days" to "It's a low price to pay for high self-esteem"—what else but the need to be loved could motivate someone to do this to herself? *She never gave herself a chance*, Marcus thinks, *to be loved for who she is, flaws and all.*

His watch feels like a shackle around his wrist, immediate punishment for his presumed superiority.

"I'm in the business of helping anxious passengers." Jonelle sneaks a fingernail into the pocket that conveniently calls redundant attention to her breasts. She pulls out a small white card and hands it to him:

Jonelle Jenkins
Aeroanxiety Specialist
thAIRapy spa @ Newark Liberty International Airport

Marcus's heart sinks with the revelation that she *is* a clinical therapist, perfume spritzer, and masseuse all in one. He had wanted Jonelle to surprise him, to teach him a lesson about false first impressions. Against his better judgment, he tries to salvage the conversation by asking a question. "Do you always target clients like this?"

Jonelle's mouth widens, better for showing off a full set of custom veneers. "Only when they look as anxious as you do."

Marcus stands up to his full height for the first time during the conversation, stretching well over six feet tall. "How anxious?" He needs to get an objective opinion.

"Bordering on terrified," she says. "You want to move forward, but you can't. You aren't brave enough."

Marcus nods in reluctant agreement, and Jonelle is encouraged by his gesture of approval. She edges one step closer, body-slamming Marcus with the full impact of a heavyweight perfume that evokes a nineteenth-century opium den. "You're trembling," she says. When Jonelle gently presses her hand into his palm, Marcus yanks his hand away and stuffs it into his pocket. The sudden fierceness of this gesture makes Jonelle gasp in a rather unwholesome way. "Well!" she cries out, taking a step backward to collect herself. "Well!"

"I'm sorry," Marcus says. "My issues are beyond any therapy."

"If you need me," Jonelle says breathily, gesturing down the concourse, "I'll be right there."

Marcus's eyes are drawn in the opposite direction of her hand, back to Jessica. The women who were on line in front of her are exiting the Clear Sky customer service center en masse. Some are sobbing, others are grimacing; no grievances have been resolved to their satisfaction. It's Jessica's turn to talk to the Clear Sky customer service center representative.

All at once it hits Marcus like a shaft of light in a darkened tunnel. The way out! The next step! Why didn't he think of it before? He had all the information he needed and still wasted all this time.

Jonelle has freed the heart charm from the D-cup danger zone and is now zipping it along the gold chain, back and forth against her breasts. "Ahem," she hints, unaware that Marcus's side of the conversation is irretrievable.

Marcus pauses just long enough to pay her a compliment. "I like your necklace," he says.

Jonelle hasn't had a chance to say thank you when Marcus waves a perfunctory good-bye and turns his back on her. Jonelle clickety-clacks in retreat as he pulls his cell phone out of his back pocket and dials the phone number on the closest Clear Sky Airlines poster. (This one, for nonstop service to Paris, reads: THE CLEAR SKY FORECAST? 100% CHANCE OF . . . ROMANCE!) He presses certain numbers as he is told. He waits and waits some more.

When he finally gets a Clear Sky sales representative on the line, he asks, "When is the next flight out of Newark to St. Thomas?"

fourteen

"When is the next flight out of Newark to St. Thomas?!"

As far as Jessica is concerned, the sing-in was a smashing success. It worked well enough to get the Tristate Chapter of the Barry Manilow International Fan Club out of the Clear Sky customer service center and bring Jessica to the front of the line. But she's still a few footsteps from the counter and has blurted the question too soon, with barely a glance at the person to whom it was directed. The Clear Sky customer service representative coaxes her to come closer with a shiny pink fingernail.

Jessica does a double take. *Wait. Is that . . . Sylvia?* she asks herself. *Or have I been here so long that all Clear Sky employees are starting to look alike?*

On another day, a surprise doppelgänger wouldn't be a cause for alarm. But in light of everything that has already happened today, Jessica is starting to question her sanity. She turns to ask Garanimals whether she noticed a shift change while they were waiting on line, only to discover that Garanimals is gone. At some point during Jessica's conversation with Hope, or perhaps after, while in the midst of her gastronomic voyage to Donutopia, Garanimals was replaced by an assortment of new and unhappily waylaid travelers. Jessica is a bit surprised that Garani-

mals cut and ran without one last farewell poke. Hadn't she and Garanimals bonded? Briefly, of course, but in the intense way that soldiers
invoke, you know, in the trenches against a common enemy? Apparently
not. Jessica is feeling irrationally slighted by Garanimals's brisk disregard.

"Please step forward," says the woman who looks exactly like
Sylvia, the Clear Sky gate agent who has already spurned her once today.
It is only when Jessica gets within a few inches of the counter that she
can read the employee name tag—SYLVIA—that confirms this is indeed
the same woman she squared off against at Gate C-88 and not her
(more) evil twin. Jessica thinks it's odd that Sylvia didn't bother to mention at any point during the finger-in-the-air cartography that a two-
hour stint at the Clear Sky customer service center was the next shift of
her rotating schedule, one designed by the Clear Sky Airlines Employee
Satisfaction Task Force in the effort to relieve monotony and help alle-
viate the long-term psychological damage inflicted by hour after relentless hour of air rage.

"Hello again!" Jessica's sugarcoated teeth are gritted into a deranged
smile. All her donut energy is being exhausted by this smile, and it isn't
nearly enough. This smile is a grueling effort; she can feel the tension
straining muscles well below her neck. Her shoulders are carrying more
than their fair share of the weight of this smile. She might develop bursi-
tis from this smile. "So, I'm still hoping to get to St. Thomas!"

Though Jessica was too busy licking smudgy frosting off her fingers
to notice, it was Sylvia who'd had the unenviable task of informing the
Tristate Chapter of the Barry Manilow International Fan Club that they
were stuck in the city of Newark indefinitely. Sylvia is not ready to move
on without a gripe or two, even though it's totally unprofessional and
frowned upon in the official *Clear Sky Customer Service Center Handbook*, the same one that advises employees to be impersonal yet polite
with all disgruntled passengers.

"You're not one of those fan-clubbers, are you?"

"Noooooo," Jessica insists.

When Sylvia looks heavenward and mouths *THANK GOD*, she
is revealing more personality than is recommended in the *Clear Sky*

Customer Service Center Handbook. To Jessica, this Sylvia is nothing like the brusque robot at Gate C-88, so she chuckles at the gesture to keep up the unexpected camaraderie.

"Such a fuss over Barry Manilow's Final Farewell tour. Ridiculous!" Sylvia's tone is light, but five decades' worth of frowns undermine any effort at turning them upside down.

"I totally agree with you," Jessica says, running her tongue over her teeth. She can feel the erosion of tooth enamel already. Why did she eat that donut?

"I've never been much of a fan of his, to be perfectly honest," Sylvia says.

Jessica is tempted to force a segue. *Me, either! Though that "Copacabana" song is kind of fun to dance to at weddings, don'tcha think? And speaking of weddings, I'm hoping you'll be able to get me to my best friend's wedding . . .*

But Sylvia doesn't let Jessica get a word in edgewise. "Final Farewell? Ha! That's what they all say. Didn't Cher's farewell tour go on for five years? And what about that Céline Dion? Hasn't she gone into retirement three times already? It's just a ticket-selling scam."

"You're right!" Jessica says, again too eagerly, having chosen forced politeness over her other options.

"Say what you want, but that Céline Dion sure can sing. She's sure got some pipes. But Barry Manilow? Meh!"

"Meh!" Jessica mimics.

Sylvia nods, simpatico, and wiggles her fingers over the keyboard. Jessica is now confident that Sylvia will do whatever is in her power to get her on the next flight to St. Thomas.

Of course that's when, as if on cue, Jessica's phone starts singing. *You know I can't smile . . .*

Sylvia frowns, and her hands freeze. "I thought you said you weren't a fan." She obviously feels betrayed by Jessica in a meaningless, minuscule way that is not unlike how Jessica still feels after being abandoned by Garanimals.

"I'm not!" Jessica glances at the caller ID and sees that it's a text message: NO WORRIES!!!! XO, B&P

The number of exclamation points undermines the message. Jessica is more desperate than ever to get on the next flight.

"I got this phone for work a few years ago, and I still don't know how to use it. I'm not really techy, and this thing has more buttons, bells, and whistles than I know what to do with."

Sylvia's face is unchanging.

"Anyway, a girl I know programmed this ring tone as a joke because an old boyfriend once tried to win me back with a Barry Manilow toilet seat cover."

Jessica stops midsentence, not only because she sounds like a lunatic but because she's caught herself in the kind of public overshare that she finds so distasteful. She hates being on the inadvertent receiving end of these types of conversations. In Manhattan one can take unwilling part in conversations about infidelity, abortions, genital infestations, all out loud, in public, without shame, on a daily basis. It's commonplace, she knows, and she feels like an anachronistic curmudgeon for wanting to adhere to some outmoded sense of propriety and discretion. Whenever she overhears one of these shameless conversations, she can't help but look at the oversharing narcissist and think, *I don't want to know this about you.* Jessica doesn't want Sylvia—or anyone on line behind her, for that matter—knowing about Sunny.

"Let me start over," Jessica says.

She explains her problem: She missed her flight to St. Thomas. And her goal: To get on the next available flight. As well as the complications therewith: The flight she missed was itself a change to the original reservation, which means that the airline is under no obligation to make yet another change, with or without the hundred-dollar surcharge. Sylvia takes this all in and—with newfound professional resolve—starts clicking away at her computer. "Ms. Daring?"

"Darling," Jessica corrects. "With an L."

"Oh, right!" Sylvia says, squinting at the screen. "I need a new prescription." She types, then stops. "Darling with an L. That's quite a name to live up to." Sylvia, bless her, clearly does not know about the porn star and how she's chosen to live up to the Darling name. "It's like the family in *Peter Pan!*" Sylvia yelps, her fingers still hovering over the keys. "What was the girl's name again? Not Tinker Bell. You know, the girl in the family."

"Wendy," Jessica answers, as she has many times before. "Wendy Darling."

"Right! Wendy Darling! Thank you!" Sylvia says, finally touching her fingertips back down on the keyboard. "That would have bothered me all day. I wouldn't have been able to get anything done."

"You could have Googled it," Jessica says.

Sylvia waves at the computer dismissively. "Not here. No Internet connection. Clear Sky wants us cut off from the outside world so we can concentrate on serving customers . . . like you!"

Jessica laughs politely, sticking to that game plan for getting this done. She congratulates herself on her sense of restraint and maturity, thinking about how a younger, less patient Jessica Darling might have resorted to huffing and puffing and blowing the whole thing out of proportion. But the mere fact that she is so proud of her progress points to just how tenuous her grip on maturity really is. Did Garanimals pat herself on the back for not throwing a hissy fit? No. She just whipped out her cell phone and went into problem-solving mode without causing a ruckus or putting up a fuss. Full-fledged grown-ups shouldn't celebrate themselves for resisting behavior unbecoming of a toddler. Jessica's getting there, but she hasn't arrived yet.

"I don't like Google," Sylvia says. "Call me old-fashioned, but I like getting all my answers the hard way, by racking my brain! I swear, my son can't think thirty seconds into the future. Everything is now now now, with all that texting and instant-messaging nonsense. I don't think his generation knows how to think for themselves in any way that makes sense."

"They can think for themselves, and they do," says Jessica. "They just choose not to share those thoughts with you."

Sylvia fixes Jessica with a skeptical look. "Are you a teacher or something?"

"More of an 'or something' than a teacher," Jessica says. "But I hope to change that." She realizes she could end the conversation here, but she's compelled to push it further, to defend all the Girls who aren't here to defend themselves. "Texting makes sense to your son. He doesn't want it to make sense to you. That's the whole point. Didn't you pass coded notes in class when you were his age?"

"I did," Sylvia concedes, before regaining momentum, "because *we* wanted to keep things private. But that's not how it is nowadays, with everything on the Internet. None of these kids want privacy. They're all addicted to attention. Nick dropped out of college and thinks he deserves to be famous for doing nothing. He didn't have a job until I forced him to get one. Argh!" Sylvia slaps a hand to her forehead.

Jessica's eyes spin around in their sockets. Sylvia's comments are indicative of precisely the kind of collective character assassination that gets the Girls all riled up. And no one fought back against the youth bashing more fiercely than Sunny.

Dearest Mom and Dad,

I'm writing this letter to apologize on behalf of the Look at Me! generation. We think we deserve the world's undivided attention. We demand it! While I have yours, I will use it to make a confession: You are right.

The world is passing through troubled times, and yet we think of nothing but ourselves. Today's teens love luxury. We want it all and we want it now and heaven help you if you don't give it to us. We are the biggest culprits in this culture of excess, the most fickle consumers, the biggest contributors to the global garbage pileup resulting from our disposable society.

We have bad manners, contempt for authority, and show disrespect to our elders. We contradict our parents, chatter before company, and are tyrants over our teachers. We have no reverence for parents or old age. We talk as if we know everything, and the wisdom of our elders is passed off as foolishness. I can only speak for myself when I promise: No more!

I understand why you see no hope for a future dependent on the frivolous youth of today, for we are reckless beyond words. When you were young, you were taught to be discreet and respectful of elders, but teens today are exceedingly wiseassed and incapable of showing restraint. As a girl, I offer an extra apology for being forward, immodest, and unladylike in speech, behavior, and dress.

By the way, this letter is a plagiarized mash-up of quotes attributed to Plato, Peter the Hermit, Hesiod, and vintage Dear Abby that I found on the Internet. So, um, I guess my generation isn't any more spoiled, entitled, or narcissistic than teens who lived hundreds or thousands of years ago . . . or those who grew up in the 1960s and '70s, for that matter, LIKE YOU.

Your daughter,
Sunny

P.S. This cut-and-paste approach is intentionally ironic. Thank you.

Jessica's eye roll, as fantastically executed as it was, barely registers with Sylvia. As an overworked mother of a bitter son not much younger than Jessica, she has developed a high tolerance for parental disdain as a means of survival.

"We can put you on a flight that leaves tomorrow morning at nine A.M., connects in Miami, and gets you into Charlotte Amalie, St. Thomas, at one P.M."

Jessica is already shaking her head in protest. "The wedding is tomorrow morning," she pleads. "Is there any flight that can get me there tonight? I don't care how late."

"Ooooh!" exclaims Sylvia. "A destination wedding! How fun! Who's getting married? I love weddings! I wish my son would get married."

Jessica sighs before responding, wondering if she passed up her best opportunity by eschewing the "Copacabana" segue. "Two of my oldest and dearest friends."

The description is inadequate. Bridget and Percy aren't merely her friends, they are the two people who make her "believe in love. Not just love but love in all its mutinous mutations over time." Over the course of their nine years together, Bridget and Percy have taunted lovesick cynics like Jessica by "serving as flesh-and-blood proof of the impossible: Two young people can fall in love, stay in love, and continue to choose loving each other over everything and everyone else . . . *and still be deliriously happy with that choice*." (Again, all quoted passages come from

Jessica's sermon.) It's the last part that seems to trip up other long-term couples, like her parents, who fight monotony by traveling all over the world, or her sister's husband, who fought monogamy by philandering all over the city until her sister finally came to her senses and dumped his trans-fatty ass for good.

"Well, the last flight out today leaves in three hours," Sylvia explains. "It connects in Miami and will get you to St. Thomas by ten P.M. tonight."

Jessica flexes and poses like a victorious prizefighter. "Yesssss!"

"It's overbooked," Sylvia buzzkills. "I'll confirm you for tomorrow's flight, but you could try standby for the one that leaves today."

"What are my odds of getting a seat that way?"

Sylvia gives her a thumbs-down and a full-face frown.

"So what you're saying is, I can only hope there's someone like me who is stupid enough to miss her flight."

"Yep," Sylvia says with a shrug. "Someone like you."

Someone like you. Jessica's wayward attention drifts yet again. She thinks about someone like herself, as she was during hospital visiting hours last night. She remembers the shaved head (Jessica prays for the opportunity to joke about a whole new awkward hair-growing-out phase) halved by one-sided train-track stitches; the unresponsive face, unrecognizable and grotesque from bruising and swelling (another joke: about how she's lucky she looks good in purple); the thin, small body (more childlike than ever) attached to too many tubes—breathing, feeding, excreting—connected to too many machines keeping her alive for too many hours already: thirty-six.

Jessica glances at her new watch, a gift from her mother, who, in one of the more harmless intergenerational differences of opinion, still believes that it's unprofessional to check one's cell phone for the time. It's almost two P.M. It will be near dark here in Newark when the next plane to St. Thomas takes off. Two days ago, in another time zone, Jessica's watch would have been three hours behind, requiring three twists of the tiny dial to catch up. And if she were in yet another time zone, it would be evening right now. Or tomorrow. Time is fluid and flexible, a made-up construct. Isn't that the kind of logic that has alcoholics lining up their glasses at all hours of the day? *Hey, it's five o'clock somewhere.*

"So, Sylvia," Jessica says, leaning in to the counter. "Can you point the way to the closest bar?"

fifteen

Marcus inhales. Clasps his hands together, swings them over his head and pushes them palms-up toward the ceiling. He exhales.

A high school senior in her first-choice college hoodie, sweatpants, and Sherpa boots giggles all over herself as she snaps pictures of Marcus on her camera-phone.

Marcus drops his entwined hands behind his neck and squeezes the sides of his head with his jutting elbows. He inhales again.

The girl texts a friend: **hott**

His hands break free. He exhales again.

The friend replies: **iwhi**

He shakes his hands out in front of him chest-high, his fingers all blurry from the flapping. Inhales once more.

The girl texts back: **omfg ita**

If Natty were here, he would tell Marcus to stop swinging his dick around like a lasso.

"I'm just stretching," Marcus would say.

"The jailbait would say otherwise," Natty would argue. "This is classic lasso-dicking."

"No, it's not."

"Yes, it is." And then Natty would smile wickedly and say, "Didn't your anthropology professor teach you *anything?*"

In fact, she did. She lectured Marcus about all sorts of flamboyant courtship displays throughout the animal kingdom. The Argentine lake duck swings its long, thin penis to lasso females cowboy-style. Frigate birds inflate their throat sacks into bright red heart-shaped balloons.

Hippos take huge, pungent dumps, then twirl their tails helicopter-style to spread the scent. Moose soak their beards in urine. Bower birds build elaborate maypole towers out of twigs and twine. Painted turtles grow out their toenail claws, then swim laps to show off the wake. Hedgehogs run in frenetic circles. Prairie dogs square-dance. Frogs sing. Elks bugle. Many primates—with whom humans share 98 percent of their DNA— flash engorged rainbow-colored genitals.

Marcus Flutie stretches.

"Lasso dick."

Whenever Natty said it, Marcus would punch him in the chest much harder than necessary if it were just a meaningless joke. The truth is, despite his denials, Marcus knows his poses attract more attention than standing still. Whether he assumes these yogic positions in public in spite of or because of this knowledge is something not even Marcus can answer. But he senses that he's being watched right now. The teenage girl has shuffled away, having been summoned by her parents. But perhaps Jonelle is keeping her eye on him, readying herself to return under the pretense of admonishing him for his rudeness—*how could you just ignore me like that?*—when in reality, her rehearsed hostility is just an excuse to talk to him again.

"Pardon me," says a commanding male voice.

Marcus turns to face two Port Authority policemen who had been watching him. With his salt-and-pepper mustache and sandbagged eyes, the first officer appears older than he really is. Marcus would be surprised to hear that he's still a few decades from retirement and is only a few years older than his brother, Hugo, who just turned thirty. The second officer is shorter and thick with overcompensatory muscles, especially around the neck. He's new to the beat, still passionate about his job, and will pounce if provoked. He reminds Marcus of a pit bull trained to kill.

"Is there a problem, Officers?" Marcus looks them both briefly in the eye before settling his gaze on the more coolheaded-looking officer.

"We were going to ask you the same question," the pit bull says with a menacing smile that warns, *I will Tase you if I have to*. He narrows his eyes, trying to size Marcus up.

Have I been acting suspiciously? Marcus wonders. *Or did Jonelle report me to the police as revenge for rebuffing her advances?*

"No," Marcus says. "There's no problem here." He has conditioned himself to keep responses brief in these types of situations.

The officers exchange looks. The pit bull's fingers twitch at his sides, just itching to pull his gun out of his holster. The first one asks in a measured tone, "Can we please see your identification and flight information?"

Marcus can't help but think that even the first officer, so polite with his "please" and "pardon me," wouldn't hesitate to handcuff and haul him off to a holding cell. Fortunately (or not), he has had a lot of practice with negotiating his way out of situations like this. Just as Marcus is unfazed by attracting the attention of strange females, he is equally accustomed to being subjected to impromptu interrogations by police officers, security guards, and other keepers of the peace.

"No problem," Marcus says, reaching into his back pocket for his wallet. He flips it open to his driver's license photo. The policemen examine the man in the photo (thinner, somehow older at twenty-two than he is at twenty-six, with an unfortunate Al-Qaedan beard) and compare it to the man standing in front of them.

"And your flight information?" the first cop asks.

"Of course," Marcus says, patting his pockets until he finds evidence of his flight from New Orleans, the only proof he has right now that he still has reason to be here. He hands over the halved boarding pass with no further explanation. Marcus knows better than to put up any protest, especially when the officers are harassing him for no reason. No reason can turn into a night in jail very quickly.

The first officer takes a look at Marcus's document, then hands it to his partner for appraisal.

"This flight landed hours ago," the pit bull says, his voice rising. "You have no reason to be here. Only valid ticket holders are permitted to remain in the airport. We can issue you a citation for loitering."

Marcus has been threatened with the same charge more times than he can count. He is a habitual loiterer. Though today it's intentional, a consequence of watching Jessica from afar, his loitering is usually accidental, an unplanned ambulatory meditation during which he gets so caught up in his thoughts that he forgets what he's doing (walking somewhere), where he is (leaning against a lamppost on Nassau Street), or how long he's been there (a half hour). How many times has he been shaken back into consciousness by a man in uniform who assumes Marcus is under the influence of alcohol or another, more illicit mind-altering substance? How many times has he shown up late without an acceptable answer when asked where he's been and why it took him so long to arrive?

"I'm waiting for a friend whose flight is late."

Marcus immediately regrets this lie because he doesn't like to lie. He doesn't like to lie on principle: The truth should always suffice, and if it doesn't, well, that's his own fault for getting himself into such a morally questionable position to begin with. But he also doesn't lie for practical reasons: He can never keep his lies straight.

Now that he's already lied, he sees no choice but to commit to it. "I'm supposed to stand here by this telephone bank until she arrives, but—" Marcus cuts himself off midsentence, unwilling and unable to embellish any more than that.

"What flight is your friend on?"

This is exactly why Marcus doesn't like to lie. One lie always requires another, and another, and it's all too much for him to handle. Marcus's heart speeds up. He can feel a bead of sweat dropping from his armpit, trickling, tickling its way down his torso, slipping past his waist-band.

"Your friend must have provided her flight information, correct?"

Even the first cop is tensing up, his fleshy cheeks popping in and out with the clenching and unclenching of his jaw as he looks Marcus over. The cop doesn't know what this guy is up to, but there's something not quite right about his story. He thinks the guy is under the influence of something, but he's not sure what. Marcus wonders if it's too late to backtrack from his first lie, or whether he's skilled enough to compound that lie with another. He recalls Natty's warning: *Ten more seconds, and you've crossed the line between bittersweet reunion and restraining order.* The second cop is ready to lunge.

Marcus spots a movement out of the corner of his eye, a figure in all black exiting the Clear Sky customer service center. He points with his whole arm.

"That's her," he blurts, unleashing a chestful of pent-up air. "That's who I'm waiting for." Marcus is at their mercy.

It's the first cop who makes the decision. "Then let's go have a talk with your friend."

sixteen

*W*hat a day, Jessica thinks as she heads to Hwy. 9 Bar & Grille. *This day has been so . . . so . . . ?*

Jessica fumbles for the right word and, in failing to find it, wonders whether she should bother with the alcohol. She feels as if she's functioning in a sort of dream state already, one comparable to early stages of drunkenness when the five senses are on the way to not making much sense at all. Jessica doesn't drink much anymore—last night was an exception. Abstaining is easy because Jessica has a rule against drinking alone that goes all the way back to a video about PROBLEM DRINKING in seventh-grade health class. DRINKING ALONE was number two on the list of signs that you were a PROBLEM DRINKER (after DRINKING TO GET DRUNK). Jessica went on to ignore other warnings on that list (DRINKING TO GET DRUNK, DRINKING TO THE POINT OF VOMITING, DRINKING TO THE POINT OF PASSING OUT, etc.) but rarely broke the rule about drinking alone. Her sloppiest inebriations were always in the company of others. She was a *social* drunk, personable, not pathetic, and certainly not problematic, even on those collegiate morning-afters when she woke up without panties, the stench of fresh puke in her hair. When she travels by herself, there's no company of others to drink with. So she doesn't. Except on the one occasion she did bring company back to her hotel room in the form of Len Levy. That night she did drink. A little too much.

"Miss!"

Jessica hears the shout and assumes it's directed at someone else because she's a "ma'am" now.

When she drinks in the company of others, it's usually over a meal, in which case she orders the appropriate beverages to go with the food on the table: margaritas with burritos, sake with sushi, bold reds with pasta, sangria with tapas. Oh, how she wishes she were already on St. John, clinking cocktail glasses full of tropical fruity beverages with her best friends. She doesn't regret visiting Sunny in the hospital, though she does regret the unfortunate consequence of her actions: the possibility that she might miss Bridget and Percy's wedding altogether.

Jessica might feel less guilty about her delinquency if she knew for sure that Sunny had benefited from the visit. Her mom and dad (whom Jessica had never met in person and who seemed more sympathetic than their daughter's essays made them out to be, though in this situation, even the most cretinous parents would be transformed into good people worth rooting for) encouraged Jessica to talk to her as she always would. They believed that their daughter could still hear, if not respond to, visitors' conversations, and that such interactions were crucial for stimulating her injured brain and could be the difference between a full recovery and a semivegetative state.

"Hey, Sunny," Jessica had whispered, looking at the blips on the heart-rate monitor instead of her. "You know, I rearranged my travel plans to be here, so the least you can do is wake up."

No one else was in the room, but Jessica shrank with shame all the same. The joke felt crass, forced. And worst of all, unfunny. Sunny definitely would have called her out on it. "With all due respect, Ms. Darling," she would have said, "that lame joke is why the baby Jesus weeps."

Jessica had known going into the visit that Sunny wouldn't be able to contribute to the conversation. Yet deep down, Jessica had hoped for a cinematic miracle that was not going to come, at least not while she was sitting beside Sunny. That delayed realization made the rest of the brief visit almost too much for Jessica to take. She stayed only until Sunny's beleaguered parents returned from a quick dinner in the hospital cafeteria, a ten-minute respite from a round-the-clock vigil.

She asked them to please call her cell phone at any time—night or day—if there was a change in Sunny's status. They promised someone would call her, if not them. There were, after all, a lot of people who would need to be called. Jessica has been waiting for that call ever since.

Sunny's mom escorted her by the elbow to the elevator. As Jessica stepped inside, her mother said, "Thank you for coming by. Sunny thinks the world of you."

The doors closed before Jessica could return the sentiment.

And it was that final fleeting glimpse of Mrs. Dae's torment that had driven her to drink too much last night. The first time since the last time she drank too much, which is a time she also prefers not to think about but for entirely different reasons.

"Miss! Miss!"

Jessica knows Sunny was plugged in to her MP3 player when it happened. She just knows. But what song was she listening to? What was the last thing she heard before that driver blew through the stop sign, plowed into her in the crosswalk, and just kept going? It's questions like these that drove Jessica to the bottle last night. Not the questions, per se, but her fear of never having an opportunity to hear them answered.

So what's her poison? Jessica has no idea. She drank her mother's zin because that was all her parents had in the fridge. It's been so long since she was in a bar that she can't settle on what to order once she gets there. She recalls a time when she tried to impress or maybe intimidate the opposite sex with her masculine requests for brutal shots of whiskey. She'd tip her head back, down the shot in a single gulp, shake off the fire in her chest, place the shot glass mouth-down, then wait, never too long, for a male onlooker to order another round. Now, just a few years later, she's embarrassed by the very idea of that lonely girl at the bar who wasn't fooling anybody. Not even herself.

"MISS!"

The insistence of this voice, and the impression that it's gaining on her, is what compels her to slow down. *Maybe I've got the face of a "ma'am" but the ass of a "miss,"* she muses. In retribution for the compliment she's just paid her ass, she's now half expecting a kind stranger to tell her that she's tucked the toilet seat cover into her jeans and it's trailing behind her like an unhygienic peplum. This is what she's thinking when she turns to see two Port Authority police officers flanking . . . Marcus Flutie.

The earth rumbles.

Collapses beneath her feet.

The stable foundation she has painstakingly constructed since their breakup (and hastily reassembled after their earlier run-in) has been instantly and powerfully unmoored.

She wobbles in her sneakers.

She wants to shout, "Don't panic, everyone! It's just my world being pulled out from under me!"

She searches through the rubble for a rational explanation that will explain this second run-in with Marcus Flutie in as many hours, digging for a grounding bit of evidence that will help her recalibrate and retain a semblance of control.

"Excuse me, miss," the first officer says. "This man claims to know you. He says he's waiting for you."

Marcus is still here. And so is she.

"Do you know this man? Or do we have a security issue here?" barks the pit bull.

"No," Jessica croaks, still reeling. The answer isn't the right one, and alarm careens across Marcus's face. She zeroes in on that split seam in Marcus's sweater, the tiny thread. Jessica thinks of a song she hasn't heard in years by a band she was never *that* into, though she did think the lead singer was tortured and adorable in a geek-cute kind of way, a way, it is worth noting, that Marcus Flutie himself is flaunting these days. What were the lyrics? *If you want to destroy my sweater . . . Hold this thread as I walk away . . .*

That tiny thread from a cashmere sweater she suspects—no, knows for certain—was purchased by an ex or current lover becomes the metaphorical tether to which Jessica decides to grab.

"No, this is not a security issue." Jessica clutches a hand to her throat, clears it. "Yes, I know him," she says more firmly. "His name is Marcus Armstrong Flutie." She then turns to the first officer, switches on a smile. "And he's with me." She pivots toward Marcus, puts her hands on her hips, and says in perfect exasperation, "Where have you been? I've been waiting for you forever."

"I was waiting for you," Marcus says. "The whole time."

Marcus holds up his palms in apology. Jessica can feel in her cheeks that her grin takes the risk of going a little too far, a little too eager to please, as if she's a tuneless naïf desperate for fame who has just auditioned for a community theater production of *The Sound of Music* and knows Maria is out of the question, and Liesl is a long shot, but maybe, just maybe, she could be one of the nuns in the abbey, and oh, if the directors just give her this shot, they won't regret it, she will wrest every bit of emotion out of her one line . . .

Jessica's imagination takes off on this nonsensical flight of fancy if only to escape where she is right now. She returns to the tiny thread, clings to it, holds on.

"Okay," the first officer says. "You've found each other. Now get on with it."

The cops stand their ground, clearly waiting for Jessica and Marcus to make the next move.

"Riiiiight," Marcus says slowly. "Let's get going."

"Yes," Jessica says in a stilted voice. "Let's."

After a moment of hesitation, Marcus steps toward Jessica and takes his place beside her. She shifts, turns in the direction she was originally headed, and puts one foot in front of the other.

"Thank you," Marcus says under his breath. "I'd be headed for a holding cell if it weren't for you and your innocent face. They didn't even ask to look at *your* documents."

"What did you do?" Jessica asks, eyes straight ahead.

"I was loitering."

Jessica's eyes flicker in his direction. "Loitering?"

"Loitering."

"Loitering?" Jessica asks again, this time with a hint of a laugh. "There are thousands of people passing through this airport, and they stop *you* for loitering."

"Apparently, I'm a conspicuous loiterer," Marcus answers. "Though less so since I shaved the beard."

Jessica's mouth twists. She had hated The Beard, and not just because of its regrettable jihadist insinuations. She had resented that Marcus chose to keep the wild, shamanic beard after his return from the desert, especially when she told him that it scrubbed her skin raw when he ravenously descended on her mouth or parts southward. She wondered at the time if it was intentional, if he was making her wear him like a hair shirt, yet another form of penance for her careless infidelity at Columbia, a betrayal that had already resulted in two years of silence between them. The fact that she even entertained such ideas about this person she was supposed to love proved just how dysfunctional that relationship had become, which, in her mind, was all the justification she needed for saying no and letting him go.

So, yes, you might say The Beard is a loaded subject. She resists the urge to ask him when he shaved it off. "The dreads are gone, too." This is what she says instead.

Marcus rubs the short tufts of hair on his head. "Hm," he murmurs, then nods soberly as if verifying this truth—the loss of his foot-long dreadlocks—for the very first time. They are marching forward in tandem, him right behind her, matching step for step, when he asks, "Where are we headed?"

She slows down just enough for him to catch up. She glances behind and waves at the policemen who are still watching them from a distance. "I don't know, but let's keep moving."

And that answer, for now, is just fine with him.

seventeen

Jessica doesn't say anything as she leads Marcus across Concourse C. She can't resume talking until she's found a place to sit, somewhere away from the swarms of travelers, somewhere she can settle down and focus on upholding her half of the dialogue.

The content of this conversation with Marcus is difficult for Jessica to fathom. Where to begin? The conversation will require her total concentration, which won't be easy, since her mental competence has already been compromised by emotional trauma, pink wine, insomnia, and monounsaturated oils. She is grateful to have somewhere to go—back to Gate C-88—in two hours because it means their reunion will be finite. She can give her side of the narrative (whatever it may be) a beginning, a middle, and yes, an end. The fateful hypothetical—*what if you see Marcus again?*—has at last presented itself. And now it's up to Jessica to give their story a resolution that she hopes will satisfy both Marcus and herself.

Jessica spots the neon sign for the Hwy. 9 Bar & Grille, pauses, almost turns toward it, then reconsiders. She doesn't want to drink in front of Marcus. She doesn't want alcohol to lower her defenses, loosen her tongue, lull her into saying things she doesn't want to say. She's not sure what she wants to say to Marcus. She wonders how long she could get away with not saying anything at all. Marcus has already tested his own mettle in this regard, having famously embarked on a silent meditation that lasted his twenty-second year. She doesn't doubt that he could outlast her in a silent battle of wits by disarming her with a quarter-smile.

Jessica isn't moving, so Marcus stops, too. He takes this moment of stillness to look at her, to confirm yet again that it really is her. She really is here. He contemplates her profile and notes that there is a sprinkle clinging to her jaw, a tiny pink speck desperately holding on for dear life. The sight of it makes him grin, but it's his own laughable personification of and identification with the sprinkle that makes him snort out loud.

"What's so funny?" Jessica asks. Her tone is more cautious than caustic.

All of this, thinks Marcus. *Not ha-ha funny but strange funny. The Queen's warning, hearing your name, getting run over, stalking you from afar, almost getting hauled off for loitering, being rescued by you, Jessica Darling, standing inches away from me with a pink sprinkle dangling from your pale cheek, an innocent patch of skin that I'm not allowed to reach out and touch . . .*

"What?!"

He is standing there, staring at the sprinkle, forgetting to speak. "There's a sprinkle stuck to your face," he finally says.

"There is?" she says, frantically wiping all around her face with her hand, yet still missing the spot. "Where?"

He wants to free the sprinkle with his fingertip but thinks better of it. He points to the same spot on his own jaw and rubs. She mimics the gesture, and the sprinkle falls to the floor.

"There also appears to be a smudge of frosting in the corner of your mouth."

"What?" she yelps, licking all around her mouth like a slobbery pup. "I can't believe Sylvia didn't tell me!"

"Who's Sylvia?"

"The Clear Sky customer service representative," Jessica quickly answers. "I was talking to her for, like, ten minutes, and she didn't bother to tell me I had food all over my face."

"And," Marcus says, directing her attention downward to the rubber tip of her Converse sneaker, "on your shoe."

Jessica looks down, stomps her foot and grunts. Powerless to resist the overwhelming paranoia about her deteriorating appearance, she must make an immediate detour to the nearby bathroom. "I need to use the ladies' room. Can you wait?"

"*Wait* is a synonym for 'loiter,' " Marcus replies, making Jessica smile, if not with her mouth, then with her eyes. "I've already set a precedent."

"What I mean is, I don't know what your travel plans are, if you have to be anywhere else—"

"I don't have to be anywhere else." Marcus waves her concerns away with his palms. "I've got time."

"Are you sure?" she says in a rush as she frisks into the bathroom, not waiting to hear the answer.

"As long as it takes," Marcus says when she's out of earshot. "I can wait."

eighteen

The donut, it seems, was the least of Jessica's problems.

"Oh my God," she groans, shivering at her cadaverous complexion in the bathroom mirrors. "I look like a hemophilic vampire." She splashes cold water on her face, then gently slaps pink into her cheeks with her fingertips.

A pretween girl wearing a pink tracksuit and matching slip-on sheepskin boots approaches the sink next to Jessica's. The girl is all aglow with a tropical suntan that debunks Jessica's hastily cobbled theory that the fluorescent bathroom lighting is responsible for her skin's greenish, ghoulish cast.

"Impothible," the girl lisps.

"That's nice of you to say," Jessica says to the girl, genuinely touched by the reassurance.

"Vampirths can't be seen in mirrorths," she explains, the speech impediment the result of a second mortgage's worth of orthodontia. "No reflethion."

"Oh," Jessica replies.

"You juth need a makeover," the girl says over the toilet-flushing cacophony.

"Amber!" shouts a shrill voice from one of the bathroom stalls. "What did I tell you about talking to strangers?"

Amber glares at the closed door, then twirls her finger cuckoo-style for Jessica's benefit. *Crazy*, she mouths.

"I can see you!" admonishes the mother. "Through the crack in the door."

"Ewwwwww," says Amber. "Thath dithguthing! Talking to me while you do number two. Groth!"

Jessica hears the unmistakable sonic boom of a mother biting her tongue.

"She'll be in there *foreeeeeever*," Amber whisper-whines. "Sheth got irritable bowel thyndrome."

Jessica recoils from this news—a classic overshare—then recovers. "You should be nicer to her."

Amber responds with a calisthenic eye roll.

Jessica tries to shut out the mental image of Amber's mother's inflamed colon. She turns back to the mirror, and what she sees is barely an improvement. *This* is not how she wants to look during her reunion with Marcus Flutie, all puffy-eyed and hollow-cheeked, with a decomposing nose and leprositic lips. She agrees with Amber's assessment, but she is not one of those travelers who have invested in miniatures of every imaginable high-end toiletry and beauty gadget. Jessica remembers waking up midflight from LGA to LAX to the sight (winged elbows), sound (*cracklesnap!*), and deeply unsettling smell (charbroiled human hair) of the passenger squeezed next to her in the middle seat trying to flatten her frizz with a travel-size rechargeable wireless straightening iron. That woman would have been adequately prepared for a surprise run-in with her ex-boyfriend in the middle of Newark Liberty International Airport. But Jessica is not. With the exception of a tiny pot of Be You Tea Shoppe–brand lip balm, all her makeup and ancillary grooming products are stowed in the suitcase she reluctantly checked when she arrived at the airport, the suitcase that is currently making its way to St. Thomas, USVI, on Clear Sky Flight 1884, the one containing not only all the summery party clothes she needs for the wedding she may or may not get to but all the high-tech subzero outerwear required for surviving her wintertime stint in the Chicago suburbs with all twenty fingers and toes intact.

Jessica unscrews the tiny teapot of Sweet Orange Marmalade Lip Plumping Balm, dips her index finger in, and swirls it around.

"I love the Be You Tea Shoppe!" Amber exclaims as she pushes the nozzle on the soap dispenser. "I had my 1ath birthday there. Look!" She turns and booty-pops two letters sequined across her tiny butt: BU! Ah yes, Bethany had told Jessica she hopes to keep this aspect of her business alive, a clothing line to promote female empowerment, positive body image, and healthy self-esteem.

"AMBER JEWEL!" cries her mom from the stall.

Another eye roll, one that has just earned Amber a coveted spot on the U.S. women's gymnastics squad for the 2012 Olympics. "I wanted to get the Little Ladie's Luxe Life package for my birthday, but Mom thaid it wath too ethpenthive. We did the Mother-Daughter Marveluth Mini-Me Makeover inthead."

Jessica opens her mouth to tell Amber that she is in fact related to the beauty and the brains behind the Be You Tea Shoppe, and that one of the gorgeous multiculti, generation-spanning Daughter-Mother-Grandmother trios used in the brand's advertising and promotional materials (the one representing all-American blondes) is her own niece, sister, and mother. It would be intended as a fun nugget of info, something Amber could go back and tell her friends about: *Hey, I met the sister of the owner of the Be You Tea Shoppe* . . .

But on second thought, this tidbit has little positive value and could even have a detrimental effect on the young girl. Jessica can just imagine the withering replies from Amber's pretween cohorts. *Um, like, did you get any free stuff? No? Then, like, who gives a flying crap?* More likely, Amber would predict the pointlessness of sharing such a lame story with her friends back home, yet *still* end up feeling bad about herself because *she* wasn't born to a family of millionaire entrepreneurs enabling *her* to become the internationally recognized face of a brand by the tender age of seven. Jessica knows that all the Be You Tea Shoppes will shut down within the year, which only reinforces the futility of such a comment.

It's a career objective that has crossed over into Jessica's real life: No one should end a conversation with her feeling worse than when it began. In her many hours of listening to the Girls tell their stories, and listening to the Girls react to the stories they've been told, Jessica has discovered a certain tactfulness she lacked when she was younger. Just because she has something to add to a discussion doesn't mean she should. With this in mind, she puts a restraining order on her tongue, wishing she had an unopened sample of a future must-have something-or-other to offer Amber instead of a silenced anecdote.

Amber pounds the nozzle on the soap dispenser once more, rubs the cheap soap into her hands, and waves them under the electric eye to start the water. Then she begins to sing. "Happy Birthday to You." She has a high, tinny voice, befitting all the metal in her mouth. "Happy birthday to you . . ."

Jessica is stunned by this song in this place. "Is *today* your birthday?"

"No, my birthday ith in Auguth," Amber says. "Why?"

"You were singing the Birthday Song."

"Ith juth a hand-wathing song," Amber replies with a shrug. "So I wath my hanth long enough to kill all the nathy germth that make you thick. We were juth talking about birthdays, and I gueth it wath on my mind. But it workth with the alphabet thong, too."

"Oh," Jessica says, feeling sheepish. "Right."

After two years of working with the Girls, who *always* know better than she does, Jessica has also developed a talent for reading unspoken questions. She goes out of her way to pose such queries rhetorically, so none of the Girls feels embarrassed by ignorance or curiosity. Even though the youngest high school storytellers are a few years older than Amber, Jessica can see the obvious question forming in Amber's mind: *When is your birthday?*

Amber's about to ask it, too, when a toilet flushes and a stall door bursts open to reveal a permatanned anatomic impossibility in the same pink outfit as her daughter, a foolish attempt at agelessness that only draws more attention to the long decades of hard living separating the two. She is what Las Vegas would look like if it suddenly decided it didn't want to be Sin City anymore but, rather, the high-strung mom of a ten-year-old girl.

"Amber! What did I tell you about talking to strangers?"

"To not to," Amber answers in a monotone.

"You won't be happy until you get kidnapped, raped, and left for dead."

Jessica is shocked by the violent outburst and wonders if such demonstrations of maternal anxiety are the cause or effect of the woman's screeching colon.

Her daughter, however, is unfazed. "I'll get my own Amber Alert," she says tartly.

"What did I do to deserve this?" her mom snarls heavenward before grabbing her daughter by the hoodie and dragging her out of the bath-room without, Jessica notes, washing her hands first. Both mother and daughter have messages of female empowerment, positive body image, and healthy self-esteem advertised across their asses: BU!

Jessica isn't disgusted by Amber's mom; she feels sorry for her. She's just another mom trying to use rules to protect her daughter from harm. Jessica imagines Sunny reading aloud from her next essay:

Don't talk to strangers. Don't do drugs. Don't smoke. Don't drink and drive. Don't have sex. Wear a condom. Wear sunblock. Wear a seat belt. Wear a helmet. If you see something, say something. Just say no. Stop, drop, and roll. Stop, look, and listen. Look both ways before you cross the street . . .

Safety is an illusion. Bad things can happen to anyone at any time, whether you follow the rules or not. You can check left, check right, check left again before you step off the curb and into the crosswalk, but that won't stop an anonymous asshole in his shitty pickup from putting you in intensive care . . .

Jessica shakes the voice out of her head, searches inside the bag for her cell phone, and checks for any missed calls. There aren't any. She thinks back to her visit from the night before, when Sunny's parents promised Jessica that Sunny really could hear her, even if she couldn't respond. Were they delusional or optimistic? Is there a difference when your only daughter has been in a coma for three days? Jessica wonders whether it would be worthwhile to call the hospital and request that the phone be put up to Sunny's ear so she can tell her a story she's—no! not *dying*, bad choice of word—*living* to hear.

"Hey, Sunny," Jessica would say. "Guess who's waiting for me outside the bathroom door right now?"

What else is there to say? "He looks like a god." And? "I look like a gorgon because I haven't gotten any sleep since I found out about you." Then? "So get your ass out of bed, Sunny! Your coma is really taking a toll on my personal life." Finally? "I'm sorry. I can't joke about this. You are such an incredible girl. Wake up, Sunny. The world will be so much worse off without you . . ."

The phone shakes in her palm as if she's receiving a call, but she's not. Jessica decides she isn't prepared for Sunny and stuffs the phone back into one of the pockets.

She studies her face once more, trying to see herself as Marcus might see her. She acknowledges that the view isn't too pretty, and she knows there is no way she can pull herself together. There will be no "marveluth" makeover, no transformative miracle to be found in a tiny teapot. This is what she looks like today, even if it isn't a fair representation of her attractiveness on any other day. And because Jessica won't be seeing Marcus again anytime in the near future, this is the image he'll be left with. This is how he'll remember her.

Rather than lament the unfairness of the situation (*Why couldn't I have run into him last week? I totally had my shit together last week*), Jessica gamely accepts her ugly reality and even divines an advantage to playing up her contagious appearance: It will diffuse any hint of sexual tension between them. Not that she's allowed herself to acknowledge any attraction so far. But Marcus is Marcus, after all. Someone who can sexualize just about anything, even the removal of a sprinkle from one's cheek. Someone who has made prudence in thought and action even more difficult by having the nerve to look better than ever.

And it's been, what, almost two years since Jessica had sex? Doesn't she have needs? But consider the curious circumstances of that last lay: exes fucking for old time's sake. Sex recycling is common practice among consenting adults of a certain age, so Jessica's one-night stand with Len Levy would hardly seem worthy as a source of guilt and regret—that is, until it spawned a nerdcore breakup anthem of guilt and regret. Jessica has lazily surrendered to familiar temptations before and has suffered extraordinarily awkward postsex consequences. She chalks it up to a lesson learned and will not let it happen again.

She is intentionally careless with the lip balm, smearing it all over her decaying nostrils and dry lips, hoping it makes her look even less sexy than she did before she entered the bathroom.

"*Happy birthday to you,*" Jessica sings as she washes the sticky goo off her fingers, her voice echoing in the suddenly empty, eerily quiet bathroom. Then she gets serious with the greasy face in the mirror. "*You* are not sixteen anymore."

The words have barely escaped her lips when her eye catches the coin-op feminine product dispenser. This inspires another protective layer of subterfuge.

Aha! she thinks. *I'll fake my period, too!*

This is not the first time Jessica has faked her period. The first time she faked her period, she was (ahem) sixteen years old and motivated to do so for very different reasons. When she was a sophomore in high school, she stopped menstruating. Since she was a virgin with a vacuum-packed hymen, this wasn't cause for contraceptive alarm; however, her mother feared the pubescent reversal could be the sign of a more serious medical problem. To assuage her mother's fears, every twenty-eight days, Jessica dramatically doubled over in cramps and ostentatiously disposed of (unused) tampon applicators in trash cans all over the house. Jessica Darling was the Meryl Streep of bogus menses.

Now she loudly pounds the machine with her fist, waits for a minute to pass, then at last emerges from the bathroom to find Marcus unmoved from his spot.

"I had a fight with the tampon dispenser," Jessica explains.

A puzzled look passes across Marcus's face.

"I won. I got what I needed. For you know. My *period.*"

Marcus is more confused than discomforted by this menstrual non sequitur. He senses that Jessica is awaiting some sort of response. He relents in the form of a simpleminded "Okay."

Jessica follows up with a theatrical, tubercular cough. "Oh, and I have a cold," she says through her nose. "A nasty one, too. You should probably keep your distance."

"Okay," Marcus says again, this time taking a giant step backward for effect.

nineteen

They resume walking, destination undecided.

"I missed my flight," Jessica explains, remembering to talk through her nose. "I've got two hours–ish until I find out whether I can get out of here on standby." She pauses. "Wait, why are you here? Shouldn't you be at school?"

Marcus doesn't hesitate. "No classes right now; it's the reading period before finals." He goes on to say that Princeton sticks to the old-fashioned system of administrating final exams after the students return from winter break. "I've only got one in-class exam, and it's not until next week. So I don't have to be on campus right now."

"Does that mean you're coming or going?"

This time Marcus takes a few steps forward before responding. "Both. And neither."

Jessica has to physically restrain herself from throwing up her hands in exasperation and fleeing in the opposite direction. Two seconds into their first conversation in over three years, and he's already speaking in typically cryptic tongues.

Marcus is nearly knocked over by the waves of angry energy. He knows he must choose his next words carefully. "A trip to New Orleans. Overbooked. Next flight leaves tomorrow."

These obfuscating half-sentences aren't lies. (There *was* a trip to New Orleans. There *was* an overbooked flight he looked into. His next flight *does* leave tomorrow.) But they don't reveal the full truth. (He *returned* from New Orleans. The overbooked flight *is* the one leaving in two hours, which Jessica has little hope of getting on. Tomorrow's flight *is* the same as Jessica's, departing for St. Thomas.) To his relief, his misleading explanation seems to satisfy Jessica, who nods as if she understands.

Marcus knows the next question is risky. But he can't quell his curiosity. Why is she—and now *he*—headed to the Virgin Islands? A winter getaway is the logical answer, but he suspects it's not the right one. Jessica doesn't seem to be in a frivolous-vacation frame of mind.

"What about you? What's in St. Thomas?"

"Well, I'm actually headed to St. John, but I have to fly in to St. Thomas and take the ferry—" Jessica stops dead, chokes on her breath, coughs for real. "Wait. How did you know I was flying to St. Thomas?"

Marcus feigns nonchalance. "It's kind of funny, actually."

Jessica turns to stone.

"Not ha-ha funny, but . . ." He doesn't bother filling in the rest when he sees a thick layer of permafrost forming over her already hardened surfaces. "I heard your name announced. 'This is a final boarding call for Clear Sky Flight 1884 with nonstop service to St. Thomas, U.S. Virgin Islands. Final boarding call for passenger Jessica Darling.' "

Her face warms, softens. He heard her name. She recalls her first impression of the accident, how it had seemed as if he chose that exact spot on the floor as if waiting for her. In a way, he *had* anticipated her arrival. He had heard her name.

Both Marcus and Jessica silently ask themselves the same questions at the same time. How would she have reacted to the sound of *his* name? Would she have allowed herself to believe it was him? Would she have looked for him? Or kept on running? The answers come easily. If it had been up to her, they would not be standing together, face-to-face, right now. They both know it.

"You really heard my name?" she asks, though she knows he's telling the truth. "When?"

Marcus takes off his glasses, then rubs the lenses with his shirttail—a bit of sprezzatura before answering. "About a minute before you ran me over."

Before Jessica can respond, Marcus announces, "There's Starbucks!" with more enthusiasm than the observation requires. For the first time, he speeds up and passes her. "You get their table," he says, gesturing toward a departing couple, "and I'll get some herbal tea for what's ailing you."

Jessica, dazed and disoriented, bumps into several customers as she wends her way toward the just-abandoned bistro table in the corner.

twenty

Marcus is stymied by the quotidian task at hand.

Jessica can't decide if Marcus is affecting her constitution or if she's really coming down with something through hypochondriacal power of suggestion.

Marcus makes his way to the head of the Starbucks queue and orders herbal tea and a muffin for Jessica Darling as if this isn't the most miraculous thing that has ever happened.

Jessica shivers as he approaches the table, her teeth chattering with a fever or something else.

"I got you the healing tea," he says, handing her a venti. "The barista promises that it has restorative properties, especially when consumed with this vitamin-C-packed cranberry-orange muffin."

"Thanks," Jessica says, remembering to sniffle. Then she clutches her lower stomach and groans. "I hope this combination works for, uh, cramps."

"You're welcome." Marcus tampers down a tiny lip tic. "I sure hope so, too."

He sits. She sits. He sips. She sips. She speaks. "You drink espresso?"

"I guess I do," Marcus replies, regarding the cup as if he'd never set eyes on it.

"Since when?"

"Around the same time I shaved off The Beard."

This will be a treacherous conversation. A simple question about his caffeine intake has already transgressed into dangerous emotional territory. Jessica catches herself nervously sliding the cardboard heat sleeve up and down her paper cup. It's a gesture that all of a sudden strikes Jessica as accidentally and overtly hand-jobby. She lets go of the cup, reaches for a napkin, and fake-blows her nose. "And when was that?" she asks.

I can wait, he says to himself. *I can wait*. "That's a story I don't want to tell right now."

Jessica relaxes into the cold, hard curve of the plastic seat, relieved that Marcus is as skittish as she is. "*You* brought up the subject of The Beard." She is emboldened by his nervousness. "Twice."

The corners of his mouth twitch upward again, still resisting the pull of a full smile. She, too, is taking careful note of the words passing between them. "I suppose I did," he admits without offering an explanation for why he might have done so. "But let's talk about something else instead."

"Okay," Jessica says, hands shaking slightly as she brings the cup to her lips. "Let's."

And for the next two hours, they do.

part two: during

one
(together vow)

"You didn't answer my question."

"What question?"

"Why are you headed to St. Thomas?"

"Oh! *That* question."

"Was there another question?"

"[Cough.] There are *always* other questions, Marcus. [Cough.] But to answer this specific question, Bridget and Percy are getting married!"

"Married? That's fantastic!"

"It is."

"You must be so happy for them."

"I am! They're so great together. They always have been so great together."

"Please congratulate them for me. Although . . ."

"What?"

"I thought they had decided not to get married. Or am I remembering wrong?"

"No, you're remembering it right. They changed their minds. Actually, Bridget changed her mind. Percy was always for marriage, even if he pretended to be against marriage for a while, just to make Bridget happy. But after so many years together, he couldn't deny the truth anymore, that he was a traditional guy who wanted a traditional wedding with some, if not all, of the traditional trappings. A ceremony on the beach was a middle-ground . . . uh . . . uh . . . ?"

"Compromise? Or is that too negative?"

"Compromise. Yes, that's the word I was searching for, I guess. *Compromise*. If you think about it and break it down, it's really not all that negative. 'Com' is Latin for 'co,' meaning 'together.' And '*promise*' is, of course, 'promise,' a vow. Together vow."

"Together vow."

"That doesn't sound so bad, does it? Actually, that's pretty damn good. I should add that to tomorrow's sermon."

"*Sermon?*"

"Did I forget to mention that I'm performing the ceremony tomorrow? Or I'm supposed to, if I ever get down there."

"You? Of all people?"

"Yes, me. Go ahead and mock, but I'm a woman of the cloth now, ordained over the Internet by the Universal Ministry of Secular Humanity."

"You?!"

"It's a fake church for atheists, Marcus."

"That makes perfect sense."

"Then why are you looking at me all smirky like that?"

"You don't see any *irony* in this situation?"

"Irony? What's so ironic?"

"It's not your lack of faith in a higher power that makes you an unlikely minister for a marriage ceremony. It's your lack of faith in m—"

"My public speaking skills?"

"Er, right. That's *exactly* the irony I was referring to."

"You know what's really ironic? After Bridget and Percy booked this out-of-the-way and out-of-pocket destination wedding, I told them that the RSVPs would serve as a barometer of who matters and who doesn't. They would know for sure who their most devoted friends and family members were, you know, the ones willing to take off from work and go into debt to fly their asses down there, the ones who cared enough to *show up*."

"That *is* ironic. But I'm sure they know you're there for them, Jessica, in spirit if not in body."

"Yeah, I know. I've heard it already. But I'm still pissed off at myself for missing the flight. And if I can't get on this flight that leaves in a few hours, then I won't get out of here until late tomorrow morning, which means I'll miss the wedding altogether, which sucks for me because I obviously really want to see two of my best friends get married."

"And to make matters worse, you're not feeling well."

"Right. [Cough. Cough. Sniffle.] These cramps are, uh, *hell*. Ow."

"It looks that way."

"Anyway, it's not like their wedding is a huge affair, just family members and a few select friends. Two dozen guests, tops. So my absence won't go unnoticed."

"I'm sure your absence would be felt even if they had invited five hundred guests."

"Is that supposed to make me feel better?"

"What I meant is that you're not easily missed."

"Uh, *thanks*? I'm so annoying that no one misses me when I'm not around?"

"No! That's not what I meant at all! I meant 'miss' as in 'overlook.' Not 'miss' as in 'regret . . . the . . . absence . . . of.' "

"Uh, okay."

[Pause.]

"I'm fairly certain that my year of silence permanently affected my ability to talk like a normal person. I approach language almost like a nonnative speaker."

"A Lacanian theorist would have a field day with you."

"A what?"

"Forget it. Continue."

"Well, I feel like I'm speaking ESL all the time. Or English as a third or fourth language: 2007 LOLcat translated from phonetic Chinese via Babel Fish."

"So you sound like . . . a bad tattoo?"

"Ow. Now I'm the one who's hurting."

"Oh my God. Why did I say that?"

"Really, it's okay. I'm not in too much agony over here."

"I'm so sorry!"

"I'm kidding, Jessica. You don't have to apologize."

"I really have no idea what possessed me to say that."

"Can I do something?"

"I guess that depends on what it is you want to do."

"I want to get it out there: This is not an easy conversation."

"Really? I thought I was the only one having a tough time."

"What? Are you kidding me? We've only been talking for a few minutes, and I'm already sweating my balls off."

"Perhaps you should take off that gorgeous sweater of yours."

[Pause.]

"Feel better now?"

"My shirt is still sticking to me, but yes."

"Look, I appreciate your honesty, Marcus. I'm nervous, too."

"You don't look nervous. You're not biting your lip."

"I'm not what?"

"You're not giggling or nibbling the corner of your lip. That's a dead giveaway that you're nervous."

"That *was* a dead giveaway. I've outgrown the habit. I don't do that anymore."

"Oh."

"So I may not be gnawing on my lip, but it doesn't mean I'm unfazed by how surreal this is. I mean, how is it possible that I'm sitting across the table from you at Starbucks right now? How does a conversation with you even start? There's so much to say. And so much more we could say but maybe shouldn't. And discerning the difference is difficult indeed."

[Pause.]

"Uh, that last sentence was unintentionally singsongy."

"I noticed."

"Thanks for not calling attention to it, Marcus."

"I was tempted to, but I refrained. I didn't want to make you more self-conscious."

"Thanks again. I appreciate your altruistic avoidance of acknowledging my annoying alliteration."

"Ha."

"So."

"So let's just accept that for the duration of our conversation . . ."

"The next hour and forty-odd minutes . . ."

"No matter how careful we try to be, we will both say things we'll want to take back immediately. I will most definitely say more regrettable things than you will. But let's agree not to beat ourselves up about it when it happens, okay? Let's not get tangled up in regrets this afternoon. Let's just . . . talk."

"Talk."

"Just talk."

"I'm sorry, but—"

"No apologies."

"Right. I'm sor—"

"You're apologizing again!"

"Oh my God. I was, wasn't I? [Cough.] It's just that, well, I had a lot on my mind today even before I ran into you. My brain is overloaded. I'm having a hard time processing everything that's happening."

"I can relate to that."

"It's like I'm coming down with prosopagnosia, or something."

"Proso-what—?"

"Prosopagnosia. A brain disorder that makes it impossible to recognize objects or people. Oliver Sacks. _The Man Who Mistook His Wife for a Hat._"

"Interesting. Are you taking meds for the cramps? And your cold?"

[Cough.] "Sure."

"Does it help with the pro-so-pag-no-si-a?"

"No. [Cough.] The meds are definitely not helping at all."

two
(stranger things)

"So what's in New Orleans?"

"Oh. Just some work that I'm doing."

"What kind of work?"

"I spend my breaks as a volunteer for various long-term restoration projects."

"Wow. I'm impressed."

"Don't be. Save it for the locals who have been working all day, every day, since the levees broke."

"Is it really that bad down there, even after all this time?"

"It hasn't been that long, Jessica. Only four years, which in the grand scheme of things is only a blip. It's the *b* in *blip*, and a lowercase one at that. But we're so shortsighted here in this country. We're all about quick fixes, and New Orleans will be anything but."

"I'm sorry."

"No more apologies, Jessica."

"Right. I mean, I didn't mean to sound so ignorant, but I guess I am."

"It's not your fault. I didn't know how bad it was until I went down there and saw it for myself. How else would you know? There are too many other fucked-up things in the world vying for the public's attention. New Orleans isn't newsworthy anymore. The media has lost interest, but the problems haven't gone away in the absence of attention. The poorest communities aren't much closer to reconstruction today than they were in the weeks after the hurricane hit. Entire neighborhoods are boarded up and abandoned. Families are still cramped in their FEMA trailers, with limited access to schools, doctors, grocery stores—the basics for survival. It's devastating to see it all firsthand, to talk to these people face-to-face."

"How did you get involved?"

"Through a class."

"Oh, really? So what's . . . I mean . . . uh . . ."

"What's what?"

"Uh . . . I was about to ask what your major is."

"And you hesitated because?"

"I'm not sure, exactly. Maybe because it's been a few years since I've asked anyone that question. I mean, in college it's kind of an icebreaker. You know, 'Where are you from? What's your major?' You don't have any reason to ask that question when you aren't in school anymore. It changes to 'Where do you live? What do you do?' "

"I see. So you are far too mature to ask me about my major."

"I didn't mean it that way! Only that I was suddenly aware of asking you a very collegiate question, one that I haven't had any reason to ask anyone since I graduated."

"I see."

"So?"

"So . . . what?"

"You're going to make me ask it, just to make me ask it?"

"Ask what, Jessica?"

"Your major."

"Take a guess."

"I really have no idea."

"Just guess."

"I don't want to guess, Marcus."

"Why not?"

[Cough.] "I just don't."

"I'm a . . ."

"Philosophy. You're a philosophy major."

"Hmmm . . . philosophy. That's interesting."

"Am I right?"

"Wasn't one of your college boyfriends a philosophy major?"

"Uh, yes. And for the record, I only had one college boyfriend. Not boyfriends, plural."

"Two."

"One."

"Two."

"One!"

"One—*him*—plus one—*me*—equals . . ."

"Oh! [Cough.] I wasn't counting *you*."

"You weren't counting me? Why don't I count?"

"You weren't a college boyfriend, Marcus."

"We were together during college."

"If together means three thousand miles apart!"

"A technicality."

"And we got together *before* college."

"So?"

"So that puts you in a different category."

"And what category is that?"

"Marcus, if I knew the answer to that, this conversation would be a whole hell of a lot easier, wouldn't it?"

[Pause.]

"So guess again."

"Marcus, this is silly."

"Just one more guess."

"Why?"

"I want to hear how you think I've spent the past three years."

"Women's studies."

"Now, *that's* funny."

"Seriously, Marcus, it seems like something you would do, choosing a major that's ninety-nine-point-nine percent female just for the fun of being the point-one exception."

"Tragically, Princeton offers only a *minor* in women's and gender studies. Which is why I went with my second choice."

"Which is?"

"Public and international affairs."

"Public and international affairs. Duh. I should have known that all along. I mean, it makes sense, considering what you said about your work in New Orleans."

"The class I referred to earlier, the one that took me there, was called Disaster, Race, and American Politics. After spending fifteen weeks discussing and debating all the many ways our federal government has screwed our neediest citizens, a bunch of us were inspired to take our lessons beyond the classroom. We needed to see the devastation for ourselves and do something about it."

"Good for you."

"Some of us were self-conscious about the idea of going down there at first. I know I was. Oh, how nice. A bunch of privileged Princeton students going to New Orleans to help poor black folk and unburden themselves of their liberal guilt. Oh, and won't it look nice on their grad school applications? Or when they run for public office? But then I decided that anyone who thought that way was an asshole."

"So true."

"Why should I let some closed-minded asshole stop me from help-ing?"

"You remember Cinthia Wallace, right? She used a multimillion-dollar inheritance to start Do Better and has had to face a lot of that kind of cynicism. Like, how dare she start up a philanthropic collective with that money? Isn't someone with her socialite credentials supposed to, I don't know, mainline that money?"

"Someone of her station avoids needles. She'd snort the cash. Or smoke it."

"Right. Anyway, people tend to be very suspicious of anyone who supports the greater good. It's assumed that you're working some angle."

"There might be some truth to that. My motivations aren't purely altruistic. There's a lot about New Orleans I identify with."

"Like what?"

"Like the idea of rebuilding a place that most people had long writ-ten off as morally corrupt and hopeless, despite its gifts."

"Uh . . . you know, I actually heard a little about your volunteer work from a friend. Paul Parlipiano. But I didn't know how reliable the information was so . . ."

"Paul Parlipiano. Yeah, I remember him. We were on the same house-gutting crew. It was over a year ago, I think."

"That sounds about right."

"I had no idea of his name. I knew who he was through you, but I don't know if I ever met him in person. He recognized me right away, which came as a surprise to me, considering I was elbow-deep in mold, wearing a biohazard suit and a respirator."

"I'm not surprised. Paul's, like, a savant with names and faces. There was one time when I was attending the Summer Pre-college Enrichment Curriculum in Artistic Learning, otherwise known as SPECIAL, remember?"

"Not really. Was that the same summer I was attending the Middle-bury In-Patient Adolescent Rehabilitation for Addictions and Associ-ated Treatment Issues?"

"Otherwise known as?"

"MIPARAATI."

"*Mi para ti*. Me for you."

"*Mi* . . . *para* . . . *ti* . . . Me . . . for . . . you . . . You're right."

"*Sí, señor*. No one ever pointed that out before?"

"No. Never. Most experts would frown upon it as a rehabilitative philosophy. You're supposed to clean up because you want to, not because anyone else wants you to. *Mi para mi*. But it definitely works as a personal philosophy, the idea of giving yourself over to others."

[Pause.]

"How did we get on this subject?"

"We were talking about Paul Parlipiano, and I started telling you about the trip I took to the city when I was at SPECIAL."

"Oh, right."

"For the record, it *wasn't* the same summer. You were in Middlebury the summer before."

"Where was I during your SPECIAL summer?"

"I have no idea. Which was kind of the whole point of getting out of Pineville for six weeks."

"Ah, yes. I see."

"Anyway. I took a trip into the city, and I ended up standing next to Paul Parlipiano at this tiny coffee shop near the Columbia campus. He knew who I was right away, even though I hadn't seen him in, like, two years. Then again, it's probably hard to forget someone after she's puked on your shoes."

"You puked on Paul Parlipiano's shoes?"

"I was sixteen years old and drunk. I've gotten much better at holding my liquor since then."

"I hope so. You'll be happy to hear that he didn't mention the puking. He was like, 'Oh, you're Marcus Flutie, aren't you? I graduated from Pineville High a few years ahead of you. I'm Jessica's friend from Columbia.' He seemed like a good guy. We only hung out briefly. We went to a bar later that night, but he left the city the next day."

"Wait. What? You went to a bar?"

"Yes."

"Where people, like, go to drink alcohol?"

"Yes. That's what people usually do in bars."

"You hate bars."

"I hated bars when I was the only person not drinking in them."

"You drink now?"

"Socially."

"*Socially?*"

"And in moderation."

"You drink now. *Socially and in moderation.* I can't believe it. Since when? Oh my God, no. Don't even say it. I know the answer already. Right around the same time you shaved off The Beard."

"I won't say it because you said it for me. But you're right. And this time I didn't bring it up."

"You sort of did. By mentioning going to a bar with Paul Parlipiano, you knew I would ask about the drinking."

"I didn't know that for sure. I thought you might ask what we talked about."

"Okay. I'll play along. What did you and Paul Parlipiano talk about?"

"Drywall. Socialism. Deregulation as the root of all financial evil."

"Sounds like Paul."

"Brad Pitt. Protesting the Beijing Olympics. Bioremediation."

"Same save-the-world Paul."

"What heterosexuals can learn through homosexual experimentation."

"Wha—? You're not serious."

"I am."

"No!"

"Yes!"

"Marcus! Paul Parlipiano . . . *hit* on you?"

"He didn't outright proposition me. But he did spend a disproportionate amount of time trying to convince me that the research against bisexuality—the idea that you're either gay, straight, or lying—was all wrong. And you know Paul better than I do, so you're aware that he's a very persuasive debater."

"My high school crush-to-end-all-crushes almost had man sex with my ex."

"Almost?"

"Do you hear that sound? Do you? That is the sound of my heart exploding."

"*Almost?!*"

"Well, you *are* drinking again. How am I to know whether or not you've gone back to indiscriminate sex and all your other vices?"

"Indiscriminate *man* sex was never one of my vices. And for the record, I have not gone back to indiscriminate *female* sex, or drugs, or whatever other vices you might be referring to. I've learned to enjoy a few drinks every now and then among friends. That's it."

"Is that, you know, *healthy* for someone with your history?"

"I was never addicted to drugs or alcohol. Tobacco, maybe, but I kicked that habit, too. There were plenty of students at Pineville High who were far more messed up than I ever was. But I was more conspicuous, for whatever reasons."

"The same reasons that make you a conspicuous loiterer."

"Right. So my flirtation with self-destruction was harder to ignore, I guess. And I didn't do anything to dispel any myths that might have circulated around town. The less I said about myself, the easier it was for everyone else to spin their own fabulist versions of Marcus Flutie, which was fine by me. Anything to keep up the attention-getting poet-addict-manwhore mystique that was the primary conceit of my teen years."

"Well, it sure worked."

"Too well, Jessica. It worked all too well."

[Pause.]

"I don't think Paul was really into you."

"You don't? I'll try not to be insulted."

"If he was really into you, he wouldn't have given up so easily. I'll tell you who he's really hot for: my mentor. Remember Samuel Mac-Dougall? The writer? To bring this conversation full circle, he was the one who taught the writing class at SPECIAL that took the trip to New York City where I met up with Paul Parlipiano at the coffee shop."

"I just saw his latest book in the airport gift shop."

"*The Rainbow Parachute.*"

"Right. If he's selling in the airports and supermarkets, he must be doing okay for himself."

"Paul has been smitten with Mac for years. They met at my graduation party a few years back, and Paul has been semi-stalking him ever since. I mean, Paul actually signed up for one of his creative writing seminars, which I couldn't believe, because there is *nothing* creative about Paul in the least. My friend Dexy from college still refers to Paul as, like, the worst gay sidekick ever. So it was kind of funny to watch serious Paul turn into a giggly teenage girl. I mean, he was exactly like me at seventeen, when I was taking Mac's summer writing program and got so obsessed and was all, like, *got it bad, got it bad, got it bad . . . I'm hot for teacher!* It's really the first time I ever saw Paul act so irrationally, which was a refreshingly shallow change from Mr. Weight of the World."

"Did anything ever happen between them?"

"Nope. Mac rebuffed Paul's advances, citing that it was unethical and kind of shady for a teacher to have intimate relations with a student half his age."

[Throat clearing.] "Unethical and kind of shady. Of course."

[Pause.]

"So that must have been strange, bumping into someone from Pineville in the Lower Ninth Ward."

"Stranger things have happened, Jessica."

"That's true. Give me an example."

"An example?"

"A strange-but-true story. I love strange-but-true stories."

"An example of a strange-but-true story . . ."

"Come on, Marcus. There are so many to choose from."

"Don't rush me. Let's see . . . all right. I've got one. Ready?"

"Hit me."

"A Detroit man named Figlock was walking down the street. A baby fell out of a high window and landed right on top of him. Both survived. A year later, Figlock was walking down the same street. The same baby fell out of the same window and landed right on top of him. Both survived *again*."

"Yawn. If his last name were Babycatcher, then I'd be amazed. And I've heard that one already, anyway."

"An American woman was shopping in a used bookstore in Paris. She spotted a copy of her favorite book of short stories from her childhood—"

"Yeah, yeah. She opened it up to the front page and found her name written on the inside in her seven-year-old handwriting. Gimme something else. And don't insult me with the JFK–Abraham Lincoln connection, or how the twenty-dollar bill predicted September eleventh."

"I wouldn't dream of insulting you, Jessica. Not on purpose, anyway, and not so early into this reunion."

"Quit stalling. I'm still waiting to be amazed."

"Why is it that we've all heard these same strange-but-true stories?"

"It's like a form of religion, Marcus. The existence of unbelievable possibilities make us believe in the impossible."

"Ha! And you've accused *me* of spouting pseudo-philosophical bumper-sticker wisdom!"

"That was painfully bad, wasn't it? I'm sorry, it must be the pseudo-ephedrines talking . . . Or, uh, the Midol. I'm sorry."

"Jessica!"

"What?"

"You don't even realize you're doing it."

"Doing what?"

"Apologizing all the time."

"I'm— Oops! I did, didn't I?"

"For the rest of this conversation, I'm charging you a dollar every time you say 'I'm sorry.' "

"A *dollar*? How much money do you think I have?"

"Then you better mind your tongue."

"Mind your tongue?"

"Oh, man. Now, *that* sounds like a badly translated tattoo."

[Pause.]

"That was a joke, Jessica. I was making a joke."

[Pause.]

"I was just thinking that if you got 'mind your tongue' as a tattoo wrapped around your other arm, it could also be read as 'tongue your mind.' "

" 'Tongue your mind.' That's certainly evocative. I can just picture someone licking a brain, can't you?"

"I can. It's gross—yet oddly . . ."

"Sensual."

"Right."

"More *provocative* than evocative."

"Ow. Ow. Ow."

"Another wave of cramps?"

"Oh yeah. It's a menstrual tsunami in my uterus. Oh, I'm being totally gross, right? TMI! Ewwwwwwww!"

"Not at all. The female reproductive cycle is a beautiful thing. A wonderful, miraculous—"

"Are you stalling, Marcus? Because I'm still waiting."

"For what?"

"For your best strange-but-true story."

"Oh, right. Hmm . . . How about this one? Seventy-year-old Finnish twins were hit by cars while riding their bicycles. Two separate accidents on the same road. They lay comatose in adjoining hospital rooms, then died seventeen minutes apart—exactly the same amount of time between their births."

[Violent coughing fit.]

"Are you okay?"

[Still more coughing.]

"Your bullshit detector is *whoop-whoop-whooping*. You're right, Jessica. You got me. I made up that last part about the seventeen minutes, but the rest is true."

[Cough.] "No, that's not it."

"What? Are you okay? Did I say something wrong?"

"No. Just. This cold. And. Ow. These beautiful, wonderful, miraculous cramps."

"Are you trying to get me to apologize so *I* have to pay *you* a dollar?"

"Oh, so it goes both ways?"

"Of course it does. That's just fair play. So I'll ask again. Did I say something wrong? Because I won't apologize even if I did."

"You didn't say anything wrong."

"Are you sure?"

"I'm sure."

"You don't seem too sure."

"I'm sure. Uh. I was just trying to remember something."

"What?"

"A quote Mac shared with me. ' 'Tis strange—but true; for truth is always strange.' "

"Point taken: The Finnish twins story was strange but true enough as it was, without embellishment. I won't exaggerate the truth again."

"And if that quotation sounded like a bumper sticker or a bad tattoo, don't blame me."

"Who's to blame?"

"Lord Byron, I think."

"Aha! Byron is the fall guy! The scapegoat! Jessica, for the rest of this conversation, let's blame it on Byron."

"Blame *what* on Byron?"

"All of it. Anything. Everything."

"On Byron?"

"Yes, Byron."

"Why Byron?"

"Because he's the one to blame."

"For what?"

"All of it. Anything. Everything."

"I see. So Byron is the de facto asshole of assholes."

"Now you're getting it!"

"At least our nonsensical non sequiturs have literary roots."

"Want to know why this conversation isn't making any sense?"

"Let me guess. *Byron.*"

"Bingo."

[Pause.]

"So, not to put, uh, you know, undue emphasis on this particular topic or anything . . ."

"Feel free to put due emphasis on whatever topic you want, Jessica."

"Because I can always blame it on Byron."

"Exactly."

"So having a drink every now and then is part of the whole Buddhist middle-path approach to life, right?"

"I was never a Buddhist."

"Right. Are you still a deist who studies— What was it again?"

"Vipassana meditation. And not really. After years of trying, I had to own up to the fact that I'm not really the meditation type. It's too passive. I've come closer at finding inner peace through action. Doing something instead of trying to contemplate nothing. That's part of what my work in the Gulf Coast is all about. We tear houses down to the studs so they can be built again. Paul and I talked about this—the benefit of manual labor is that you can see the results right away. You tear out a door frame with a crowbar, and it's gone, you know? It's real progress, not just theoretical."

"It's the very opposite of the navel-gazing philosophy major I mistook you for."

"I wasn't going to point that out."

"That's why I didn't want to guess."

"*What's* why?"

"You know how I hate to be wrong . . ."

"Right."

"I didn't want to find out just how totally wrong I could be."

"The next time you make a mistake? *Byron.*"

"Right, I'll pin it all on Byron."

"Things will go a lot more smoothly, Jessica, if you just blame Byron."

three
(fair question)

"Oh! I'm vibrating! I mean, my phone. It's vibrating. Where is my phone? I can never find my phone."

"Isn't there a special pocket for your phone?"

"There are, like, thirty-six special pockets for my phone."

"But if you put it in the same pocket every time, you'll always know where it is. You need a system."

"A system. Gee whiz, Marcus. I never thought of that. And— Oh! I've found it. It's already stopped. Let's see . . . Oh . . ."

"Who was it?"

"Just my sister."

"Are you avoiding Bethany?"

"Not avoiding, per se, just not going out of my way to talk to her."

"Is there something going on?"

"Oh, no. Well, not really. I know why she's calling, and it's not, like, an emergency situation or anything, so . . ."

"Why is she calling?"

"She's just calling to wish me a happy b—bon voyage. It's nothing. No big. Sister stuff. You know."

"Not really. But, er, okay. How is Bethany, anyway?"

"Bethany is a happy divorcée."

"She split with what's-his-name?"

"G-Money. And yes. Two years ago."

"I can't say I'm surprised. He was always a bit of a . . ."

"Douchenozzle?"

"Well, yeah."

"The divorce is the best thing that's ever happened to Bethany— and Marin, for that matter."

"Marin! How is Marin?"

"Marin is *awesome*. And get ready, because this is going to freak you out."

"I'm ready."

"She's turning eight in June."

"Eight?"

"Eight!"

"Oh, man. I remember when she was born! How did that happen?"

"*Life* happened. You want to see her picture?"

"Yes."

"Here it is."

"Wow. She's a little knockout, isn't she?"

"She's really, really smart, too. But you can't really see that in the picture."

"Hmmm."

"What?"

"This is going to sound crazy, but I swear that I've seen this picture before."

"You've probably seen it in the advertising for the Be You Tea Shoppe."

"Advertising?"

"Oh yeah. Before the stock market tanked, Marin's face moved a few hundred thousand units of Chamomile Lowlights hair extensions to the six-to-nine-year-old starter market."

"That's it! I walked past Marin's picture hundreds of times. One of those Shoppes used to be up on Nassau Street. It was MILF HQ until it went out of business."

"That makes perfect sense. Princeton was precisely the type of high-end, upscale, affluential community targeted by Wally D's/Papa D's Retailtainment Corp. But a venture like the Be You Tea Shoppe was doomed in this economy. All the Shoppes will close by the end of this year."

"Wow. That's too bad."

"Yeah. Too bad."

"You seem oddly pleased by your sister's failure."

"I've got mixed feelings on the subject of my sister's failure."

"Elaborate."

"On the one hand, I was very proud of Bethany and how hard she's worked to turn this strangely anachronistic concept into a hip, profitable business. It was really doing well until, you know, the global economy collapsed. I mean, in an age when eight-year-old girls could go to a spa and get a Teeny-Weeny Tweeny Bikini Wax, who knew there'd be a market for girls happy to hang out and have tea parties and get mani-pedis with their moms? Or their grandmothers? But now, well, such luxuries are considered gauche. Which is a shame because working outside the home gave Bethany a sense of purpose and self-confidence that, quite frankly, shocked the hell out of me."

"How so?"

"I'll be the first to admit that I always saw my sister as being . . . well . . ."

"Shallow?"

"Yeah, shallow. No depth. Talking about the weather could strain the limits of her intellectual terrain. Or so I thought. Because it turns out my sister is perhaps one of the most complicated people I know."

"Go on."

"In her adult life, there's always been a certain duality to her personality. She could be at once completely reasonable and—though this isn't PC to say, I'm going to say it anyway—like, retarded."

"Jessica . . ."

"Hey, I would have apologized before I said that, but I didn't want to give up a dollar. But seriously, Marcus, I've sometimes wondered if there's an insidious mini–monster virus snacking on her brain cells. Remember the ten-thousand-square-foot *biodegradable* dot commune? Or when she wanted to hire *strippers* to sell a product called Donut Ho's?"

"I see your point."

"But walking out on G-Money took *balls*. I was so proud of her. So many of her friends stay in unhappy marriages because they're so afraid their lives will fall apart. Bethany really saw it as an opportunity to rebuild. And I've always admired how she's raised Marin, now more than ever. Like when she and G-Money were still together, she got a lot of shit from the MILFs—remember the Only the Best MILFs?—for not having another kid."

"I thought lots of families in the city have only one."

"Oh no, not in Bethany's circle, where four is the new two. Or, as I like to put it, four is the new stretch Hummer. It used to be that the poorest families had the most children so they could be put to work on the farm or whatever. But now mass procreation is the must-do. It's, like, the ultimate marker of economic success and prosperity. 'Even in a worldwide recession, we can afford private school for four kids! Can you?' "

"That's messed up."

"You have no idea. Bethany made it pretty clear that she's done with one. Marin satisfies all her maternal urges, which has made her a pariah among the MILFs. Like, they cannot understand why she wanted to bother with this business of hers when she got the brownstone and wife and child support in the settlement to still keep up with everything OTB."

"Only the Best."

"Right. Only now in these uncertain financial times, OTB is less ostentatious and more sanctimonious. When the MILFs aren't bragging about their kids—'Darwin is the only child in his preschool who can request paper, not plastic in six languages'—they're bitching about them—'Curie's orphan obsession has gotten totally out of hand; we have to sponsor yet another starving child from Appalachia'—in a way that's even more smug and annoying than the in-your-face praise. They don't seem all that interested in doing or talking about anything else."

"And Bethany?"

"To my surprise, she's totally over it. You know what she said to me? That every opening of a Be You Tea Shoppe was like having another kid. And I knew what she meant. That she's grateful to be a mother and wouldn't trade Marin for anything else in the world, but was eager—is *still* eager—to do something else with her life."

"So what's the problem?"

"I just wish she had chosen an industry that didn't promote a superficial value system that serves to only undermine her own daughter's sense of well-being."

"Don't most little girls pretend to be grown-ups? Didn't you play with makeup and costumes when you were little?"

"Sure I did. But I played with my mother's or Bethany's hand-me-downs. It wasn't all corporatized and out of control. At least Bethany drew the line at letting crazy mothers pay for the removal of their prepubescent daughters' nonexistent pubic hair. But what she considers harmless fun is still . . . I don't know . . . troubling to me. I mean, what six-to-nine-year-old needs lip plumpers and lowlights?"

"Plumpers? Lowlights? I have no idea what you're talking about." .

"Right! Exactly! You're a man, so your brain isn't cluttered with this superficial garbage. I didn't feel such intense pressure to pretty up and dumb down until I hit middle school. Today's girls start conforming to sexist stereotypes much, much earlier than that. Do you know what youth market analysts call this phenomenon? The HIM Effect. The Hormones in the Milk Effect. Girls are growing up so much faster. It's depressing that girls Marin's age—and younger!—are already wasting so much brain space worrying about their looks when they could be doing something far more worthwhile with their time and energy. Do you think the boys in Marin's class are so preoccupied with their appearance? No way!"

"They're too busy beating the shit out of one another."

"You're right! Maybe when conspicuous consumption is back in style, Bethany can exploit male aggression and tap into the boys' six-to-nine starter market. 'Roids 'R' Us! Get Juiced! Try the Andro Stack Wacky Pack!"

"You've put a lot of thought into this."

"More than you know. Marin is so smart and sharp in a way that, quite frankly, kind of scares me, because I don't want to see her lose the spark that makes her special. She's one of the coolest people I know, by far the most levelheaded person in the family."

"She was always a bit of a sage, wasn't she?"

"Absolutely! She can just cut through all the bullshit and get right to the truth of the matter."

"I remember one time—she must have been around four years old—she was talking about wanting to invent a robot sister doll. And when I told her it had already been invented, she said, 'Darn. By the time I'm old, everything will be done already.' And I could only agree with her, feeling exactly the same way in my twenties as she did at four."

"You're not serious."

"I am."

"Stop it. No, you're not."

"Yes, I am. What are you talking about?"

[Coughing.]

"What is it, Jessica? Are you okay?"

"Uh, yeah. It's just . . ."

"What?"

"You weren't there for that conversation."

"What do you mean?"

"That was a conversation *I* had with Marin. Not you."

"You're wrong. I remember that conversation clearly."

"You remember *reading* about that conversation *in my journal*."

"What?!"

"I wrote about that conversation with Marin in my journal. One of the two notebooks I kept during your orientation week at Princeton, you know, the week before we—"

"Whaaaaa—?"

"The notebooks I wanted you to read to help you understand why . . . you know . . ."

"I remember the notebooks. But I also remember having been there for that story—or at least I thought I was there for that story."

"You're confusing my history with your own."

"Are you . . . sure?"

"I'm positive."

"I . . . I think you're right . . . I . . ."

[Pause.]

"Don't worry about it, Marcus."

"That's just really . . . unnerving. It makes me question how many of my memories might be stolen from someone else."

"You loom large in Marin's memory, so you must have had a few meaningful conversations that actually did occur."

"I . . . ?"

"She still asks about you sometimes."

"Really? What does she ask?"

"Oh, uh. Just . . . how you're doing. That sort of thing."

"And what do you say?"

"I say I don't know how you're doing because we're not together anymore."

"And what does she respond to that?"

"She . . . uh . . ."

"I'm sorry, I shouldn't have asked that."

"*You* shouldn't have apologized. I will gladly take a dollar from you now."

"Fair's fair. Here you go."

"Thank you. It's a fair question, Marcus, and I'll answer it. Marin wants to know why we can't still be friends, even if we aren't boyfriend and girlfriend anymore, because her mom and dad got divorced but still talk to each other. And I tell her that sometimes it's just not possible to go back to being friends, but you appreciate the relationship for what it once was. That breakups are sad but part of growing up."

"You've always been so honest with her."

"I'm honest because I'm not a very good liar." [Cough.]

"I know that."

[Pause.]

"Are Bethany and G-Money involved in new relationships?"

"Uh, yeah. Why do you ask?"

"I imagine it would be easier to make the transition to friendship if you've already moved on to someone else."

"I imagine it would."

[Pause.]

"It's kind of funny, actually."

"What?"

"Well . . . Bethany got back together with a high school boyfriend."

"I-ROC Jerry? The one who only listened to Def Leppard?"

"Oh my God. I told you about I-ROC Jerry?"

"In the notebook. Either that or I'm coopting another one of your memories as my own."

"He's E-Car Jerry now, the most successful distributor of eco-friendly personal transport on the East Coast."

"No shit."

"Yes shit. In fact, I think he sold Leonardo DiCaprio a private jet that runs entirely on human waste."

"Ha."

"Thank you. So anyway, my sister was newly divorced, hadn't gone on a date since 1994, and started trawling the Internets for ex-lovers. One e-mail led to another e-mail, which led to a face-to-face reunion over coffee and . . ."

"The rest is romantic history."

"Uh, right."

[Extended pause.]

"I'll be happy to provide Marin with a status update."

"You can tell her I'm doing just great and that I think about her, too."

"You do?"

"Of course I do."

"Really?"

"Yes, Jessica; I think about it all."

four
(happy enough)

"So . . . How are your parents, Marcus? Your dad?"

"Thanks for asking. That's . . . nice."

"I wasn't asking to be nice. I don't do things just to be nice."

"Right. Because Jessica Darling would *never* live up to her last name by doing *anything* just for the sake of being—*bleurg!*—nice."

"I asked because I want to know."

"I was joking, Jessica. My dad is fine. Although he seems to think that surviving prostate cancer gives him a license to ride his motorcycle like a reckless maniac. But what can I do? I'm just his son, right? I can tell him that he's a danger to himself and everyone else on the road, but he doesn't have to listen to me."

"Yikes."

"Yikes is right. But overall, my parents are happy, I guess. At least that's what they tell me on the phone. I don't see much of them since they moved."

"My mom told me when their house was up for sale. She actually asked me whether it would be appropriate for her to offer her services as an accredited home-staging professional."

"Oh, man. At least she asked."

" 'At a discount, Jessica! I or one of my associates would provide the Fluties the full Darling's Designs for Leaving experience at a fraction of the price.' "

"You sound exactly like your mother when you do that. I mean, I haven't heard her speak in years, but wow. Your impression. It's eerie."

"I've had years of practice."

"I'm sure your mother meant well."

"I *know* she meant well. My mother always means well; she never intentionally tries to mortify me. In this case, I think she saw it as a way to help out your parents, to do them a favor to make up for . . ."

"For what?"

"For any [cough] stress our relationship might have caused you, and them [sniffle] by extension."

"Hmmmm."

"But they obviously sold the house without the benefit of the full Darling's Designs for Leaving *experience*, as my mother put it. Where are they now?"

"They spend summers at my brother's campground in Maine, swimming, fishing, spoiling their grandchildren. They spend winters in a stucco bungalow located in an over-fifty-five community in Key West. I can't believe I have parents old enough to retire to Florida. What are yours up to?"

"My parents? After thirty-whatever years together, they've discovered the key to marital bliss."

"What's that?"

"Never spending enough time together to get on each other's nerves."

"Come on, Jessica."

"I'm not being judgmental here."

"It sounds like you are."

"I'm not. I'm not judging them. I mean, I used to, you know, think it was pretty dysfunctional that my parents got along better when they never saw each other. But . . . uh . . . until I've been married as long as they have, I'm in no position to say what's a healthy relationship and what's not. So big whoop, when my mom is at her office, my dad is at home. When my mom is at home, my dad is on his bike. Is it weird that when they do choose to spend time together, it's rarely at the condo but on a cruise ship thousands of miles away? Maybe. Maybe it *is* really, really weird. But it works for them, and they seem happy enough, so . . ."

"Where do they go? Anywhere interesting?"

"Places that no one in their right mind would ever go to for a vacation."

"Like where? Iraq? Somalia?"

"Like Canada."

"Canada? What's so bad about Canada?"

"There's nothing, like, intrinsically bad *abooot* Canada. But it *is* cold. I don't know; it's just not the first place I think of when I think of a vacation. The country I considered fleeing to during the right-wing reign of terror? Yes. Vacation destination? Not so much."

"Norway used to be my top choice for expat escape fantasies. It consistently ranks number one in the world for overall quality of life."

"Have you been there?"

"Of course not. That's what makes it the ideal escape fantasy. I don't know enough about it to be discouraged by the imperfections."

"Like how it's dark, like, half the year?"

"A quarter. Between November and January. But who minds staying inside in the dark for three months when all the women look like Britt Ekland and all the men look like Dolph Lundgren?"

"Woooooow. College has done wonders for you, Marcus."

"How so?"

"You're far better equipped to drop inane pop culture references than you were three years ago. Nice work with the Ivan Drago reference."

113

"Hey, I figure lowbrow is my only way to go. How can I possibly compete with someone who oh-so-casually name-checks Jacques Lacan, Oliver Sacks, and Lord Byron?"

"Aha! So you *do* know what a Lacanian theorist is!"

"Er, yes."

"You don't need to be so modest, Marcus. And I'll bet you watched *Rocky IV* in a senior seminar at Princeton."

"How did you know? Popcorn Flicks and Hollywood's Promotion of Cold War Stereotypes in Reagan-Era America. I got an A."

"Oh, I'm sure you did. Ha. Unfortunately, any points gained for creativity are deducted for accuracy because Dolph Lundgren isn't Norwegian."

"What?"

"He's a Swede, Marcus. And for the record, so is Britt Ekland."

"They are?"

"Definitely. But it's okay. You can blame Byron for the error."

"I will, thank you. *Damn you, Byron!* And I suppose you know from Swedes from all those years living in the former bowling alley."

"I *still* live in the former bowling alley of the Swedish American Men's Athletic Club. And yes, it has made me an expert in Swedish trivia."

"I thought you had to move out after a year."

"We were supposed to leave when Manda's aunt returned from Europe with her family. She's on the lease but hasn't come back to the U.S., so we're still there."

"You still live with Manda?"

[Cough.] "Oh, no, no, no. I haven't talked to Manda in, uh, ages . . . [Cough.] A very long time. I actually see more of Sara and Scotty—you know they got married, right?"

"I didn't."

"Well, they did. After Destino and before the twins, Donatella and Dolce."

"Donatella and Dolce?"

"Named after the designers, of course."

"They've got *three* kids?"

"Oh yeah, and a long list of D-names for hypothetical fertilizations, divided by categories."

"Categories?"

"The actor D-names, like Demi and Denzel. The sports-page D-names, like Deion and Danica. The stripper D-names, like Diamond and Desire. The stripper D-names that are also cities, like Dallas and Dakota."

"Dakota isn't a city."

"Um, *I* know that. But you try interrupting Sara when she's babbling about her brood. It's impossible. And because her family is all she ever talks about, it makes it very easy to uphold my side of the conversation."

"So you see them a lot?"

"I've seen Scotty once or twice since their wedding. He works for Sara's dad in some capacity. I've been told what he does, but it's one of those job titles—junior vice president of marketing strategery—that goes in one ear and out the other. I always seem to run into Mrs. D'Abruzzi-Glazer when I'm doing errands for my parents. The Mrs. must park her SUV in the Pineville Super Foodtown lot every morning, just waiting to descend upon unsuspecting members of the Pineville High Class of 2012 to tell them all how getting accidentally knocked up at twenty-two was the best thing that ever happened to them both."

"Maybe it *is* the best thing that ever happened to them."

"Did I sound like I was being sarcastic?"

"Well, no. But you tend to take a cynical view of such things."

"What things?"

"Other people's happiness."

"I won't deny that. But in this case, I have no reason to be a cynic. Sara says she loves being a mom, Scotty loves being a dad, and they can't wait to have more kids. She appears to be fully consumed and completed by her role as a wife and mother, and that's great for her. Even when she's being totally Sara and all patronizing and obnoxious—'You're still young! You have plenty of good eggs left in you! All this will happen for you, too, sweetie!'—I'm still happy for her. I'm happy that she's found domestic bliss in the 'burbs. I'm probably happier for her and Scotty than

115

I am for most people, if only because theirs is a type of happiness I don't want for myself."

"Ever?"

[Cough.] "Not right now."

[Pause.]

"What was the name of Manda's partner, the baggy-pants, break-dancing gangsta who didn't conform to the gender binary?"

"Shea. Why do you ask?"

"I thought I saw her when I was in the city a few weeks ago. If it was her, she's a bike messenger. Just as her face registered as familiar, she took off."

"Wait, you saw her in the city, as in New York City?"

"Yes."

"The same city that you hated and never wanted to visit? The same city that provoked debilitating anxiety attacks?"

"The same."

"So am I to assume that *the city* is something else you've learned to appreciate socially and in moderation?"

"Something like that. Only I wasn't there for social reasons. [Throat clearing.] So was it Shea? Is she a bike messenger?"

"I have no idea. Manda and Shea moved out after the first year. It's just me and Hope until Ursula decides to kick us out."

"Ursula! Oh man, this conversation is really getting nostalgic. I haven't thought about her in years."

"You probably blocked out her memory. A common post-traumatic-stress response."

"She accused me of housing cockroaches in my dreadlocks."

"Yes, well, I assure you that she's as charming as ever. Why, just the other day, she told Hope how she's come to love us like the daughters she never had. 'You almost make me regret getting all zose abortions.' "

"Almost. That's classic."

"So Hope and I still live in the same apartment, but we have our own rooms now. No more bunk beds for me! I bought a big-girl bed of my very own."

"Your parents must be proud."

"Oh yes. *Very* proud. They've put a picture of my big-girl bed up on the refrigerator. Not me, just the bed."

"What parent wouldn't? I wish I could see it for myself."

"The picture on the refrigerator or the bed?"

"For the sake of propriety, I'll say the picture."

"Good answer, Marcus. Good answer."

[Pause.]

"So . . . how is Hope?"

"Well, she dropped out of school."

"She did? Why? I thought she wanted to get her master's in art therapy. If there's anyone meant to work with disaffected youth, it's her."

"Ow."

"You okay?"

"Damn cramps."

"You sure?"

"I'm *sure*. Uh. Anyway. Hope never *really* wanted to work with kids. Graduate school was just her fallback plan. She really wanted to be an artist."

"I guess that makes sense."

"Cinthia bought a few of Hope's paintings to decorate her new apartment, which is really like the equivalent of six apartments stacked on top of each other. You met Cinthia once or twice, right? So you know she's a force of nature, someone who can singlehandedly cultivate or kill a trend without even trying. She threw a housewarming party, and a bunch of her well-connected friends saw the paintings and just had to get one or two or a few for themselves, and, well, Hope's career just kind of blew up from there. She didn't really see the point in continuing her education. She wants to open up a gallery that showcases and sells the work of young artists who wouldn't otherwise have opportunities to do so."

"How many people can say they're making a living doing what they would do for free?"

"I know, right?"

"Good for her."

"Yeah. It is. It really is. She's totally in love, too."

"The same boyfriend from college?"

"Nope. She broke up with— What was his name? Oh my God. I've forgotten that guy's name. I totally overheard him engaging in the most intimate of acts with my best friend in the top bunk, and now I can't even remember his name. How bad is that?"

[Throat clearing.] "Oh, I can think of worse things to forget."

"This is really going to bother me. I'm tempted to call Hope right now and ask her. 'Hey, Hope, what was the name of your college boyfriend, you know, the one you used to quietly have sex with in the top bunk in the middle of the night when you thought I was asleep?' W-W-W-ade? It starts with a W, I think. W-W-Wyatt? Oh, what does it matter? He's long gone. They broke up not too long after . . . uh . . . They broke up a few years ago. It was, like, the most mutual, untraumatizing breakup in history. As far as I know, they still . . ."

"Still what?"

"Keep in touch."

"I see."

[Cough.] "So. Uh. Yeah. Hope's ex-boyfriend—Christ, what's his *name?*—even introduced Hope to her new boyfriend, which made him feel better about his own new girlfriend, who I think was also a friend of Hope's at RISD."

"It sounds very incestuous. You'd think with six billion people in the world . . ."

[Pause.]

"Uh. Yeah. So. Hope's been seeing the new guy, Jonas—hey, at least I can remember *his* name—for a few months now. He's a sculptor. Together they're like this perfectly adorable artsy urban couple that advertisers should use to sell an edgy, ethical, eco-friendly product. Like a so-ugly-it's-cute little car that gets a hundred miles to the gallon. Or something like that. Dammit, it's right on the tip of my tongue . . ."

"See? This is why you need to mind your tongue, Jessica."

"Christ. I don't know why this is bothering me so much. *What was that guy's name?*"

"So the sculptor. The new guy. He's a good guy? You like him?"

"I don't know him all that well, to be honest. But he calls when he says he'll call, shows up when he says he'll show up. He pays his own rent and hasn't been caught in any compromising positions on MySpace. So I guess by today's relaxed dating standards, that makes him a good enough guy. He makes Hope happy, which is what really matters, right?"

"You and Hope are still close, though, even without the bunk beds?"

"Oh yeah. We're still very close, though my job requires a lot of travel, so I don't get to see her as much as I'd like to. I was looking forward to catching up with her in St. John. She's down there already. I'm sort of jealous."

"About her getting down there before you?"

"Right . . . Wynn! His name was Wynn! Oh, thank God. I feel so much better now."

"I'm glad."

"The whole world can collectively exhale."

"What a relief."

"Yes, I can finally move on with my life."

five
(nothing meaning something)

"Oh, man, forget Byron. *I'm* the asshole."

"Why are you giving me a dollar, Marcus?"

"Advance payment for my apology."

"What apology?"

"This one: I'm sorry that I haven't even asked what *you're* doing. You mentioned traveling a lot, and I realized I had absolutely no idea what you're doing."

"Oh."

"Oh what?"

"Nothing. You don't have to ask me about my job just to be . . ."

"Nice?"

"Right. *Nice.*"

"I'm asking about your job because I'm curious to hear what you've been up to for the past three years."

"You really have no idea what I've been up to?"

"No, I don't. Why, should I? Are you notorious?"

[Cough.] "No!" [Cough.]

"What?"

"Nothing. Let's talk about my job."

"Are you going to make me guess first?"

"Do you want to?"

"In the interest of fair play, sure."

"Okay. Go ahead and guess."

"Let me think. You travel a lot. And . . . let me see . . . well . . . you really haven't provided any other clues."

"Go with your gut."

"My gut. Okay. My gut tells me you're doing something involving psychology and writing. Some sort of research, maybe? Involving travel . . . hmmm . . . You're studying . . . I don't know . . . demographical differences in narratives?"

[Pause.]

"Am I close?"

[Long sigh.] *"Marcus."*

"What?"

"Nothing."

"Seriously, Jessica. *What?*"

"Oh, come on, you know what."

"I honestly don't know."

"If I say something that makes me sound like an asshole, I can blame it on Byron, right?"

"Sure."

"When you guessed about my job . . . No, I don't need to say this to you. It's nothing."

"I swear I've never heard someone speak so much of nothing when she obviously means something."

[Pause.]

"Have you Googled me?"

[Pause.]

"No. I haven't Googled you."

"Not once?"

"No."

[Pause.]

"I choose to believe you."

"You should. Because I'm telling you the truth."

[Pause.]

"Have *you* Googled *me*?"

[Sigh.] "I confess that I have, though not recently. I quit cold turkey because it was always so . . . anticlimactic. You're, like, one of the last un-Googleable people left on the planet. Or you were when I last tried it. Anyway, getting back to your guesses, you could make a killing as a mind-reader."

"I didn't read your mind."

"I know that! But you did what any fake psychic does. You used what little you did know about me from what I had said throughout our conversation, and you made educated guesses based on those clues. Then you carefully watched my body language in response to those clues and made more educated guesses. It's all Professor Marvel, *Wizard of Oz* bullshit."

"So you don't believe in clairvoyance. You don't believe that anyone can accurately predict events in the future."

"No reputable scientific study has ever supported the idea of a sixth sense."

"Hmmm."

"Hmm, what?"

"So I take it that my guess was pretty close, huh?"

"I'm the cofounder and head of development for the Do Better High School Storytellers project, a nonprofit creative writing and mentoring program."

"Jessica!"

"What?"

"That's amazing!"

"What? My job? Or your guess?"

"I was referring to your job. Though my guess wasn't that far off, was it? No wonder you thought I Googled you."

"Though you missed the part about how *I'm* the one who works with disaffected youth, not Hope."

"Are you annoyed about that?"

"About what?"

"The assumption that Hope was the one working with disaffected youth and not you."

"Why would you ask that?"

"The furrow in your forehead. The tone in your voice."

"I'm MMS-ing, okay?"

"Mmmmmm?"

"Mid-menstrual-syndrome-ing. And what? You don't think there's enough disaffected youth for the both of us? There's plenty, I assure you."

"By all means, assure me. Tell me more, because I'm already very impressed."

"Oh, don't be too impressed. The whole thing wouldn't even exist without Cinthia's Do Better seed money."

"Jessica, stop being so modest. That's just an underhanded form of apology. I'll have to charge you a dollar if you do it again."

"Well, it's true! Without Cinthia's money, the idea wouldn't have survived long enough to even qualify as an epic fail."

"Did Cinthia conceptualize this program?"

"Uh, no. I did."

"Did Cinthia strategize? Organize? Put those concepts into practice? Make them a reality?"

"No, no, no, and no. That was all me, too. With a team, of course."

"A team assembled by who?"

"Okay. You've made your point. I am a *genius*! And you don't even know what I actually *do* yet."

"You're right. Tell me."

"Basically, I travel to high schools all over the country that have applied for and won High School Storytellers grants. Priority goes to schools that have lost funding for arts programs because of budget cuts."

"There are far too many to choose from, I'm sure."

"Hundreds. And we're still pretty small; there's only a half-dozen of us mentors so far. We work with the students a few times a week for about ten weeks—a marking period. Between us all, we can only hit about twenty schools a year."

"Still, Jessica, you're doing something, which is better than nothing."

"Except when nothing means something, right?"

"Ha! Of course."

[Pause.]

"Since you're so good at guessing games, guess what school, of all the schools in the entire country, was the first to benefit from the Do Better High School Storytellers project?"

"Pineville High?"

"It was no accident, of course."

"Jessica, there are no accidents."

"Wait. What? Did you just say there are no accidents? How can you really believe that, Marcus?"

"As a fan of strange-but-true stories, Jessica, I would think that you, too, would believe in a causally connected reality."

"Spare me the quasi-Bodhi-shitty wisdom, Marcus."

"What wisdom?"

" '_There are no accidents. We are all life, and all life is limitless. One is all and all is one. I am he as you are he as you are me and we are the walrus, goo goo g'joob.'_ "

"I was actually referring to Jung's notion of the collective unconscious."

"Woooow."

"What now, woooow?"

"Woooow, now look who's getting all highbrow."

"You're mocking me, aren't you?"

"Just a little bit."

"See what I get for trying to elevate myself to your level?"

"Perhaps you should stick to the *Rocky IV* references from now on."

"I'll keep that under consideration. However, since you're a lover of strange-but-true stories, I'm sure you know this one: Carl Jung has a patient who dreams of a rare golden scarab, then a scarab flies in through his office window."

"Yes, it's a fantastic if timeworn strange-but-true story, Marcus. But you don't believe in accidents? Really?"

"I believe . . ."

"You could tell me a million strange-but-true stories, and they still cannot prove that we experience everything in life by cosmic design. And you know why, Marcus? Because there *are* accidents. Horrible, tragic accidents that hurt innocent people who don't deserve it."

[Pause.]

"If I said something wrong, Jessica, I'm sorry."

[Pause.]

"You owe me a dollar."

[Pause.]

"Seriously, Jessica. You seem upset. I'm sorry."

"*Seriously*, Marcus. You really suck at the no-apologies game. You owe me another dollar."

"Jessica . . ."

"Just drop it, okay?"

"Here's your money."

"Thank you."

"You're welcome. I guess."

"And fuck you, Byron, wherever you are."

six
(intriguing slush)

"Now, Marcus, what was I saying before everyone within earshot rolled their eyes at the pretentious turn in our conversation?"

"Pineville."

"Oh yeah. How I ended up back at Pineville High. Even after all these years, Cinthia still feels so guilty about *Bubblegum Bimbos and Assembly-Line Meatballers* and how it, you know, immortalized our high school as a symbol of all that's dumb and debauched about suburban youth. She kind of forced me to go there first as a way of making up for past sins."

"I haven't been within a half-mile of that place since we graduated. Oh, man, that must have been . . ."

"Surreal. You thought navigating the cafeteria was treacherous? There's a little place called the teacher's lounge, my friend, and it is where the human spirit goes to die."

"I can't even imagine. Are our old teachers still there?"

"I think the Class of '02 might have forced them all into early retirement. Except for good ol' Miss Haviland, who is still giving power to the young people, still rocking our nation back to its revolutionary roots one Honors English class at a time."

"You know, in retrospect, she really wasn't all that bad. She was just trying to motivate us, which is more than I can say for just about every other teacher I had."

"I know. And once I got to know Haviland as, like, a real person, she's actually pretty cool in a crazy-hippie-lady kind of way. I actually felt kind of bad about nicknaming her Miss Havisham for all those years. But there was no mistaking her gratitude for the infusion of funds. Pineville had eliminated all its expendable arts programs. No more music, no more drama, and no more extracurricular writing, including her beloved newspaper, *The Seagull's Voice*."

"And we thought Pineville sucked when we were there."

"I assure you that it sucks even more now. But at least I helped get the newspaper up and running again, both in print and online. It sounds totally corny, but . . ."

"What?"

"I feel like I made a difference, you know? Because for me, writing for the high school newspaper . . . Oh, forget it."

"No, I won't forget it, Jessica. Go on!"

"Writing for that stupid paper . . ." [Long sigh.] "Changed my life."

"How so?"

"Ugh. I hate to even say it because it's so . . . I don't know . . . *melodramatic*. But . . ."

"What?"

"*The Seagull's Voice* gave *me* a voice."

"You always had a voice, Jessica. You just weren't encouraged to use it until then."

"Okay, right. It's true that before Haviland forced me to write for the paper, I only bitched about the tragic indignities of high school life in my journals or in letters to Hope. But writing those editorials when I was sixteen, seventeen . . . it was the first time I found the courage to speak out loud about issues that were important to me."

"Why are you laughing?"

"Because working with teenage girls for the past two years has helped remind me how *everything* matters so much when you're sixteen years old. A whispered secret is an opera. A one-word text is epic. A dirty look is drama, drama, *draaaaaamaaaaa*. Every minute of every day is *so* intense in a way that fades with time. I knew for sure that I had gotten *really fucking old* when thinking about all those vitally important issues from my sophomore year only made me embarrassed for my former self."

" 'Homecoming King and Queen: Democracy at Its Dumbest.' "

"Oh my God, Marcus. You *remember* that? I barely remember that!"

" 'Vegetable Medley Mayhem: A Food Fight Against Cafeteria Tyranny.' "

"That wasn't even one of my best."

"Your best? That would have to be the first one you ever wrote: 'Miss Hyacinth Anastasia Wallace: Just Another Poseur.' "

"I have to agree with you on that, if only because some would say it's still topical ten years later."

[Pause.]

"Before you wrote that editorial, I thought you were . . ."

"What?"

"Oh, never mind."

"Oh, never mind my *ass*, Marcus."

126

"Intriguing."

"Intriguing."

"But . . ."

"There had to be a but."

"Icy."

"Intriguing but icy?"

"Yes."

"Like wasabi sorbet!"

"Okay, like wasabi sorbet. But after that editorial . . ."

"Mount Everest!"

"*Fine*. You were like Mount Everest."

"A polar bear! A polar bear . . . uh . . ."

"With a Ph.D. in the semiotics of snow. Are you finished yet, Jessica?"

"Uh . . . I think so. Yes."

"After that editorial, I wanted to get to know you better."

"Warm me up? Make me melt? Reduce me to a pool of, uh, intriguing slush?"

"I'm officially ignoring you now, Jessica."

"No, go ahead. Finish what you were going to say."

"That editorial inspired our first real conversation, remember? You were limping home on crutches, and I offered you a ride home in the Caddie?"

[Cough. Cough. Cough.] "The Caddie! How is the Caddie?"

"The Caddie has passed on."

"It died?"

"That car was almost forty years old. Its time had come."

"I am shocked by how sad this news has made me. You must have been devastated when it rode off into the big ol' scrapyard in the sky. You *loved* that car."

"I did. But I've loved and lost before, so . . ."

"So."

"We could have a moment of silence, if that would make you feel better."

"I think it might."

[Moment of silence.]

"See? You *can* still feel things intensely. You know, even though you're *so fucking old*."

"Har-dee-har-har."

seven
(turning point of view)

"So, Grannypants, what do you do with your disaffected youth?"

"I'm one of those half-dozen mentors, of whom I am by far the least qualified. They all have M.F.A.s and Ph.D.s, but I've got the rich philanthropist friend willing to drop major coin on a whim."

"You're apologizing via modesty again."

"Well, it's true. My comparative lack of education is one of the reasons I've applied to graduate school."

"Really. Where? If you don't mind me asking."

"Teachers College. It's the graduate school of education—"

"At Columbia. Yes, I know."

"Then you're familiar with it?"

"Yes. [Throat clearing.] I am."

"Anyway, we work with a school staff member; it's usually the favorite English teacher or adviser of the school newspaper. At Pineville, it was Haviland, of course. That staff member selects twenty students—five from each grade level—to participate in a ten-week after-school writing seminar that culminates with a public reading and collection of the Girls' work in an anthology."

"So they're all aspiring writers?"

"Some are. Other Girls are encouraged to come because they're considered high-risk and can benefit from narrative therapy."

"All girls? You keep saying 'girls.' "

"A habit. The program isn't exclusive to girls, but, like, the vast majority of the participants are girls. As a former teenage boy, why do you think that's the case?"

"I don't know. Because teenage boys are idiots? As you pointed out earlier, I would have joined _because_ the vast majority of the participants were girls."

"Of course you would have! Which would have done wonders for your . . . What did you call it again? Your 'poet/addict mystique'?"

"You forgot 'manwhore.' But yes, it would have been great for that, only if I didn't actually participate. I would have needed to show up at every single session for ten weeks but never say or do or contribute anything."

"Right! But then on the very last day, you would have raised your hand. And the room would've fallen silent, all eyes and ears on you. And you would've opened your mouth and uttered something totally random and absurd. Something like . . . 'Blame Byron!' "

"Something exactly like that."

[Pause.]

"So how does your psychology background factor in to all this?"

"It's therapeutic creativity. Risk prevention through personal expression."

"Ah, yes, arts and crafts are a crucial component of any rehabilitation program. You should have seen the set of _Super Mario Brothers_ statues I made out of Popsicle sticks."

"Really?"

"Yes, really. It wasn't easy, because we had to use this special nonintoxicating glue substitute that didn't stick together very well. I suffered for my art."

"I didn't even know you played _Super Mario Brothers_."

"I didn't. But others did. I knew I could trade them for contraband cigarettes."

"_Really?_"

"Yes, really, Jessica. Why do you find this so hard to believe?"

"I don't find it hard to believe your stories. Your stories are very credible. I just find it hard to believe that I've never heard them before."

129

"I guess the subject of *Super Mario Brothers* never came up."

"I guess not."

[Pause.]

"So, risk prevention?"

"Oh, right. So, humans are, uh, uniquely adapted for narrative constructions. Studies indicate that we begin to see ourselves as characters in our own life stories in adolescence, with key periods serving as different chapters. The most dramatic events are presented as the key scenes to the overall plot, the high points and low points of one's life story. You remember the inscription to the journal you gave me? You said, 'The tales we tell ourselves about ourselves make us who we are.' "

"I did?"

"You did. So you understand the concept. But storytelling not only defines who we already are, it also has the power to determine who we will be."

"Interesting."

"When faced with major decisions, adults turn to their personal historical narratives as a guide. Teenagers, however, have far fewer volumes to choose from in their autobiographical library—they haven't lived through as much success and failure and . . . ugh."

"What?"

"I'm taking this right from the Do Better High School Storytellers mission statement. I hate when I catch myself sounding like a Power-Point presentation, like I've forgotten how to think and speak for myself."

"It's okay, go on. I want to hear about this."

"Basically, we encourage teenagers to recount the past in a way that will help them make more informed choices in the future."

"What do they write about?"

"Everything."

"Can you give me an example?"

"Uh . . ."

"Not the whole thing, obviously. Just the gist."

"I don't know."

"Oh, if it violates some sort of ethical code of confidentiality . . ."

"It's not that. It's just. Uh. Well . . ."

"I don't want to put you on the spot."

"You're not putting me on any . . . uh . . . spot. There's no spot for me to be put on. Or, uh, rather, I mean there's no spot on which I can be put. On which you can put me."

"Now you're really talking like a bad tattoo."

"It's a plague."

"A contagious babble."

"Spread by a Byronic sneeze."

[Pause.]

"Okay. My favorite essay was a mockery of the genre. A girl wrote about flipping over on a hammock, falling on her face, and becoming anosmic."

"What's that?"

"She lost her sense of smell."

"Oh. Anosmic. Good word. Like you're anosmic right now."

"What?"

"Because of that nasty cold of yours. Which seems to be doing much better, I must add."

"It [sniff] comes and goes."

"Right."

"Anyway, the essay concluded with something like 'She learned two invaluable life lessons from this experience. She might have lost her sense of smell, but she gained a sense of self. After all, she was never the type of girl who would stop to smell the roses, but now she wouldn't have to pretend that she was.' "

"That's pretty good."

"It's not the best part. The kicker was 'And the other lesson she learned was this: Never fuck in a hammock.' "

"Ha!"

"It's even funnier when . . . when . . . uh . . ."

[Pause.]

"Jessica?"

"Huh?"

"You just kind of stopped in the middle of a sentence."

"I did?"

"You did."

"I *did*. I'm so sorry, I'm just really dis—"

"Distracted, I know. Now give me a dollar."

"A dollar? For what— Oh, dammit. Here it is."

"Thank you."

"You're still down by two."

"This conversation isn't over yet."

"No, it's not."

"How's it going so far?"

"What? The conversation?"

"Yes. The conversation. Are you enjoying yourself?"

[Pause.]

"Yes, I am."

"I am, too."

[Pause.]

"Is it going the way you thought it would?"

"No . . . and yes."

"Meaning?"

"I didn't really know how it would go, but in that unpredictable sense, it's going exactly as I thought it would."

"I'm in full agreement."

[Long pause.]

"Now look what's happened."

"I know! Our in-the-moment analysis of our conversation brought it to a dead stop."

"Let's avoid getting meta-conversational again. Let's just talk."

"Sure. Let's just talk. There's just one problem."

"What's that?"

"I totally forgot what I was talking about. I lost my train of thought."

"You were talking about the girl who had never fucked in a hammock."

"Right, her. Her . . ."

"And the essay was funny because . . ."

"It was funny because, uh, she had never even kissed a boy when she wrote it. Hey, excuse me for a moment, okay? I'm just going to check to see if I missed any calls."

"Are you expecting to hear from someone?"

"Sort of. Maybe. But . . . nope. No missed calls."

"Do you need to make a call? I don't mind."

"Do I need to make a call? Uh, no. It's fine. I can wait. It's . . . perfectly fine. Perfect."

[Pause.]

"Do they only write personal essays, or . . . ?"

"No, no. We do exercises in all kinds of forms and genres. Non-fiction, fiction, screenwriting, poetry. But as an introductory writing exercise, we ask them to recount a turning point in their lives."

"Like the classic first-person college application essay."

"No, actually. The first-person essay has become such a cliché, you know? By the time they hit high school, they've already written so many first-person turning-point essays that they've run out of turning points. That's why we make them write that first assignment in the third person."

"Third person? Why?"

"Brace yourself for another two-hundred-and-fifty-thousand-dollar word."

"Two hundred and fifty thousand?"

"The average sticker price of four years at an Ivy League college."

"Oh. Okay. Consider me braced."

"Prosopopoeia."

"It sounds just like the last quarter-million-dollar word."

"That was 'prosopagnosia.' This is 'prosopopoeia.' "

"Well, no duh."

" 'Prosopopoeia' is a literary device in which a writer speaks as another person."

"Okay."

"Research has shown that when you tell a story in the omnipotent third person, it creates a buffer between the narrator and the character in the story, even when the story is autobiographical and the protagonist is a version of yourself. Still with me?"

"I'm still with you."

"That shift in point of view helps painful stories feel less painful. You become an objective observer of all the Sturm und Drang and not the unfortunate person going through it. Therapeutically speaking, we hope the writer can actually learn something about herself and how she goes about making certain life choices . . . Ugh. I'm sorry, this is all from the mission statement again."

"Gimme a dollar."

"Dammit. Here you go, Marcus. Don't spend it all in one place."

"Thank you. What a shame. You were on such a roll."

"Now we're even. Deadlocked."

"It's not a game, Jessica."

"It's not?"

"Oh, well, I suppose it is."

[Pause.]

"I was waiting for you to call me the Game Master. Were you tempted to call me the Game Master?"

"I judiciously refrained. That's so senior-year-of-high-school, isn't it?"

"You've evolved."

"Oh yeah, I've totally, *totally* evolved. I'm, like, way, way more mature than to resort to high school taunts."

"Even for nostalgia's sake?"

"*Especially* for nostalgia's sake. Now, what was I saying earlier?"

"The third p—"

"Oh, right. The third person. We call this writing exercise the turning point of view. The change in narrative perspective triggers an internal psychological shift that allows you to see past decisions in a whole new way. It's similar to when you see a friend making a huge mistake and it's just so obvious."

"Yet at the same time, you're blind to your own foibles."

"Right."

[Pause.]

"What about happy stories, Jessica?"

"Happy stories?"

"Yes. Happy stories with happy endings."

[Long sigh.] "Unfortunately, Marcus, there aren't enough of those. But . . ."

eight
(doth protesting)

"Hold that thought—now *I'm* vibrating. Let me see who it is. Oh, never mind."

"Who was it?"

"No one I need to talk to right now, either."

"Anyone I know?"

"Do you remember meeting my roommate, Natty?"

"The freckle-faced little boy from Alabama?"

"That freckle-faced little boy from Alabama is all grown up. He's a Rhodes Scholar."

"That *child* is a Rhodes Scholar? Oh my God. *I'm so fucking old.*"

"*You're* old? I'm ten years older than my lab partner. She barely remembers boy bands."

"That is a serious gap in her knowledge. How did she even get in to Princeton?"

"I know. She knew very little about the rivalry between the Backstreet Boys and *NSYNC. I had to educate her."

"That's important work."

"Indeed."

"So you and Natty are still friends."

"Yes. He's my best friend at school. He can be an immature, er, dick, for lack of a better word, but that's just part of his charm. He's like the pain-in-the-ass little brother I was but never had."

"Talk about strange but true."

"You don't know the half of it. Natty's parents waged a campaign to have me kicked out of school."

"Are you serious?"

"Serious. Of course, that only made Natty even more determined to be my friend, as these parental social interventions tend to do."

"How did they try to get you kicked out? And why?"

"Why? They hated me on sight. And really, who could blame them, right? The Addisons of Alabama had spared no expense in molding their son—a mediocre student and hopeless athlete—into the very model of an Ivy League superachiever. They knew how much time, effort, and money it took to win a coveted spot in Princeton's Class of 2010. One look at my dreads, my tats, my terrorist beard, and they were one hundred percent convinced that I was an impostor admitted to Princeton under fraudulent pretenses. There had been a few cases of older students with untraditional backgrounds faking transcripts and test scores to get into top schools, and Dr. Addison was damned before he was going to let another one besmirch his alma mater's good name."

"What happened?"

"They hired a private investigator to run a background check."

"No!"

"Yes. My academic record has more holes than a paper target at a firing range. One incomplete after another. The Addisons tried to argue that I never technically graduated from high school and was therefore ineligible for enrollment as a first-year student."

"Obviously, nothing came of it, right? Because you're still graduating this spring."

"Princeton investigated my application and ultimately stood by my acceptance."

"That's a relief."

"It should have been."

"What do you mean?"

"A big part of me agreed with the Addisons. I *was* a fraud. I had willfully deluded myself into thinking I was anything other than a deviant low-life dreg. They were right! I didn't belong in the Ivy League!

I didn't deserve to walk among their privileged ranks! And why would I even want to?"

"Marcus, you're being way too hard on yourself."

"I second-guessed my reasons for applying in the first place. What was I hoping to gain from a diploma from Princeton that I couldn't get anywhere else? Sure, a Princeton diploma is a passport to opportunities, but I was motivated by far more than job prospects."

"Validation, maybe? That you had transcended your trashy roots? I felt that way after I got in to Columbia. After all, our town had semi-famously become the representation of dumb, debauched suburban youth."

"Maybe. But more of a redemption, I think. Applying to Princeton made me both a con artist *and* the conned."

"How so?"

"I knew the Office of Admissions would come all over itself at the sight of my application. See? The American meritocracy is not a myth. I could serve as living proof that anyone who works hard enough can rise above his station into the upper tiers of society. Which, of course, is total horseshit. Because the moment I found myself among the elite, the elite—as personified by the Addisons—wanted no part of me. I kept asking myself: *Does being here make me a better person, or even a different person, than who I was before?* I felt like a fool, a millennial Fitzgerald simultaneously trying to fit in to and fight against the hypocritical foundations of the American class system."

"Uh, wow. To quote you from earlier: You've obviously put a lot of thought into this."

"And to quote you right back, Jessica: more than you know."

"You said yourself that a lot of that dregginess was an exaggeration."

"A lot but not all. Despite my best efforts to be the biggest fuckup I could be."

"I don't believe that you went out of your way to make bad choices when you were a kid."

"I beg to differ, Jessica. I was held back in kindergarten. Do you know why?"

"You sexually propositioned the lunch lady?"

"That was fifth grade."

"Late bloomer."

"No, I was held back for being an underachiever. I was this close to being a kindergarten dropout."

"Just like the book."

"There's a book?"

"Yeah, there's a book. *Kindergarten Dropout: Underachiever at Six, Unwanted at Eighteen, Unemployed at Thirty, Dead at Sixty.* Or some crap like that. It's a huge best seller. I've seen the MILFs poring over it at Bethany's place."

"You're kidding."

"I'm not. I wish I were. I think the child psychologist–slash–author–slash–evil genius appeared on *Dr. Frank Show* a few years ago. You obviously predate the book and the hysteria that followed it."

"Gee, I'm so proud to be a part of the slacker vanguard. Let's just say I scored extremely well on a pre-K IQ test, and my parents thought I wasn't living up to my expectations in kindergarten. So they held me back to teach me a lesson, I guess. I needed a strong dose of discipline to rise to the standards of my IQ test. The only lesson I learned was that I was bad."

"You *weren't* bad. You were probably just bored."

"You're right. But I grew up feeling like I was always already in trouble for one reason or another. After a while I decided to live up to that rebellious reputation, since I was getting punished for it anyway. And guess what? It turned out that I was very, very good at being bad. Too good. And now, years later, that disreputable label still clings to me, Jessica."

" '*We are what we pretend to be. So we must be careful what we pretend to be.*' "

"Exactly. That's exactly right. Who said that?"

"I can't remember who said it first, but I heard it from Mac—you know, Samuel MacDougall—years ago, and I never forgot it. He has a habit of offering inspiring quotations for every occasion. I wish I could remember who originated the pretend-to-be quote. I like to give credit where credit is due. Especially when I come off sounding like a bumper sticker."

"Or a bad tattoo."

"Vonnegut! Kurt Vonnegut!"

"Now you can move on with your life. *Again.*"

"Yes, I can. Okay. So what I don't get is . . . you were under eighteen when you got in the most trouble, right? You were a minor. Aren't those youthful indiscretions considered privileged information? How could the Addisons access any of those records?"

"They had ties to the Bush White House. My kindergarten report card was clearly a matter of national security."

"You're kidding."

"Barely. That's the irony of the situation; they couldn't even get their hands on the worst of it. They couldn't get police reports or rehab charts or any psychiatric evaluations from that time period. Just my Pineville High transcripts."

"They probably bribed Brandi in the guidance department to get those. Do you remember Brandi?"

"I can't say that I do. Which one was Brandi?"

"She looked like she was auditioning for the role of Nympho Hood Ornament in an eighties hair-band video."

"Hmm . . . I saw so many counselors and therapists and psychiatrists between the ages of twelve and eighteen that they kind of blend together."

"Brandi was the only one I was ever forced to talk to. I guess that's why I remember her so vividly."

"Why did you have to talk to her?"

"My tenth-grade chem teacher thought I was suicidal."

"You were suicidal?"

"No. I just enjoyed writing suicidal lyrics on my book covers."

"Who doesn't at sixteen?"

"Exactly. But my suicidal song lyrics were misinterpreted by my chemistry teacher as a desperate cry for help. So I had to go down to guidance and talk to Brandi about my *feelings.*"

"Oh, man. Talking about feelings is *the worst.*"

"The worst. But it turned out not to be a complete waste of time."

"How so?"

"Well . . . uh . . . Oh, never mind."

"What? You can't stop now. That's not fair."

"Do you remember bumping into me right outside her office?"

"Me? And you? Outside her office?"

"You don't remember that?"

"I'm trying to remember, Jessica."

"Oh, come on, Marcus. You remembered the titles of my editorials and our conversation in the Caddie. You remembered a story about Marin that you didn't experience firsthand. You can't remember this?"

"Honestly, Jessica, I can't say that I do."

[Cough. Sniffle.] "Oh, it's no big deal." [Sniffle.]

"I'm sorry, Jess—"

"Ha! Pay up, sucka!"

"Did you just trick me into apologizing?"

"Maybe, maybe not."

"Here. Now you're one up."

"Thank you. And for the record, I probably wouldn't remember seeing you outside her office, either. Only . . . well . . . that's the first time I ever wrote about you in my journal."

"Really?"

"Really."

"And what did you have to say about me?"

"Hmmmm . . . I think I said that crackheaded girls who didn't know any better thought you were sexy. Then I went on for many, many paragraphs doth protesting too much about how I just didn't understand your appeal."

"Doth protesting too much. That's classic. I do believe that sums up a lot."

"About what?"

"About . . . oh, wait, hold that thought. My phone is vibrating again. It's Natty again. Only this time he sent— *Dude*."

"What?"

"He sent a picture. Do you want to see it?"

[Pause.]

"Those are two of the biggest, fakest, roundest tits I've ever seen. Where was this picture taken?"

"New Jersey Transit."

"Oh, nice. And did you see the message? 'Venn Diagram: Ho/Hot.' And look, he included an adorable little emoticon rendering of big, fake, round tits just in case we didn't get the joke. Such clever use of parentheses as a visual aid. No wonder he's a Rhodes Scholar."

"You won't get another dollar out of me, Jessica. I'm not making any apologies for his behavior."

"Well, you told me he was an immature dick. It turns out he's sexist, too!"

"Sometimes, yes. He is. But that has nothing to do with this picture. He sent it because he's looking out for me."

"Because he knows how much you appreciate a ginormous silicone rack?"

"No. He's trying to embarrass me by association. He sent that picture to protect me."

"Protect you? From what?"

"Not what. Who."

"Who?"

"From you."

"*Me?* Why me? And how does he even know you're with me?"

[Throat clearing.] "Er, he knows because I told him."

"When?"

"Right after you ran me over but before you rescued me."

"You called him?"

"I . . . told him. I needed to tell someone about it, to confirm that it had actually happened. Why, you didn't tell anyone? Didn't you say you talked to Hope earlier? You didn't say anything to her?"

"Uh, no. Actually, I didn't. But like I said, Marcus, I'm really, really distracted today. My brain is going in too many different directions."

"Oh, sure, I can see how you could forget to mention seeing me for the first time in three years. I can see how that would slip your mind."

[Pause.]

"So, Natty doesn't approve of me, huh?"

"Not you as a person, just you as a . . . concept. He was there for everything that happened. And everything that happened afterward. [Throat clearing.] He's really the best friend I've ever had."

"Better than . . . uh . . . oh . . . ?"

"I assume that by 'uh . . . oh' . . . you mean Len?"

"I was trying to remember who else you were friends with."

"There haven't been too many. There was Hope's brother, of course."

"Right."

"After Heath died, my options were limited. Len was the first one in our class who was willing to give me a chance, to get to know me. I'll never forget that. And he was a good friend for a while . . . until . . ."

"Until . . . uh . . ."

"Let's put it this way. It's hard to be friends with someone when . . ."

"You've got [cough] competing interests?"

"That's one way of putting it."

[Pause.]

"Well. Uh. I never thought you and Natty would get so tight. I had my doubts about your lasting a semester in the same room."

"What about you and Manda?"

[Cough. Cough. Cough.] "What about me and Manda? What do you know about me and Manda?"

"Nothing. Just that you were improbable roommates for that year in Brooklyn."

"We were hardly friends. Even on our best days, she was more like an amusing adversary than a friend. We lost touch. I haven't seen her since Sara and Scotty's wedding back in 2008. Anyway, I have no idea what she's up to or where she is, and I don't really care. So, no. Not friends. Not then. And not now. And really, not ever and— Why are you laughing?"

"No reason."

"Seriously. Why are you laughing?"

"You won't think it's funny."

"Try me."

"Oh, Jessica. You're doing it."

"Doing what?"

"Doth protesting too much."

"I am not!"

"You are."

"Am not . . . Stop laughing!"

"I'm laughing because the more you say that, the more you're doing it."

"Why would I doth protest too much about Manda? There's nothing to protest."

"I don't know why you are doth protesting. I only know that you are."

nine
(arrested development)

"Do you hear that, Jessica?"

"Christ! That's *my* phone again. Where is it?"

"Am I hearing what I think I'm hearing? Is that? Could it be?"

"Dammit, where is my phone? I can never find it when I need it."

"Is that Barry Man—"

"Yes! It's Barry Manilow, okay? I have a Barry Manilow ring tone. I keep mashing the wrong buttons on this damn thing today. I must have accidentally taken my phone off vibrate when I checked the message from Bethany. Get over— Oh! Here it is. Oh . . . It's from Hope. She sent a picture of . . . OMIGOD! ACK!" [Laughter.]

"What's so funny?"

"It's hard to explain."

"Let me see."

"I'm warning you, it's kind of . . . uh . . ."

[Laughter.] "Donkey porn?"

"It's an inside joke!"

"And you had the nerve to accuse *my* friend of being a pervert?"

"I accused him of being a sexist, immature dick. Not the same thing."

[Pause.]

"What if I make an apology for obnoxious behavior that legitimately deserves an apology? Will I still owe you a dollar?"

"All such exemptions will be made on a case-by-case basis. Why? To whom do you owe an apology?"

"Hope."

"Hope? For what?"

"I wasn't being fair to her earlier. I shouldn't have been so eager to mention that she dropped out of school when she's kicking the art world's ass right now. I'm happy for her new relationship, too. But to give this apology its due respect, I will confess that, yes, it did rub me the wrong way when you assumed Hope was the one so altruistically toiling for disaffected youth. Hope deserves better from me. Especially when she has so bravely faced her great fear of donkeys just to make me laugh. So, Hope, I'm sorry I was an undermining bitch. It was worth losing a dollar to apologize out loud."

"Keep your money."

"You sure?"

"I'm positive."

[Pause.]

"You could call her."

"I could, but . . ."

"You don't want to talk to her in front of me, do you?"

"What?"

"You avoided your sister, you avoided Hope . . ."

"What are you *talking* about?"

"You don't want anyone to know that you're here with me."

"Woooow! Where did that come from? You're—"

"Presumptuous. Who am I to jump to such conclusions about you? Especially when I haven't spoken to you in three years? Who am I to do that?"

"Actually, I was going to accuse you of being stuck in arrested development."

"Stunted at seventeen."

"Which means you, Marcus Flutie, are still the Poet/Addict Man-whore. And I, Jessica Darling, am still the Cynical Girl Who Has It All and Yet Has Nothing at All. And that makes Hope the Idealized Best Friend Who Isn't Around Anymore and Would Never Understand My Relationship with Marcus Flutie."

"Is that your subtle way of telling me I'm wrong?"

"Right."

"Then why not call her back, if not to apologize, then at least to thank her for the donkey porn?"

"I figure I've got limited time to talk to you, and you know, I *live* with her, so . . ."

"You can talk to her anytime, but who knows when you'll ever see me again. This is a one-time-only opportunity. It's now or never again."

[Cough.] "Uh, right."

"May I ask you a serious question, then, since our time together is limited?"

[Pause.]

"Jessica?"

"Uh . . . yeah . . . uh . . . okay. Sure. Shoot."

[Dramatic pause.]

"Why is Barry Manilow your ring tone?"

"Ha! *That's* your big question?"

"Yup, that's it."

"Whew. I was worried there."

"Obviously. But why?"

"I was just worried that you'd ask something I wouldn't be capable of answering."

"Such as?"

"Marcus, we have done a commendable job at keeping this conversation within a certain comfort zone. Let's not ruin it by trying to . . ."

"To what? What do you think I'm trying to do?"

"I don't think you're trying to do anything . . . yet. Which is why this conversation has been so pleasant. But with the time ticking . . . What time is it any— huh. That's strange."

"What?"

"My watch stopped."

"The battery?"

"I don't know. I just got this watch yesterday from my mom for my—I mean, it's brand-new."

"Do you have to wind it?"

"*Wind* it? I have no idea. Ask me to churn butter or wire a telegram while you're at it. Seriously, who wears watches anymore, anyway? . . . Hey, *you're* wearing a watch. What time do you have?"

[Throat clearing.] "It doesn't."

"What do you mean, it doesn't?"

"This watch doesn't tell time."

"It's broken?"

"No, it's . . . It's not a watch that tells time. It doesn't have hands or numbers."

"What? Let me see. This watch doesn't have any hands. Or numbers."

"I told you."

"Well, duh, Marcus. *Duh.*"

"I know. Duh."

"I mean, really. Duh. What is this? Some pretentious statement about the illusory nature of time? How it's just an artificial construct created by humankind to make sense of the natural world? Duuuuuuh."

"I'm not disagreeing with you. It was a gift."

"That's the biggest dumbass gift ever."

"Again, I completely agree."

"*Then why do you wear it?!*"

"Why do *you* have a Barry Manilow ring tone?"

[Long pause.]

"How about this, Jessica? You tell me the story of the ring tone, and I'll tell you the story of the dumbass watch. Then we'll be even."

"No, I'll still be ahead by a buck."

"Ah, but the conversation isn't over yet."

"But time is ticking. Or it would be if you wore a functional watch."

"Need I remind you that your watch isn't working, either? This isn't merely a case of arrested development, Jessica. We have officially stopped the arrow of time."

[Pause.]

"Why are you looking at me like that, Jessica?"

"Like *what?*"

"Like you want to stab me with a spoon. Or beat me with your dis-carded tea bag."

"Why do you *think* I'm looking at you like that?"

"I don't know."

"Well, then I don't know, either."

ten
(yes)

"Okay. I guess I'll start."

"And with such enthusiasm, too."

"Woo-hoo."

"So much better, Jessica."

"The story is only half as long as it would normally be because you already know the first part."

"Which part?"

"The part about you tracking down the absurdly awesome, one-of-a-kind, not-for-sale decoupage Barry Manilow toilet seat cover I once coveted at an outdoor art festival and giving it to me as a get-back-in-my-good-graces gesture after vanishing in the desert for two years."

"*Jessica.* I did not vanish. You knew where I was. I sent—"

"The postcards. The crazy-making one-word postcards. I . . . WISH . . . OUR . . . LOVE . . . WAS . . . RIGHT . . . NOW . . . AND . . ."

"*And* I gave you the toilet seat cover not as a reconciliatory gesture but because it was Christmastime and I had always regretted not buying it for you when we first saw it."

"You see it your way, I see it mine. And this is *my* version of the story. You can tell your *Rashomonic* version another time."

"*Rashomon.* Oh, man, you really are a—"

"A highbrownnoser."

"Ha! That's exactly what you are. And quite a wordsmith as well."

"Thanks, I think. So, how did you find the one-of-a-kind not-for-sale decoupage Barry Manilow toilet seat cover?"

"There's this wondrous new invention called the Internet."

"Har-dee-har-har. But how did you persuade, ah, what was the name of the crafter-slash-Fanilow?"

"Lorna."

"*Lorna.* How did you persuade Lorna to part with it once you found it?"

"I have my ways."

"Seriously, Marcus. She was dead set against selling it. She said it was her masterwork."

"I traded sexual favors."

"Of course you did."

"Once a manwhore . . ."

"You're not going to tell me, are you?"

"I'll tell you. But I thought *you* were telling the stories right now, not me."

"You're right. I am."

"Do you still have it?"

"Have what?"

"The Barry Manilow toilet seat cover. That's what we're talking about, right?"

"Are we? Because I'm losing track."

"We are."

"It was stolen, Marcus. Remember? When Hope and I were supposed to go on that road trip. We had it in the backseat as sort of, I don't know, a good-luck token, I guess. A lot of good it did us, huh? It was stolen, along with the diaries you had given me to read and everything else in the car. Remember?"

"I do remember now. Yes."

"For the longest time, I thought it would turn up."

"What?"

"All of it. The toilet seat cover. Your diaries. Everything I had lost."

"Everything that was stolen, you mean."

"Lost. Stolen. What does it matter when it's all gone? Why did they have to take everything? Why not just take our money and credit cards? Why take a box of notebooks? Why take a toilet seat cover? Who would want such a thing?"

"Besides you."

"Right. Besides me. Actually, I know someone else who would have wanted such a thing. [Cough.] I mean, who would want it still. [Cough.] She still wants it."

"Jessica? You okay?"

[Cough.] "Fine. Just perfect. [Cough.] Two years ago one of the Do Better girls thought it would be funny to hack my multipurpose cell so it would only respond with a Barry Manilow ring tone and I've had it ever since. That's the story."

"That's the story."

"Actually, she's the same girl from the story about the hammock."

"Oh. What's her name?"

"Her name?"

"She's come up in conversation quite a bit, so I'm just curious. What's her name?"

[Pause.]

"Her name is Sunny. Sunny Dae."

[Singing] "*Sunny day, keeping the clouds away* . . ."

"It's a good thing she's not here right now. She *hates* it when people do that! She would tae kwon do your ass and . . ." [Coughing.]

"Jessica? Are you okay?"

[Pause.]

"We are the only people talking right now. It's weird, right? All this noise, and yet you look around and no one is talking. It's all texting or Twittering or Tetrising."

"Why are you changing the subject in such an alliterative manner?"

"That's a gorgeous sweater, Marcus. Don't forget to put it back on before you leave. It would be a shame to lose a gorgeous sweater like that."

[Throat clearing.] "Thank you. Why are you changing the subject?"

"Is it cashmere? It is, isn't it? And not some cheapo Wal-Mart nineteen-ninety-nine cashmere, either. That's, like, shorn from the underbelly of embryonic Mongolian lambs."

"I really don't know."

"Where does one get a sweater like that?"

[Pause.]

"I know what you're doing, Jessica."

"You do?"

"You're changing the subject for my benefit."

"I am?"

"Sure you are. There's something about your story that could hurt my feelings, but you didn't realize it until you were already in the middle of it."

"Uh . . ."

"I appreciate the gesture. I do. And I'll gladly let you change the subject if you think it will be so damaging to my psyche."

"Uh, thanks."

"However, your change of subject is sort of : . . . dangerous."

"Dangerous?"

"Because the story of the sweater is related to the story of the watch."

"It is?"

"Of course it is, don't act so surprised. You're a woman. You were following a hunch. You're curious, and yet you realize that these are stories you may not want to hear."

"I bet those stories overlap the story of how you learned to drink."

"Socially and in moderation."

"And, of course, the already legendary story of The Beard, or rather, the shaving of The Beard."

"And the more incidental shaving of the dreads, yes."

"What about your glasses?"

"The glasses?"

"Are they part of any of these stories?"

"No, they have nothing to do with the sweater or the watch or anything else. I was getting horrible headaches. I thought it was stress. Or from reading too much. It turned out that I was nearsighted."

"I like them. The glasses. They suit you. Your face."

"Well, thank you. I . . . oh . . ."

"What?"

"Nothing."

" 'Never have I met someone for whom nothing so obviously meant something.' "

"Touché, Jessica."

"So?"

"Okay. [Throat clearing.] I was thinking how I wish you, too, were wearing a new pair of glasses."

"Why?"

"So I could say they suited your face. So I could pay a compliment to your appearance in a way that wouldn't embarrass you. And I can see by the flush on your cheeks that I've embarrassed you anyway."

[Pause.]

"Thank you, Marcus."

"You're welcome."

[Pause.]

"I have no idea what I was talking about, because you so graciously let me change the subject."

"For now."

"We'll . . . uh . . . see . . . about that."

"If you wanted me to tell my story first, why didn't you just say 'Hey, Marcus, go first.' "

"I don't know. Maybe I was less hesitant to tell my story than I was to hear your story."

"And now?"

"And now I've changed my mind."

"Fair enough. So you want to hear it?"

"I think I do."

"Do you or don't you?"

"Well, after all this buildup, I most certainly do."

"Even if it might . . . I don't know . . . Make you uncomfortable?"

"Yes."

"Then I'll tell you. [Deep breath.] The story goes like this. A man receives a cashmere sweater and a watch that doesn't tell time from an ex . . . er . . . *ex*."

"An ex, er, ex?"

" 'Girlfriend' isn't quite right."

"*Lady* friend? Or is that too silver fox? How about 'lovah'?"

"Ah, love, Jessica, had very little to do with it."

"I see."

"This ex also encouraged the man to trim his beard and dreads but not cut them off completely."

"I see."

"And he did."

"I see."

"With her, the man learned to drink socially and in moderation. Then they . . . then *it* . . . ended. And he shaved off the beard and the dreads down to the skin. He still wears the sweater because it's a warm sweater and it's cold outside. But the watch—he wears the watch . . . He wears the watch as a reminder."

"Of what?"

"Her."

"Oh. I see."

"And . . . er . . . [Throat clearing.] That's the story."

[Pause.]

"Marcus?"

"Yes, Jessica?"

"I'm sorry, but that story sucked."

"I know it did. There was one really excellent part about it, though."

"What's that?"

"Your apology! *Pay up!*"

"Damn. Now we're even."

"Yes, I suppose we are."

[Pause.]

"What time do you have to be at the gate?"

"According to my cell phone, I should probably start heading over there any minute now. I guess we've run out of time. We'll never get the full, uncensored versions of each other's stories."

"Oh, that's okay. I don't mind if those stories go unfinished right now."

"Right now."

"I didn't mean to invoke the postcards. It was an accident!"

"Aha! I thought there was no such thing as accidents!"

"That was definitely one of the more regrettable things I said during the course of our conversation. I didn't even mean it at the time. I just wanted to have an excuse to bring up Jung. You know, go nose-to-highbrownnose with you."

"So if that was just one of the regrettable things you said, what were some of the others?"

"Don't you have places to go?"

"Now who's changing the subject?"

"I suppose it's easy for you to talk about my regrets when you don't have any at all."

"Even if I did, I wouldn't apologize for them now. And I don't want you to start apologizing, either. Not when we're finally all evened up. I wouldn't want you to be . . ."

"In your debt?"

"Technically speaking, yes."

"Oh, Jessica . . ."

"What?"

"For having passed the hours in such an entertaining manner, I am, I assure you, already in your debt."

[Pause.]

"I really should get going now."

"I'll go with you."

"Where? To the gate?"

"Sure. Why not?"

"I just figured we would get our awkward good-byes out of the way now, you know, so we don't drag it all out and make it even more awkward later on."

"I see."

"Because if it gets really, really awkward, all that awkwardness could undo all the goodwill engendered in our conversation."

"You think too much."

"I do. I really, really do."

[Pause.]

"So, Marcus, are you coming with me or not?"

"Are you allowing me to tempt the fates of awkwardness by accompanying you to the gate?"

"Yes. You sure you don't mind?"

"Mind? Why would I mind?"

"Well, because we're *even*."

"So?"

"If we stop talking and go our separate ways, we can be sure to keep it that way."

"Oh, no. I'll take my chances."

"Okay. Me, too."

[Pause.]

"I've changed my mind."

"What? Now you don't want me to walk you to the gate?"

"No, that offer still stands. But I may have to jump on the plane as soon as we get there. So I think I'd like to get the good-byes out of the way now before I run out of time."

"Okay."

"You know, just as a preemptive measure."

"When you put it that way, it sounds so . . . combative."

"Isn't that what we've been doing for the past two hours? Battling wits?"

"I thought we were just talking."

"Marcus, we have never *just talked*."

"True enough."

[Pause.]

"So. Uh. Good-bye, Marcus."

"Good-bye, Jessica."

"I'm glad I ran you over."

"I'm glad you did, too."

"I enjoyed catching up with you."

"Me, too."

"I enjoyed it far more than I thought I would. No offense!"

"None taken. I know what you mean. It was a nerve-racking proposition."

"And now that it's almost over, it seems stupid that I was so nervous about it."

"Hindsight is twenty-twenty and all that."

"Twenty-twenty. 'Like perfect vision' . . . Bridget and Percy . . ."

"What?"

"Uh, nothing. Just a reminder of why I really need to get on the next flight."

"Of course."

"Still, it really is too bad that we don't have more time to, you know, hang out or what— Uh . . . oh . . ."

"Or *whatever*?"

"Right. Whatever."

[Pause.]

"I know what you mean, though. I feel like we were just getting started and— Shit."

"What's wrong?"

"Shit. Shit. Oh, man. Shiiiiiiiit."

"What is it, Marcus? The police? Are you about to get hauled off?"

"Worse. Far worse. Pick up the pace, Jessica. Try to keep up with me. Stay with me."

"Why? What is going on?"

"Just walk quickly, past the thAIRapy sign."

"Why?"

"Hahahahahahahahahahaha! You are hilarious! Such a brilliant conversationalist! Go on, go on!"

"Are you mental? What is with you?"

"*You must go on.* We're walking and talking. Walking and talking. Emphasis on walking. *Go on, go on, go on.* HAHAHAHAHAHAHA-HAHA."

"Does this have anything to do with the chickie in the lab coat who's waving at you? Desperately trying to get your attention?"

"I don't see her. Nope. Just keep moving—hahahahahahaha— you are telling me the funniest story I have ever heard in my life! You are the most fascinating woman I hahahahahahahahahahahahahahahave ever met!"

"I think you could seriously benefit from some thAIRapy, Marcus."

"HAHAHAHAHAHAHAHAHAHAHAHA!"

"You know, I think *I* could benefit from thAIRapy. I always feel so out of my body when I travel. Like I'm not where I was and I'm not where I need to be. I feel totally disassociated from everything; I'm not really anywhere."

"That's good stuff, Jessica. Keep talking, keep walking. Hahhhhh . . . I think I'm safe now."

"*You're* safe. I'm clearly in the company of a madman."

"It makes sense, the purgatorial feeling. We *are* in a *terminal*, after all."

"No, no, no. You can't just pretend you weren't acting like a total maniac. Are you going to tell me what was up with your girlfriend back there?"

"Jonelle?"

"Oh, is *that* her name?"

"We . . . er . . . met earlier."

"Oh, really? I'm not surprised. According to an Axe deodorant body spray poll, Newark Liberty International airport was voted the number one airport in the nation for making a *love connection*."

"Really? Is that true?"

"Yes, from no lesser authority than the digital billboard right behind you. So, far be it from me to get in the way of you and Jonelle. I don't want to be responsible for Newark's drop in the rankings."

"Trust me, I'm not interested. She's an aeroanxiety specialist under the misguided impression that she can cure me."

"Are you anxious?"

"Since you ran over me? Extremely."

"You hide it well. Oh, wait, here's the gate and . . . This does not look good."

"That all depends on your definition of 'good.' "

"There seems to be quite a number of people who also need to get to St. Thomas this evening. Wait here while I talk to the customer service rep. Or, uh, don't. I mean, you don't have to wait for me."

"I'll wait, Jessica. It's fine. I'm looking forward to dragging this out to its maximum awkwardness."

[Waiting. Waiting. Waiting.]

"What's the word?"

"The word is: screwed. There are, like, a million people ahead of me on standby. It looks like I'm in Newark until tomorrow."

"Do you need to call Bridget and Percy?"

[Sigh.] "I already told Hope to tell them I wasn't going to make it. I was hoping to surprise them by actually arriving on time. I'm afraid if I call them right now, I'll just . . . Shit." [Sniffle.]

"You tried, Jessica."

"I know."

[Pause.]

"Well, I'm definitely not crashing in the airport overnight. I'm so over this place."

"I'm not crashing here, either."

"You're not? I figured you'd be the type to rough it. Camp out right here in the terminal, under the fluorescent lights, curled up on the crummy carpet on which millions of passengers have trod before you, using your duffel as a pillow, the recorded reminder to please maintain contact with your luggage at all times—_mantenga el contacto con su equipaje siempre, por favor_—your bilingual lullaby . . ."

"As romantic as you make that sound, hell no. I'm headed for the shuttle train that goes to all the airport hotels. I'm getting a room."

[Pause.]

"I guess I should, too."

"I hear good things about the Here hotels."

" 'If you can't be where you want to be, you might as well stay Here.' "

"Or their new motto: 'Wherever you go, Here you are.' "

"Veeeeery bumper-stickery."

"Hey, don't hold that against Here E-Dub. Let's see. Free Wi-Fi . . . high-def plasmas . . . A complimentary breakfast buffet . . . Oh, and we can get to know our fellow guests with the hottest selection of interactive gameplay . . ."

"Have you been paid by a guerrilla marketing firm?"

"I'm reading the digital billboard over there."

"Oh. Right. So. Uh."

[Pause.]

"Want to get a room?"

"At Here E-Dub?"

"Yes. Or wherever."

"Like, together?"

"Yes, together. We can pass the time. It makes sense, doesn't it? I've enjoyed talking to you. And I would prefer to be in your company instead of all alone in front of the high-def plasma TV. So how about it?"

"I don't think it's a good idea."

"Why not? You were just lamenting how it was too bad that we didn't have more time together, and now we do. Or were you just saying that to be nice?"

"There you go again, accusing me of being *nice*."

"Seriously, Jessica. Why not?"

"I don't think we should push our luck."

"Push our luck? What are you so afraid of?"

"Doing— I mean, *saying* something I'll regret."

"I haven't taken as many psychology classes as you have. But it's a well-known fact that people tend to regret the things they *don't* do more than the things they *do*, er, do. Or *say*, in your case."

"I *am* familiar with that research. And so I won't have any regrets later, I need to make something very clear now."

"And what's that?"

[Most dramatic pause.]

"We're not going to have sex."

[Stifled then unrestrained laughter.]

"There is nothing even remotely funny about what I just said."

[Another wave of laughter.]

"WHAT. IS. SO. FUNNY?"

[Throat clearing.] "You."

"*Me?* How?"

" 'We are not going to have sex.' An announcement like that says more about what's on *your* mind than what's on *my* mind."

"You did *not* just say that."

"I most certainly did."

"This is what I get for trying to handle the situation like an adult. I see I've overestimated you."

"*I'm* the immature one here? *Really?* Hey, why are we even debating this issue? What's the point? You've made it very clear to me that you are suffering through [throat clearing] your monthly cycle. Oh, and don't you have a contagious disease? Though there seems to be no signs of either of these afflictions at the moment."

[Cough. Cough. Cough.] "Your point?"

"I think I've made my point."

"You suck."

"Oh, and you accuse *me* of being immature."

"You suckity suck suck."

"All I'm saying is that you have a history of failing to make good on chaste promises."

"*What?* When?"

"I recall a certain no-sex proclamation made at my locker when we were juniors in high school. After you found that poem I had written you, the one with all the Adam and Eve imagery."

"Oh God. When I marched up to you and said, 'We will never be naked without shame in paradise.' "

"And you were wrong."

"I was only half wrong."

"Half wrong? How so?"

"We were naked without shame in Pineville, not paradise."

"Very true."

"But this time, Marcus, I promise you I won't be wrong."

"You have me thoroughly convinced that I won't be getting laid tonight. By *you*, anyway."

"Were you always such a laugh riot?"

"I am only as good as the material I'm given."

"Hear me now, Marcus. I understand that even though we're two consenting adults, we're exes with a very complicated history, and sharing a hotel room could seem like an invitation to Fuckfest 2010. But that is not the case here. And if you're thinking otherwise, you'll be better off in your own room with pay-per-view porn and a box of Kleenex."

"Is this your way of telling me that you've agreed to share a room with me?"

"Yes. I agree. But in a platonic way. Which means that you cannot and will not pull shit like that whole glasses thing earlier."

"Pull *what* shit on *what* glasses thing?"

"When you claimed that you couldn't compliment my appearance with an indirect compliment of my appearance."

"You seemed to like it when I said it!"

"But that was when I thought we were about to say good-bye."

"So?"

"So I knew that it wouldn't lead to anything untoward."

"*Untoward?* Who talks like that? You really are *fucking old*."

"Har-dee-har-har. And what's more, I've looked in the mirror! I know my current appearance is not worthy of such compliments! I call bullshit on such flattery in both form and content!"

"I, Marcus Flutie, promise not to compliment your appearance directly or indirectly from this moment onward. And I will not refute your claim that the aforementioned flattery was illegitimate because that would be a direct violation of the promise I just made."

"Just promise you won't try to make this night into something it shouldn't be."

"I promise. I guess."

"Marcus!"

"Okay! I promise!"

"Let's shake on it, then."

[Pause.]

"Yes, Jessica. Let's."

part three: enduring
(putting up with)

I. She writes

Shuttle train delays . . .
My tired tongue, too, is stuck
(Hint: Five, seven, five.)

II. He writes

So . . . we pass the time
by passing pen and notebook—
improvising verse?

III. She writes

Years ago you turned
junk mail into senryu
This game is easy

IV. He writes

Mmmm . . . spam word salads
My amuse-bouche amused you?
(And senry-who? What?)

V. She writes

(Haiku is nature
Senryu, human nature)
Yes, I laughed and laughed

VI. He writes

With me? Or at me?
(And why make a distinction
between two natures?)

VII. She writes

(Human nature, mocked.)
We were both in on your jokes
(Mother nature, not.)

VIII. He writes

(People are funny)
I'm funniest when trying
So hard not to be

IX. She writes

If not to amuse
why did you write those poems?
I don't understand . . .

X. He writes

Serious humor
Desperately trying to
Woo you, yes, you, then

XI. She writes

Stop, go, stop, go, stop
This train taunts and teases me
Just as you once did

XII. He writes

I like the way you
Fingertip-tap the paper
To count syllables

XIII. She writes

I like the way you
Silently lip-sync the words
To count syllables

XIV. He writes

So you've noticed, then
(I wonder what else you see
When you look at me)

XV. She writes

How about those Mets?
(Only what my heart can take)
How about those Mets?

XVI: He writes

Aha! Who flirts now?
Trying to seduce with words?
Breaking (y)our promise!

XVII: She writes

(I should know better
I should know better, I should
know better, I should)

XVIII: He writes

(Parentheses speak
More than we dare say out loud
Why, oh, why is that?)

XIX. She writes

Moving, moving on
At last we're getting somewhere
Wherever it is

XX. He writes

A no-tell hotel,
maybe? Where there's no telling
what will happen next?

XXI: She writes

I told you before
What won't happen anywhere
You-know-what is what

XXII: He writes

I-know-what is what
(SEX!) hath been doth protested . . .
And doth protested . . .

XXIII: She writes

Keep up the (SEX!) talk
You'll be sleeping with Byron
I'll get my own room

XXIV. He writes

No, please don't do that
One room, two beds, very chaste
Talking all night long

XXV. She writes

Try to mind your tongue
If you cannot mind your mind
We shook on it, right?

XXVI. He writes

We shook, palm to palm . . .
Shock! Our skin electrified
First touch in three years . . .

XXVII. She writes

Feet shuffled the carpet:
Static electricity
First-grader science

XXVIII: He writes

Aha! You cheated
(You never needed to cheat
Just to prove a point)

XXIX: She writes

Extra syllable?
Subtextual rebuke of
infidelity?

XXX: He writes

Subtext? What subtext?
Can you find subtext in these
Roman numerals?

XXXI. She writes

And your point is . . . what?
Besides another excuse
To talk about (SEX!)

XXXII. He writes

Everything we say
(what we don't say, even more)
has double meaning

XXXIII. She writes

Like: Are we there yet?
Are we there yet? Are we there
yet? Are we there yet?

XXXIV: He writes

Meaning: The hotel?
Or: Is this conversation
getting anywhere?

XXXV: She writes

To cheat, two meanings:
When I broke the senryule,
When I broke your heart

XXXVI: He writes

I meant the poem
(And my heart didn't break then—
but three years ago)

XXXVII. She writes

I don't know what to—
I don't think I'm ready for—
(Even though I asked)

XXXVIII. He writes

What's awkward out loud
(in parentheses or not)
On the page, less so

XXXIX. She writes

You sure about that?
I feel pretty damn awkward
Sitting here right now

XL: He writes

Why? I much prefer
this paper dialogue to
small talk in Starbucks

XLI. She writes

Small talk? But I thought
You were enjoying yourself
Or were you lying?

XLII. He writes

Lying about that?
No. But there were too many
sins of omission

XLIII. She writes

I have to agree
But there's always the risk of
too much said too soon

XLIV. He writes

Your "uhhhhs" and "nothings"
coughs, stutters, and ellipses
Spoke louder than words

XLV. She writes

As if your dropped hints
leading questions and half-truths
were any better?

XLVI. He writes

Let's start all over
No rush, we've got a long night
Take it nice and slow

XLVII. She writes

Add a few "oh yeahs"
some "day-um, girls" and that's a
baby-makin' jam

XLVIII. He writes

Well, well, Jessica
Now who brought up the (SEX!) talk?
Such a dirty mind . . .

XLIX. She writes

(I'm ignoring you.)
We're almost at the E-Dub!
(I'm ignoring you.)

L. He writes

Permission granted—
in the attempt at candor—
to say anything

LI. She writes

Hello, Lloyd Dobler!
I do not need your blessing
To do anything

LII. He writes

I only meant that
My feelings need not be spared
I dare to choose truth

LIII. She writes

Never truth or dare
With you, always truth and dare
Not sure if I'll play . . .

LIV. He writes

Then read magazines
Or listen to your iPod
Safe like other sheep

LV. She writes

Baaa! Baaa! Baaa! Baaa! Baaa!

Baaa! Baaa! Baaa! Baaa! Baaa! Baaa! Baaa!

Baaa! Baaa! Baaa! Baaa! Baaaaaaaaaaaaaa!

part four: enduring

(lasting)

one

Within minutes of keying in to Room 2010, Jessica Darling surrenders herself to the mattress. She's also helpless to the spectacle of Marcus Flutie slowly . . . slowly . . . and with great care . . . removing all his clothing. She wonders how far he will go. And how long she will watch.

He is waiting for a reminder to behave himself.

two

Jessica and Marcus are staying at Here EWR, the latest in a successful chain of boutique business hotels located as close to major airports as the Transportation Security Administration will allow. The success of this and all the properties in the Here Hotel Group depends greatly on the failings of the airline industry. Investors are banking serious money on current travel trends indicating that the number of stranded, grounded, or otherwise waylaid passengers will only continue to escalate. When forced to spend a night in a city they never wanted to visit in the first place, and given the choice between chic cheap and chiggers cheap, most airport refugees will choose the former. Jessica has spent too many nights in too many hotels to be impressed or depressed by any hospitality industry amenities or lack thereof. As for Marcus, he has just spent a week sleeping three people to a two-person tent. As long as they don't check out with a parasitic infestation they didn't check in with, both have fully embraced the motto: "If you can't get where you want to be, you might as well stay Here."

They have barely spoken since stepping off the shuttle train. It's not an uncomfortable silence, exactly, but rather a mutually accepted silence with an edge, a silence between two people who recognize that they have agreed to share roughly twelve hours in each other's company (minus whatever is lost to sleep) but have no idea how that time span—one that feels simultaneously luxuriant and meager—will be spent. Jessica worries there are far too many hours to fill with amusing anecdotes and idle gossip, especially when Marcus is pushing for truth and dare. And Marcus fears that time is too short for anything but, particularly after Jessica's professed reluctance to play along. They both try to make sense of the most perplexing aspects of their conversation thus far. (*Why didn't she want to tell me about that girl Sunny?* he wonders. *Why didn't his story about the watch make any sense?* she wonders.) They ask themselves if they should have said more (*Why didn't I just tell her about The Queen's uncanny prediction? Or the true meaning of the watch? Or Greta?*) or less (*Why did I blurt out Len's name? Why was I so snarky about Hope? Why did I keep bringing up Sunny?*).

Jessica takes a risk. She decides to say something. "It's a nice room," she mumbles, her face half pressed into a goose-down pillow.

"It *is* a nice room," Marcus replies, standing on the opposite side of the second double bed.

"I am particularly fond of the soothing palette of earth tones," remarks Jessica. "It's nice."

"I myself am quite taken with the roomy walk-in shower," responds Marcus, "and the complimentary spa-quality toiletries."

"Very nice."

"A nice room at a nice price."

"For two nice people."

"The nicest."

Jessica laughs uneasily, wondering how long they can keep this up. Marcus keeps going.

"This bed," he says, placing both hands flat on the one he has chosen. He pumps up and down a few times in quick succession, as if he's performing CPR on the mattress.

"What about *this* bed?" Jessica asks as if by rote, feeling like the straight woman paid to set up the star comic's punch line.

"It's like the gun in Act One," he says.

Jessica stares blankly.

"When a director reveals a gun in Act One, it's sure to return in a major way in Act Two."

As Jessica shakes her head, her ponytail loosens and makes a soft swish-swishing sound against the bed linens. "I assure you, Marcus, that when this bed *returns in a major way*, as you say, it will do so for the purpose of *sleeping*."

Marcus grins. "If you say so."

"I do."

The innuendo could end here. It should end here. And yet Jessica can't mind her tongue as it tongues Marcus's mind.

"By the way," she says, releasing her hair from its elastic and shaking it over the pillows. "The bed isn't the only place you're not going to have sex with me."

Marcus raises an eyebrow.

"You're also not going to have sex with me on the floor, in that office chair over there, in the shower, or in the elevator down the hall. There is no limit to the places where you're *not going to have sex with me*."

Marcus audibly swallows once, twice, again. Each time, his Adam's apple bobs up and down like a rubber ducky in high tide.

three

*S*he's testing me, Marcus thinks. *And I'm passing.*

Marcus is trying to prove he still has it in him, the ability to engage and enrage her in debate. He hasn't been knocked down yet, but her oral and written exams have certainly worn him out in mind and body. And judging by Jessica's languorous pose on the platform bed, she, too, must regroup before she can recommence the conversation.

No, not a test, Marcus reconsiders, shaking his head. *That's too one-sided. This is an intricate partnership. A grandiloquent pas de deux. I've missed this*, Marcus thinks. *I've missed you.*

"What?" Jessica asks.

"What *what*?"

"You were just shaking your head at me."

"I was?" Marcus hadn't noticed.

"You were."

"Oh."

Jessica is either too tired or too uninterested to pursue this line of questioning.

Marcus needs a shower. He hasn't had a proper washing in a week. In New Orleans he stayed with the rest of Princeton's volunteers in a tent city where conditions could be described as Spartan at best and squalid at worst. More accurately, it was the most basic of base camps, where running water and electricity were intermittently available but rarely used luxuries. Only now, in this hypermodern and sterile hotel room, is Marcus even aware of his own mammalian gaminess. He raises his arms to the ceiling and buries his nose in his own armpit. It's surprisingly pungent, considering the source of the odor is trapped under multiple layers of clothing—the T-shirt, the dress shirt, the sweater. He doubts that his all-natural stench has gone unnoticed, even from afar. All afternoon Jessica has gone out her her way to avoid touching him—with the exception of their electric handshake, of course. Perhaps Eau de NOLA Outhouse, not emotional unease, is why Jessica has kept herself at a distance. This theory is far more encouraging than it is embarrassing. The odor, after all, can be remedied immediately through a rigorous scrubbing with a battery of rosemary-mint-scented bath products. Jessica's psyche requires more complex care and attention.

She's heaped on the double bed closest to the door. Marcus is surprised she didn't bother whipping back the bamboo duvet cover first, assuming she's the type to get all paranoid about strange body fluids and shared bed linens. *Did you know that 93 percent of hotel bedspreads have tested positive for ejaculate?* That's just the sort of statistic Marcus memorized for his follow-ups to that first conversation with Jessica in the Caddie so many years ago. Conversational constructs, he called them. He had never resorted to such tactics with any other girl. No other girl had ever made him so nervous. No other girl had brought out his inner nerd.

Only Jessica, whom he always knew was superior to him in every way. His only hope at holding his own—then and now—was to throw her off balance. Hence: *Did you know that the average American spends six months of his or her life waiting for red lights to turn green? Did you know that the mauve color on your walls changed the world? Did you know that 93 percent of hotel bedspreads have tested positive for ejaculate?* He's so tempted to ask, even though he's unsure such a study of spunk exists. She might laugh *with* him in recognition of his old gambit. Or *at* him for his lame reliance on old ploys.

Jessica cocoons the duvet cover around herself. Perhaps her frequent travels have inured her to such hygienic transgressions. This would bode well for Marcus's BO. However, even if Jessica does see fit to forgive him for his ripeness, Marcus is feeling increasingly claustrophobic under all those heavy layers of fabric and dirt. He needs to shed his filthy clothes, scrub his skin, and get clean, if not for her then for himself.

"I'm taking a shower," Marcus announces. He is ready for her to accuse him of making this statement for the sole and inappropriate purpose of directing her attention to his impending nakedness. He has already decided to retaliate with an offer for her to take a whiff of the offending armpit.

But she doesn't blink. In fact, she's staring at Marcus in a heavy-lidded, dreamy way that, whether intentional or not, is more seductive than any look any woman has ever given him.

I want to tell you, Marcus thinks. *I want to tell you so much.*

four

He's testing me, Jessica thinks.

Jessica is exhilarated with exhaustion, like an ultra-endurance athlete who is thoroughly depleted after a double triathlon or other superhuman test of strength yet still *pretty! fucking! pumped!* that she crossed the finish line. Only in Jessica's case, it's like finishing a double triathlon and then finding out that what she thought was the finish line is actually not the finish line because she signed herself up for a *quadruple* triathlon and she's only halfway to the end so she better pound some carbs and chug some electrolytes and get back out there. But if his near-silence is any indication, Marcus is also in need of a respite before the next matchup, so she need not push herself just yet.

No, not a test, she reconsiders. *That gives him too much power.* This is a battle of wits between two well-matched opponents. And so far, it's a draw. *I've missed this,* Jessica thinks. *I've missed talking to you.*

Like a pro, Jessica reviews her performance, the reel of highlights and lowlights unspooling in her mind. As much as she didn't want to, she couldn't stop herself from talking about Sunny. It's so goddamn Freudian of her, to babble on about the one subject that she wants to keep sacred for herself. And isn't it just like Marcus to assume that her half-told story was all about protecting *him*? Of course, this conclusion might stem less from narcissistic than from altruistic motivations. His half-told story about the sweater, the watch, The Beard, etc., was surely edited to protect her feelings, a certainty that leaves Jessica feeling less unsettled than she'd expect from such an intimidating intimation.

Sunny would be positively thrilled to serve as a subject of discussion between Jessica and Marcus. Would it help if Jessica called right now and asked Sunny's parents to press the phone to her ear? *Marcus Flutie knows about you, Sunny. You're a story worth telling.* Would that be enough to make Sunny's eyes open? Would she grab the phone out of her mother's hand and demand, "PUT MARCUS ON THE PHONE NOW"? And if a little teaser wasn't enough to coax her back into consciousness, there was so much more Jessica could tell Sunny now than when she first considered calling from the airport restroom.

Jessica could start by telling her how Marcus pretended not to know anything about their minor impact on contemporary pop music. This is a near-impossible claim of ignorance, coming from someone who lived on a college campus that had, just three months earlier, hosted the Mighties on a double bill with a Princeton-based band named Steampunk Dandy. It's a 100 percent impossible claim of ignorance coming from someone who, toward the end of their two-hour conversation, actually quoted from the infamous song, a song that is in heavy rotation on Sunny's own iPod, without acknowledging that those lyrics (*You have stopped the arrow of time / There's no meaning to this rhyme / Because my song will never mean as much as the one / He once sang / For you, yes, you . . .*) were in fact written by (a) Len Levy (b) about them.

She could also tell Sunny how Marcus went out of his way to press her on the subject of her friendship with Manda, whom he must know was the one who ramblingly revealed their identities as the subjects of the aforementioned song to the Mighties' modest but rabid blogospheric fan base. This was a development that Sunny herself first reported to Jessica within minutes of this praecoxal post to a fansite called TheMightiest.com in response to the question from an approved commenter screen-named Len'sGirl2010: **does ANYONE know who MY SONG is about? i'm DYING to find out and Len won't tell!**

Couchsurfeminist commented: i went to high school with everyone in MY SONG. i was so fortunate to date LEN (so sweet, smart, sensitive—a male feminist!) and i am not exaggerating when i say that if any man were worth conforming to the oppressive heterosexual monogamous paradigm for, it's him. we might still be together if it weren't for my former roommate JESSICA DARLING (not the porn star, but she still exploits her body to get what she wants), who I know for a FACT is the YOU in MY SONG. JESSICA DARLING fucks LEN whenever she gets horny or bored or whenever anyone else (like me or any commenters;^*) shows an interest in him and she feels threatened that he might not worship her the way he has since the third grade because she, sadly, is only as powerful as the men who love her. the HE of MY SONG is a walking phallus named MARCUS FLUTIE who ONCE SANG a song for JESSICA DARLING before senior prom that made her spread for the first time, which was such a MOMENTOUS OCCASION because she was the only virgin left in our entire high school because she thought her TWAT was a precious jewel or a rare flower or whatever crap pushed by the patriarchy to suppress the female orgasm. MARCUS FLUTIE slept with just about every girl on the Eastern Seaboard except ME though he tried to get into my panties when i was a freshman but I turned him down because i will not disempower myself just for a few clit twitches. MARCUS FLUTIE actually proposed to JESSICA DARLING and she said no (which is shocking because what better proof of female value is there than BEING A BRIDE, RIGHT?!). anyway i guess she got all panicky that no one else would ever love her (her identity being all caught up in the male gaze) because not too long after that she briefly rebounded with Len, who was so traumatized by this last attack from her VAGINA DENTATA({**X**})—that our sweet, sensitive, sexy Len had to exorcise the demons by writing MY SONG. if you don't believe me, i've got photographic proof on my blog: http://bloggist.com/couchsurfeminist

A feminist is any woman who tells the truth about her life.

—Virginia Woolf

Jessica could tell Sunny that the worst part about Couchsurfeminist/Manda's loopily vitriolic rebuke was not how it bordered on slander but how it was totally justified and almost entirely true in essence, if not in actuality. For example, Couchsurfeminist/Manda neglected to mention that her time in the heterosexual monogamous paradigm ended immediately after Len innocently walked in and interrupted a Sapphic entanglement in Manda's dorm room. This shocking betrayal and convenient omission had as much to do with their breakup—if not more—than any lingering feelings Len had for Jessica. Jessica had been tempted, for the briefest of moments, to assign herself a screen name and defend herself against Couchsurfeminist's accusations:

NotThePornStar commented: How dare YOU of all people make such libelous smears about other people's promiscuity? You who taste-tested half the dicks in Pineville before deciding that vagina was the only meat on your menu.

What kind of example would that set? This was precisely the kind of debased public grievance-airing that Jessica tried to persuade the Girls to keep offline and private, best left for black-and-white-speckled composition notebooks. (In fact, Jessica begged a certain commenter screen-named **SunnyDaze** not to launch a counterattack to defend her mentor's honor, then overpraised said teen for being so worldly and mature beyond her years when she grudgingly agreed.) What's more, was Couchsurfeminist/Manda so far off the mark in her scathing summarization? Hadn't Jessica callously disregarded Len's feelings for her—and, to a lesser degree, Manda's feelings for Len—over the years?

As much as Jessica hated to admit it, Couchsurfeminist/Manda was right in that regard, and it didn't even matter if she portrayed herself as an innocent victim. After reading that post, Jessica understood that Manda truly believed Len could have been the Great Love of Her Life, just as she truly believed Jessica was the sole reason why it hadn't turned out that way. After all, as Jessica told Sunny and all the Girls in the program: "The tales we tell ourselves about ourselves make us who we are . . . and who we might be." If it made Manda feel better to buy in to her self-delusion, then Jessica could certainly accept the blame as penance for the very real pain she had caused. Jessica had wounded Manda; therefore, she couldn't blame Manda for pushing her revisionist history on an audience all too eager to believe it.

Jessica felt far worse about how she had mistreated Len, who really was as sweet, smart, and sensitive as Couchsurfeminist boasted. Len, who, to his never-ending credit, disavowed these online rumors. ("The song is fiction but is inspired by universal truths about breakups and broken hearts.") Len, who had never done anything wrong except for the fatal, natal error of not being born into this world as Marcus Flutie. Len, whom Jessica had conned into believing would finally have the grown-up relationship he had always wished for and always deserved. Len, who, when so callously informed otherwise ("It was just a one-night thing, Len"), coped with his pain and jealousy the only way he knew how. There's no doubt in Jessica's mind that Len is even more surprised than she is that his therapeutic outpouring has gone so very public.

Just twenty-four hours ago, Jessica couldn't think of anything to say to Sunny. But now she's convinced she could station herself by the hospital bed for hours, telling stories. If Len's song was the most prominent omission from their conversation, she could tell Sunny about how the opposite was also true, that Marcus had conspicuously asked or spoken about major and minor characters from their past—Bridget and Percy, Scotty and Sara, Paul Parlipiano and Mac, Bethany and Marin, her parents, her employer/founder of Do Better, her landlady in Brooklyn, even her AP English teacher, Ms. Haviland, for Christ's sake—before bringing himself to ask about the person he'd known longest (longer than Jessica, even) and best (though not better than Jessica): Hope. And even more revealing than his reluctance to ask about Hope was Jessica's shameful first response ("She dropped out of school!"), which was by far the most negative and least significant part of her best friend's life. Not only did Jessica still feel irrationally threatened by Hope's status as the Nice One, but Marcus had sensed as much, a truth that seemed so unfair to Jessica, as if this one stubborn flaw in her character proved she hadn't evolved at all in the three years since she and Marcus had parted ways.

Yes, Jessica could squeeze a valuable life lesson out of this unflattering confession (*I tried to make Hope look bad to make myself look better. This strategy never works, Sunny. Never.*), one that could teach her teenage mentee about the complicated dynamics of friendship between two women of any age, one Sunny could draw upon should she ever be in the position to forgive her own best friend (a girl named Leah, who, like Hope, is the shyer, more unassuming, and *nicer* of the two) the next time she does something (like being *nice* for no good reason) that tests their bond. Jessica would also have to point out—darkly, sardonically— how such tedious pedantry isn't necessary for the likes of Hope or Leah because such forgiveness comes naturally to them. Signing on as the primary beneficiary of their best friends' compassion is the great advantage to being the Not So Nice One, but also the greatest burden. That so much niceness ultimately contributes to feelings of guilt and inadequacy is something Jessica knows only too well.

Many friends and family members have tried to perform what Jessica called "interwenchions" to save her from a lifetime of bitching and bitterness. Even Marcus, who always told her that he loved her for who she was, often tried to make her see how oppressive her bad attitude could be. Though it was never said, Jessica had always assumed Marcus wished she could be just a little bit more like her optimistic, open-minded best friend. *Why can't you be yourself but just a little bit nicer?* It was this unspoken question that at the time, but even more so afterward, Jessica found so insulting, as if she didn't understand the depressing downside of going through life with such a personality defect. That she had been born with a bleak streak was inarguable. As for what to do about it, that was a question Jessica has struggled with for too many years, *still* struggles with, but less often since she started working for Do Better. Jessica was always uncomfortable with the idea of being a role model, and she still cringes at the term because anyone who allows herself to be placed atop such a pedestal is begging to get knocked off it. When Jessica voiced such objections, Sunny pointed out what should have been self-evident:

"You're a role model because you're *not* perfect. You were a mess when you were my age, but you turned out okay. You give me hope! Just don't tell anyone or they might mistake my optimism for one of those rare brain disorders you've told me about."

Imperfections weren't enough to endear Jessica to the Girls—after all, there are plenty of repugnant fuckups out there. It's her gift for storytelling, Jessica's uncanny ability to enlighten and entertain with tales of past mistakes, that made her a hero among the tart-tongued eye-rollers like Sunny. Jessica wishes she could talk to her right now, taking full advantage of another opportunity to serve by flawed example.

Jessica hadn't noticed it yesterday, surely because she was going out of her way not to take in too many specifics of the whole gruesome situation, but she wondered whether Sunny was hooked up to a machine that monitored her brain activity. Wouldn't such information be useful to Sunny's doctors? Jessica remembered studying colorful brain scans in her advanced psychology classes at Columbia, where certain zones lit up in response to different stimuli. If such a real-time mind map were possible, Jessica could have edited and embellished her tales to increase blood flow in key regions, all to Sunny's maximum medical benefit. In fact, Jessica can perfectly visualize the explosion of primary brights—Mondrian meets Pollock—in Sunny's hypothalamus as a response to the following sentence:

Marcus Flutie is slowly getting naked right in front of me. And I'm not going to stop him.

five

Marcus starts with the sweater, seizing it gently at the hem, then raising it up and over his head in one graceful, fluid movement. This sweater has meant nothing to him, really. But now it's become something more: a symbol. It's the symbol of what can't be shared, the start of stories that go unfinished. He takes the sweater by the arms and stretches it out in front of him. In this moment, the sweater and Marcus look like dance partners, about to take a grand ballroom spin. It's a bold gesture, one he would not be making if he were in this hotel room all by himself.

He clasps the arms of the sweater together, first halving it in a hug, then folding it once more into quarters. He's making a big production out of putting away this sweater, a sweater he normally rips over his head and throws into a ball on the floor, forgotten until the next time temperatures dip low enough to need it. Marcus places the now meticulously cared-for sweater on his bed, which is located three footsteps away from hers. There is an unobstructed sight line between Jessica and this sweater. He doesn't want Jessica to forget about the sweater. He's waiting for her to ask about the sweater. He's waiting for her to ask for the rest of the story, and he wants her to suffer through its telling. He's waiting for her to ask about Greta. To encourage the question, he unclasps the dumbass watch and places it right on top of the sweater as an extra visual aid. It doesn't help.

His eyes meet her silent, heavy-lidded stare. Mildly unnerved by her implacable expression, he clears his throat and turns away in a false show of modesty. The room is silent save for the muted roar of airplanes taking off and landing not far from their window. His back is to her as he begins with the top button of his tasteful blue-striped dress shirt, origin unknown. The cotton parts as he finger-picks his way down, providing a peek at the letters printed across the T-shirt he's wearing underneath. The text is revealed in a manner that might be enjoyed by lovers of word games — NT, ENTS, BENTSP, EBENTSPO, HEBENTSPOO — before the dress shirt is peeled wide open to reveal all the letters spelling out the

name of a popular Princeton ice-cream shop: THE BENT SPOON. _An anticlimactic message_, Marcus thinks. If he had known when he got dressed this
morning that he would be here in this hotel room with Jessica Darling,
Marcus would have chosen a more meaningful T-shirt, such as the red
YOU. YES. YOU. shirt he had taken off the first time they'd made love.
This was the same T-shirt Marcus was wearing when he sang the song
immortalized in Len's song, a topic that Jessica blatantly dodged even
after Marcus dropped hints so clunky and unavoidable that they could
not accurately be defined as hints.

No, no, _no_. Wearing that T-shirt would have been the wrong way
to go: red shirt as red flag. Not that he had even considered wearing it
this morning, because it sits in the bottom of a drawer in Princeton,
unworn for many months because he dislikes answering questions about
it. ("Me? Yes? Me?" was a popular line of flirtation.) Such a gesture
would have been too obvious. Too calculated. Too much of the same-
old-same-old over-the-top Marcus Flutie bullshit that drove Jessica to
distraction when they were together. Wearing the YOU. YES. YOU. T-shirt
would've validated that he hasn't changed at all over the last three years,
that he's still compelled to pull stunts to get and keep her attention.

Oh, shit, he thinks. _I'm lasso-dicking again._

At once he remembers the ticket for tomorrow's flight to St.
Thomas and wonders how Jessica might react to its existence: bittersweet reunion or restraining order? As of right now, he imagines this
$895 reconciliatory gesture sinking him into credit card debt wouldn't
go over too well. To hide the anxiety now coursing through him, Marcus
goes out of his way to appear more relaxed than ever. This masquerade is
much easier to pull off with his back to her, his afflicted face hidden from
view. He rolls his head around on his neck, releases his taut shoulders,
then, without a care in the world, shrugs off the dress shirt and hastily
tosses it aside. It clings to the edge of the duvet for a moment before slipping to the carpet on the far side of his bed, out of Jessica's view and
therefore in no competition with the sweater.

Ask me, he silently urges Jessica. _Ask me so I can tell you._

He clutches his T-shirt and jerks it up and over his head. It
launches into the air and lands in an ignoble heap in the farthest corner

of the room. Now that he is nude to the waist, his own unwashed smell is hitting him, and he knows that it will be only a few more seconds before it reaches Jessica.

He had underpacked for New Orleans, finding himself with three more days than pairs of boxer briefs. So he's not wearing any underwear. Only a pair of corduroys separates him from stark nakedness. Jessica has seen him unclothed so many times before, what should it matter now, especially when she has made it abundantly clear that there is no sex to be had? If she's so intent on chastity, seeing him naked shouldn't be a trigger for arousal. But does he dare? Or should he excuse himself to the privacy of the bathroom?

Maybe I should just ask Jessica if she wants to hear the rest of the story, he thinks. *Or maybe I should tell it without asking her first. After all, if she doesn't have to ask permission to say anything, then the same should hold for me.*

A contented moan comes from behind him, followed by a ruffle of pillows. With thumbs poised at the top of his fly, he turns toward the sound, toward her, and discovers that all questions and answers, all truth and dare, will have to wait for the time being.

Because Jessica Darling is sound asleep.

S i X

Jessica is walking along a white sand beach. Under her arm, she holds a small white-gift-wrapped box all tied up with an enormous, perhaps overcompensatory, white bow. She is wearing a familiar red T-shirt and nothing else. She isn't in much of a hurry. She's taking a leisurely stroll near the water's edge, but not so close that the tide washes away the scattershot trail of footprints that Jessica is definitely, if distractedly, following. She's so taken with the brilliance of the blue sky and the even bluer sea that she hardly notices when she abruptly happens upon the bridal party that led her here. At the center of this group is the beautiful, beaming Bridget, who is elevated several feet above the crowd by means obscured under the whitest, widest, and most wildly overwrought wedding dress in the history of wedding dresses. Despite the farcical attire, Bridget is unabashedly happy. *Woo-hoo! Nous nous marierons demain!* Percy has scaled a stepladder to reply to his future wife, also in French. *J'épouse un phénomène. Un beau phénomène.* Back on the ground, surrounding the gown on all sides, are the bridesmaids and the matron, all as underdressed as Jessica. Wearing red Crocs and a Pineville High Class of 2002 T-shirt is Sara D'Abruzzi-Glazer, who has just finished bib-tucking layers of lace under the drooling chins of the infant twins screeching on her hips. *Something new!* Sara cries out before turning her attention to the nose-picking three-year-old at her ankle. *Destiny! Use the hem as a hankie; blow the boogie-yuckies out of your nose!* Jessica winces as the toddler more than happily complies with a liquidy honk. Jessica continues to orbit the gown and meets up with Hope, who is wearing a thin paint-splattered tank top. Hope is using a large swath of satin as a canvas for her latest masterpiece. *Something blue!* Hope cries out enthusiastically as she hurls another cerulean brush-blob of paint onto Bridget's gown. *You don't think it's too derivative, do you?* Hope asks no one in particular. *Too Mondrian meets Pollock?* As Jessica progresses around the dress, she catches a fleeting glimpse of Manda backward-burrowing beneath the voluminous train. Curious to see what Manda is doing under there, Jessica uses two hands to lift up the weighty bugle-beaded fabric. She ducks her head under multiple crinolines and comes face-to-face not with Manda but with Len Levy, wearing the Mighties official fan club T-shirt. *The acoustics are. Um. Excellent,* he says. He strums his guitar and begins to sing. *Something old . . . Something cold . . . Someone I used to hold . . .* Jessica involuntarily sways to the music. *She refused his band of gold . . .* Jessica knows the chorus and can't help but sing along. *But my song will never mean as much . . . As the one . . . He once sang . . . For you, yes, you . . .* She wants to watch the whole performance and congratulate Len on his success, but she's being lulled away from his voice by an insistent tap on her shoulder. When Jessica turns around, she sees Manda kissing none other than Marcus Flutie in the sloppy, unself-conscious manner of the newly in lust. When the lascivious twosome finally break apart, Manda smiles at Jessica and says smugly, *Something borrowed*. Manda is wearing a red YOU. YES. YOU. T-shirt that is identical to the one Marcus is wearing, which makes it also identical to the one Jessica is wearing, or rather, *was* wearing, because when Jessica looks down at her body, she discovers that she isn't wearing it or anything else.

I'm naked in paradise, Jessica says.

Without shame? Marcus asks.

And before she can answer, Marcus smiles and reaches for her hands.

seven

Marcus cannot believe she's asleep. There's no way she's actually asleep. Maybe she *is* under physical duress this afternoon, maybe she *is* exhausted by the double whammy of influenza and menstruation, though he came to the conclusion very early on in their conversation that she isn't suffering from either. Jessica has always been a conspicuous liar, and today's feigned coughing and cramping were a typically unbelievable performance. Marcus is pretty much convinced that she is perfectly healthy and is just using those medical excuses as an added buffer against sexual activity. The need to resort to such dramatic measures, and her devious glee in pointing out all the places where they are *not going to have sex*, only betrays the obvious: Her determination *not* to have sex with him is only barely, by the most infinitesimal measure, winning out over her desire *to* have sex with him.

This encouraging revelation doesn't change the fact that Jessica is asleep. *Asleep.* This must be another test. Another game to play. He's tempted to belly-flop on her bed and call bullshit on this catnap, but he opts for a more tactful approach.

"Jessica," Marcus says at a volume that is half conversational, half conspiratorial. "Are you really asleep?" He expects her to crack a smile, wink open an eye, and sound off with a "Gotcha, sucka!," but she doesn't stir. "I want to tell you the rest of the story," he continues, thinking this gambit might persuade her to end the charade. "I want to tell you about . . ."

He pauses here, stoops down, gets within an inch of Jessica's face. He hovers above her a moment, studying her features for any subtle shifts that would reveal she's really awake and faking it. But her mouth is unattractively slack, her nostrils flare in and out with each breath, and her eyeballs roll beneath the surface of her thin lids. All signs that she is indeed authentically asleep. If she is faking it, this is a triumphant moment in her acting career.

Marcus stands up and guffaws out loud, not even bothering to muffle his amusement. When he considered bedding Jessica down, *this* was not what he'd had in mind. Still shaking his head in wonderment (*How can she sleep at a time like this?*), Marcus decides to go ahead with his shower.

But not without exploring a measure of last resort.

He plants himself directly in what would be Jessica's field of vision, that is, if her eyes were open. He pops open the button on his corduroys. Pauses. Then, as if in time with an imaginary burlesque drumbeat, swivels his snake hips as he begins to unzip . . . lower . . . lower . . . as low as it goes. When his pants slip to the floor, Marcus cartoonishly, coquettishly cups his privates with his hands and even mouths *Oops!* just to keep in ridiculous character. With one hand still providing obscenely inadequate coverage for his crotch, he uses the other to take hold of a trouser leg, which he then, with a great sense of pageantry, swings around in circles above his head (yes, like a lasso) before finally letting it fly. With a final showstopping flourish, Marcus ta-das! with his head flung back, feet wide-stanced, arms outstretched. Whether he knows it or not, it's nearly identical to Barry Manilow's triumphant pose on the infamous decoupage toilet seat cover at the heart of Jessica's half-told story, only the Showman of Our Time was wearing an electric-blue bedazzled spandex jumpsuit, and Marcus is starkers.

Jessica snorts and rolls over but is otherwise unmoved by this comedic lasso-dickery. Now thoroughly convinced that she's genuinely asleep (*How can she sleep at a time like this?*), Marcus retreats to the privacy of the bathroom to take his long-overdue shower.

I need to come clean, he thinks as he stands in front of the bathroom mirror, and then he laughs again, at himself *and* the situation. Knowing how much pleasure Jessica gets out of parsing double meanings, he makes a note to repeat this thought out loud later on for her enjoyment. *I need to come clean.*

He considers his naked reflection and isn't too impressed. He has always been too skinny. He can't tell the difference between his abdominal muscles and protruding internal organs. The hair on his chest is darker and coarser than the reddish-brown hair on his head, and patchy. It collects in thick bunches around his nipples, then again in the trail that would lead down, down, down into his pants if he were wearing them. But he's not, so Marcus contemplates his cock. This modicum of attention, when combined with the awareness of Jessica on the bed on the other side of the door, inspires his cock to jump up and be noticed: *Huzzah!* Yes, it's bigger than most, but not as big as the numbers ("ten inches of New Jersey Whitesnake" was the refrain that echoed loudly in the Pineville High School locker room) he's heard over the years. Like the amount of sex he's had or drugs he has done, the size of Marcus Flutie's cock looms larger in salacious imaginations than it does in reality. This exaggeration is a necessary component of perpetuating that poet/addict manwhore myth that fooled them all, from the first (a friend of his brother's, a degenerate JV cheerleader who thought it would be hilarious to seduce an oversexed thirteen-year-old) to the last (Greta), into believing that she would be the one who changed his life. All of them—however many there were—believed it. All but one. And she's sufficiently unimpressed with Marcus Flutie to fall into a deep sleep.

Marcus, now fully engorged, needs not only a shower but a cold one. He tilts the nozzle as high as it will go to accommodate his height, then turns on the water.

"Yi! Yi! Yi!" he yips, hopping from foot to foot under the icy stream in a way that resembles a Native American rain dancer, or so he has been told. He always likes the shock of that uncontrolled rush of cold water, likes making his bones crackle and his skin pucker before adjusting the flow and relaxing into warmer, more tolerable temperatures. He'll keep it cold until his cock calms down. He thinks about unpleasant subjects. Like how he'll tell Jessica about Greta.

"Natty calls her Regreta . . ."

The bad joke does little to make him go limp. He thinks more about Greta.

Greta was the one who likened him to a Cherokee under the cold water. She liked comparing him to other people, as if she could understand Marcus better by studying similar subject matter. In that vein, she assumed wrongly that this cold-shower habit was born out of a desire to conserve hot water, as many eco-minded coeds his age try to do. When Marcus explained that, no, his actions had nothing to do with saving the planet, Greta guessed again.

"Did your family have many children sharing a single bathroom?"

"Two kids, two adults, two bathrooms."

"Self-abnegation?"

"No."

"I'll figure it out."

Jessica, Marcus realizes as he bounces under the freezing rain, never noticed this dance, or if she did, never mentioned it. For all their years as a couple, they spent remarkably few days in consistent cohabitation, and Marcus has often wondered whether things would have turned out differently if they had regularly shared a bathroom _before_ he proposed. Would they be married now if she'd had the opportunity to grow accustomed to peeing while he was hopping around in the shower? Or if she'd come around to accepting the two toothbrushes in the holder as indistinguishable and interchangeable?

His cock points straight up at him accusatorially. _It's not my fault!_ it sneers. _You're the one who offered to share a room with her!_

Greta was a sociocultural anthropologist specializing in _authority and identification, kinship, sexuality, gender, historical consciousness, comparison and translation,_ and finally (at least according to her official CV), _narrative theory and the ethnographic method._ She was curvaceous and blond and in the habit of wearing low-cut embellished silk tunics in acidic brights. At forty-eight, she had earned the marionette mouth wrinkles and brow furrows that made her look her age, but not unattractively so. In fact, she had earned the red-hot-tamale symbol alongside her high rankings on RateMyProfessors.com, and was widely considered one of the more doable instructors on campus—a distinction that had been entirely theoretical until Marcus came along. Or so she claimed.

Greta's career had shown early promise but had been quickly waylaid by marriage and motherhood. Greta had divorced twelve years ago and had worked hard, researched hard, published hard to make up for lost time. Her son was a graduate student on the opposite coast, at the same university where her ex-husband, also an anthropologist, has served as the glorified cornerstone of the department for over two decades. The husband, in fact, was once Greta's professor. But she didn't talk much about the husband, and especially not the son.

"Natty says I was an Oedipal surrogate, and he's probably right."

Marcus preempts this joke, too. He strenuously ignores his resilient erection by working his armpits into a lather.

Greta taught ANT201 Introduction to Anthropology. Such entry-level classes are often the purgatorial bane of the untenured assistant professor's existence, even at a prestigious school like Princeton. But Greta liked the assignment, liked "getting them early," as she would explain to Marcus later, because she truly believed that the right teacher could turn curious interest into a lifetime calling. Her own husband had done that for her when she was eighteen, she said. The ex's influence on her intellectual life had—with the obvious exception of the genetic contribution to the creation of her twenty-three-year-old son—long outlasted his influence on her emotional life.

Marcus had enjoyed the class about as much as he enjoyed most of his classes, which was to say a lot. As his professor, Greta hadn't treated him differently from anyone else, hadn't acted inappropriately toward him in any way. He showed up every Monday and Wednesday at 10 A.M. and did the readings, took the exams, wrote the papers, learned more about anthropology than he had known before. He got an A and considered taking another, higher-level anthropology class—Human

Adaptation, perhaps?—the following semester, that is, if he could find room in his schedule. There were so many classes to take and so little time. Of course, knowing what he knows now, he wishes he had taken another class instead of taking Greta up on her offer to go back to her apartment and see a certain self-portrait of a nineteenth-century painter whom she claimed he resembled in both appearance and raison d'être.

"Natty says he's surprised she didn't offer to show me her etchings."

Another joke remembered and rejected. Marcus swivels this way and that, his hard-on cutting like a rudder through the arctic water. *It's like my cock's been winterized,* Marcus thinks. He nudges the nozzle toward H.

All the years in academia had turned Greta into a relentless questioner. Even the simplest answers were too straightforward for Greta to blindly accept without a debate. Her inquisitiveness and refusal to accept face-value truths were the qualities that first attracted Marcus to Greta; at least, that was what he told her when she asked. (Of course, this response just begged for obvious follow-up questions, to which Marcus replied "Your breasts" and "You don't need a lift" and finally "Greta, you've got better breasts than any eighteen-year-old on campus, now come over here and let me show you how much I enjoy them.") These are also traits he appreciated—still appreciates—about Jessica. Greta appealed to Marcus not only for the challenging similarities she shared with the woman he had wanted to marry, but because those qualities contributed to making Greta the very opposite of the simple, unchallenging girl (emphasis on "girl") Jessica had assumed Marcus would fuck in the effort to get over her. Marcus was Greta's subordinate. Both knew it and preferred it that way. Their relationship, such as it was, depended on that imbalance of power.

He squirts liquid soap into one hand and takes a firm grasp of his hard-on with the other, pulling back at the base, near his balls.

In all those years with Jessica Darling, she never pressed him to try to explain what had drawn him to her. He never offered such an explanation, not even in the form of cryptic postcards or elliptical lyrics, always believing that such analysis was needy, unnecessary, and impossible. He loved her because she was Jessica Darling, that's why. What better explanation could there be? And he would hope that if asked why she stayed with him as long as she did—had she been asked in the years since the breakup?—she would respond in kind: because he was Marcus Flutie, that's why.

He closes his eyes, taking slow, soapy-smooth strokes up and down and up and down and up and down . . .

Not that he would have, but Marcus never had to ask Greta what attracted her to him. She had told him straightaway.

"You look like Gustave Courbet."

"Who?"

"A brilliant nineteenth-century French painter," she replied. "Equally famous for his art—which rejected romanticism for realism—as he was for his scandalous reputation."

That was the first time Greta made the comparison, an offhand remark as he got up from his seat and went out of the lecture hall. The second time was a few months later, carnally, as she got up and off his naked lap. Only the second time did Greta provide photographic evidence in the form of the print of the self-portrait that ostensibly—but not *really*—lured him to her apartment in the first place.

"This is called *The Desperate Man*," Greta said in a tone not unlike that which she used to address her students. "This is what you looked like every day when you came to my class. Your beard is thicker, but otherwise, he could be you."

Greta handed him a heavy art book split to reveal a wild-eyed man tearing at his uncombed hair in a mad panic, his mouth half-open as if he's about to beg for help. Marcus saw only a vague physical resemblance but couldn't argue the titular comparison. He *was* a desperate man, had been a desperate man for quite some time, but never more desperate than in the moments leading up to his spontaneous marriage proposal. Proposing to Jessica had been the most desperate act of a most desperate man, a last-chance effort to hold on to something—someone—he knew in his heart was already lost to him.

Greta then pointed out the pull quote accompanying the portrait. " 'When I am no longer controversial, I will no longer be important,' " she read. "Sounds like someone I know."

Marcus's gut twisted as he looked into the face of this long-dead artist whom he resembled just enough to provide a necrophilic thrill. It was in that moment Marcus realized that Greta, for all her advanced degrees, was no better than any of the high school or college girls who had drawn similar comparisons to other tragically sexy antiheroes—Jim Morrison, River Phoenix, Kurt Cobain, Heath Ledger—all damaged madmen who could have been saved, according to the mythology, if the right woman had come along to fix him, make him whole. Marcus was profoundly disappointed in this discovery, having masochistically hoped that Greta's innate intellectual superiority, combined with a worldly lifetime of wisdom through experience, would trump his meager offerings to the relationship. And yet that disillusionment didn't stop Marcus from playing the passive role and letting Greta dominate him for several more months.

It was supposed to be just a fling. After she broke it off, he tried to win her back with phone and text sex. Once, after too much wine, he stalked the entrance to her apartment to make a libidinous proposition in person. It was foolish behavior, one that put her reputation in far more jeopardy than his own. But Greta had not, as Natty claimed, lost tenure as a result of the affair. To Marcus's consternation, however, Greta did take an abrupt leave of absence, from which she has never returned. In the years since, she has contacted him only once—via e-mail—to tell him that she had just sold a nonfiction proposal to a major publishing house. *Older Women, Younger Men: A Cross-Cultural Exploration of Cougars Through the Ages.*

It turns out that Marcus had been more ingeniously played than he ever could have imagined.

Firmer, harder, shorter strokes now. Marcus moans in self-pleasure, yes, but also because part of him wants Jessica to be awakened by the sounds of his arousal. He wants her to know. *I want you to know . . .*

In a defenseless postcoital languor, Marcus had almost made the error of telling Greta about Jessica. Jessica was, after all, the answer to the question "Why did you come to my class looking so desperate?" But Marcus had simply replied "A girl" and left the rest to Greta's imagination. Marcus didn't want Greta to know about Jessica, because Jessica had really mattered to him, and so the inverse is true about Greta. He wants to tell Jessica everything because Greta didn't matter to him. The only significant aspect of that relationship was how it ended: She broke up with him after he made the mistake of rebuffing the watch that didn't tell time. She thought he would love the watch as he had loved the decadent cashmere sweater that matched his eyes. But unlike the indulgent sweater, which at least served a purpose, he *hated* that watch for its pointlessness and pretentiousness. Later, Marcus couldn't believe he had sunk so low as to willingly subjugate himself to someone who could think otherwise.

Marcus wants to shake Jessica awake and explain himself. *I wear the dumbass watch to remind me that there will never be another Jessica, but there* cannot *be another Greta.*

Greta had enjoyed joining Marcus in the shower. In truth, the practice had always made him uncomfortable; the act of being washed by this older woman seemed more than a little ceremonial, even maternal, which reminded Marcus—inappropriately so, especially when he was going down on Greta in the shower—of the son his age whom she never saw. It had once occurred to Marcus—again, when he was on his knees, licking, sucking, servicing—that he had never showered with Jessica. That first thought quickly became an essential aspect of the whole erotic co-showering ritual, during which he would find himself making a list of things he had done with Greta that he had never done with Jessica. The list would start off innocently—*I've never slow-danced with Jessica, I've never shared a bottle of wine with Jessica, I've never sipped espresso with Jessica, I've never gone to the opera with Jessica*—before turning pornographic—*I've never rubbed a washcloth over Jessica's breasts, I've never tasted soap between Jessica's legs, I've never pressed Jessica up against the tiles and taken her from behind*—until the culmination of all these nevers made him come between another woman's legs (*Oh, Jessica*) in a passionless, masturbatory way not at all dissimilar to the manner in which Marcus has just—alone in this hotel shower, with Jessica still asleep on the other side of the door—jerked himself into ejaculatory release.

Marcus shuts off the water, reaches for a towel. He drowsily rubs his head, arms, chest, legs, his shrinking penis, dry. He's calm for the first time since this morning, when he heard Jessica Darling's name being called over the Clear Sky public address system. He cracks open the door to take a look at her on the bed. She hasn't changed positions, but he can see the duvet cover rise and fall with every breath.

He steps toward the mirror and uses the same towel to wipe off the obfuscating fog. Marcus rolls his right bicep toward the glass. If you look closely enough, and know what to look for, you might notice that the skin is darker in certain spots than it is in others. He gently traces his fingertip along shadowy hatch marks and squiggles that could be mistaken for naturally occurring freckles or accidental bruises but are neither. A shiver runs through him; even the tiniest arm hairs stand up on end. It's a response to his own touch, the delicate caresses paying respect to the ghostly remains of what was once a badly translated tattoo. Marcus pays more reverence to these near-invisible Chinese characters than he ever did when they were legible. The original needlework never meant as much to Marcus as his decision to have it erased, from his arm if not his memory.

Forever, he thinks. *Whatever.*

eight

Jessica is walking across a field of green. Under her arm, she carries a laptop. She's wearing her only suit, the dark, well-tailored, and too expensive one she bought with one of her first Do Better paychecks, the one she wears when she needs to look her most competent and professional, the one she wears when Cinthia has persuaded her to meet with potential big-money donors for the Do Better High School Storytellers project and she gives her passionate, heartfelt PowerPoint presentation about how much the program has forever changed the lives of so many young people all over the country. This is her power suit. She feels powerful in it. She's trying to get somewhere fast. The laptop is getting heavier with every step, weighing one arm down to the point that she's lurching like a humpback across the field. She'll never make it if she has to hold on to this laptop. When did she allow herself to be so burdened by technology? When did she stop using black-and-white composition notebooks and start relying on a laptop? Before she realizes what's she's doing, she sets the laptop down on the grass and keeps on walking. She feels so much lighter now, but her slingbacks are still sinking into the soft earth, slowing her down. She takes off the heels and flings them aside. Barefoot, she pushes off from her tiptoes and breaks into a run. The sky is cloudless and the sun is hot. Jessica feels the streams of sweat forming at her temples and racing down her torso. She unbuttons her jacket, slips it off her arms, and lets it fall to the ground. Picking up the pace, she tries to find a racing rhyme but gets too distracted by the *zzzp-zzzp* of fabric rubbing between her legs. She grabs at her thighs and—whoosh!—the tearaway bottoms come off with the professional swiftness of a b-baller or a stripper. Now she can concentrate on her mantra—*you yes you*—but not for long, because her camisole is chafing her shoulders. She clutches the offending straps and whisks that garment away as well. *You yes you*. With each item of discarded clothing, she is lighter, fleeter of foot. *You yes you*. She doesn't need the suit, she feels powerful without it. *You yes you*. Finally, in one impressively gymnastic maneuver—*you! yes! you!*—she leaps out of her panties without breaking stride. She bursts into a full sprint, running faster—*youyesyouyouyesyouyouyesyou*—than she has ever run in her life when—*You!* CRASH! *You!*—she runs right over Marcus Flutie in a red T-shirt, who, up to and including the moment of impact, has been standing perfectly and peacefully still.

I'm here, she pants, still sprawled on the grass. *Naked. Without shame. In paradise.*

He smiles and reaches for her hands.

nine

Marcus pokes his head outside the bathroom door to check once more that Jessica is still asleep. All evidence says yes, but he asks out loud anyway. "Jessica? Are you still asleep?"

Jessica snorts, murmurs something unintelligible, and pulls the duvet over her head.

Aha! She can hear me, Marcus thinks.

Deciding there's no need for modesty, Marcus struts out of the bathroom, across the room, toward the duffel bag propped up against his bed. As he uncinches the top of the canvas sack, he dismally remembers an important detail: There are no clean clothes in this bag. Not only are his clothes unclean, they are surely in violation of several basic health codes. They are caked in toxic demolition dust, outhouse mud, po'boy drippings, a spilled Hurricane Katrina cocktail, and other unidentifiable forms of fluid and filth. Marcus thinks it might be best to torch the whole bag and its contents and start all over again.

He debates the condition of the clothes he was wearing before the shower. The corduroys are in okay shape—they shouldn't spread any communicable diseases. He tugs them on, then stands half dressed, considering the rest of his options. Now that Marcus himself is scented with rosemary and mint, the once endurable if unpleasant stench of the T-shirt, the dress shirt, and yes, even the cashmere sweater strike him as noxious, perhaps even nefarious. He can't tolerate the thought of putting them on again, and he doubts that Jessica would come within arm's length if he did. That is, whenever she wakes up.

Should I try to wake her up? Marcus asks himself.

"Jessica?"

His voice is so needy and pathetic, it makes him recoil in shame. He's so grateful that no one else heard his whimpering. *Natty's right,* he thinks, *I need a roundhouse kick to the brain.*

At least hearing the sound of his own needy, pathetic voice has helped him realize that he doesn't really want to wake her up. If he really wanted to wake her up, he could easily do so by jumping up and down on her bed or shouting her name at full volume. He wants her to be awake, true, but he doesn't want to be the one responsible for waking her up. He also doesn't want to wait around for her to wake up. That, too, seems needy and pathetic and the ideal justification for a roundhouse kick to the brain.

Besides, he's got a plan.

On a hunch, Marcus strides over to the closet, opens the door, and—aha!—finds what he was looking for: a Here hotel–brand bathrobe. He presses his face into the plush, velvety cotton and inhales. It smells fresh, like fabric softener. He slips the bathrobe over his corduroys, ties the belt into a knot, and poses in front of the full-length double mirror on the back of the closet door. It's an unconventional outfit, yes, but less risqué than going shirtless. If asked by perplexed guests or wary employees, he could always claim that he'd gotten lost coming back from the spa or pool, or imply that his strange attire had something to do with the airline losing his luggage, which would inspire most listeners to join in with their own lost-luggage horror stories and forget about him in the bathrobe. Most people believe whatever you tell them because they want to believe.

He takes a Here hotel pad and pen to leave a note for Jessica. He pauses for a few minutes, mouthing words as he tries to come up with the right message with the right number of syllables for her to read upon waking. Once satisfied, he slides his cell phone into one pocket of the bathrobe, his key card and wallet into the other, and heads out the door.

ten

Jessica is walking through the corridors of a hospital. Under her arm, she carries her teardrop carry-on bag. She is wearing a black sweater, black jeans, and black sneakers that contrast sharply with the bright fluorescent lights and bleached-white hallway. She is looking for Sunny's room but isn't in a rush to get there. Most of the doors are closed, but she notices there is an open door farther down the hall. She thinks it's the room she's looking for, but she's not sure, because there don't seem to be any numbers differentiating one room from the next. As she approaches this room, she hears music coming out of it. It's a familiar song, but she can't place it because no one is singing the words, and she needs the words. *What are the words?* She starts humming along with the music, but it doesn't help her with the words. *Why can't I find the words?* She decides to ask the room's occupant for the words to the song, and when she pokes her head through the doorway, she is surprised to see that this is indeed Sunny's room, but the music isn't a recording, it's being played by a band of musicians who have set up all around Sunny's hospital bed for a live performance starring none other than Barry Manilow himself. Sunny is still comatose, purple, and bald, attached to a tangle of wires, including a machine that is monitoring her brain activity and projecting the multicolored images onto the wall like a lava lamp at a rave. Barry Manilow is wearing the electric-blue bedazzled jumpsuit but isn't singing—he's frozen, mouth open, microphone in hand, in the iconic pose from the decoupage toilet seat cover. Jessica wonders why Barry Manilow isn't singing and is just about to ask him to stop posing and start singing already when he suddenly breaks the pose and silences the band with a commanding wave of his sparkly arms. Then Barry Manilow says ruefully to Sunny, *I can't smile without you. I can't laugh. And I can't sing.* Barry Manilow turns away from Sunny and faces Jessica, and that's when she discovers that Barry Manilow isn't Barry Manilow but Marcus Flutie dressed as Barry Manilow.

You! Jessica shouts.

Yes? Marcus asks.

You, Sunny says, sitting upright in her bed, curiously removed from all life-support accoutrements. Her hair has grown back into the style she had before the accident, crooked self-cut bangs and all.

Sunny! Jessica cries out, dashing to her bedside.

You, Sunny repeats, this time in a scoffing *so-over-it* tone.

Me, what? Jessica asks.

Sunny flicks her irises just so. It's a gesture indicative of the weariest strain of teen disdain, when she can't even muster sufficient *ugh* to execute a full-circle eye roll.

You suck.

e|even

Marcus struts over to the elevator bank, presses G, and waits. A second or two later, he is joined by a young girl in a pink tracksuit. She is pouting in petulance but also because her mouth is overcrowded with orthodontia.

He looks down at her and smiles. "Hey," he says.

She glares up at him skeptically. "Why are you wearing a bathrobe? You look ridiculuth."

Marcus bursts out laughing, too disarmed by her candor to be the least bit offended. After all, he does look ridiculous, but only a kid would come out and say it. He decides to tease her a bit. "Don't you know? It's the latest style," he says. "I can't believe *you* left the room without wearing your bathrobe."

"It ith not," the girl replies in total confidence. "You look like a pervert." She beams as she says this, pleased with the rejoinder and herself. Her mother comes Ugging toward them.

"Amber! What have I told you about talking to strangers?" Her eyes crawl all over Marcus, taking in every detail of his appearance: height, weight, build, hair color, tattoos, scars, and/or other distinguishing physical characteristics.

"To not to," Amber says sullenly.

"It's not her fault," Marcus says. "In her defense, you can't blame her for asking why I'm wearing a bathrobe, can you?"

"No," Amber's mother says curtly. "But I can blame *you* for wearing one in the first place. What are you? Some kind of pervert?"

"I *told* him he lookth like a pervert," Amber singsongs.

The pervert comment makes Mommy proud. She throws an arm

around her daughter and brings her in for a hug that says, *That's my girl!* As the pair embraces, Marcus catches a look at himself in a nearby mirror and instantly sees the truth in their assessment. He *does* look like some kind of a pervert. What is a bathrobe but a cozier version of a flasher's trench coat?

"I'm wearing pants," Marcus explains, idiotically lifting up the hem of the bathrobe to reveal a corduroyed leg. Judging from the horrified expression on both mother's and daughter's faces, this fact only seems to further implicate Marcus in perversion.

Determined to clear his name, Marcus is relieved when Amber removes a pot of Mixed Berries and Clotted Cream Lip Plumping Balm from her pocket. Aha!

"Be You Tea Shoppe," he says as Amber pinkie-applies the translucent red gloss to her puckered lips. "I know the woman who founded it."

Now Marcus is a bathrobe-flashing perv with an unseemly knowledge of pretween beauty products. When Amber and her mother step back to keep their distance, Marcus realizes too late that such a comment won't help undo pedophiliac aspersions. Thankfully, before he can say or do anything else to sully his image, the elevator arrives on the twentieth floor. The doors open, revealing a single passenger, a middle-aged woman dressed like lunch on the African savannah, who, thankfully, seems too preoccupied with her cell phone to take much notice of him. Marcus is relieved that he won't be left alone with the appalled mother-daughter pair. He makes a sweeping ladies-first gesture with his arms.

"Oh, no," Amber's mother says in a tone that is as derisive as it is decisive. "You can go alone, dressed like that. We'll take the next one."

Marcus slinks inside the elevator. Seeing the anger in Amber's mother's face, he feels compelled to offer an explanation. "The airline lost my luggage!" he lies.

"Did they altho looth your *mind*?" Amber retorts.

The girl earns a high five from her mom just before the doors slide shut. Marcus straightens his spine, lifts his chin. He tries to assume a dignified air, like a man of leisure who thinks nothing of going about his business in a borrowed bathrobe.

"They lost my luggage, too," confides the elevator's only other passenger. "I'm on hold with Clear Sky Airlines right now. Wait—I think I've got someone—nope. Still on hold."

Marcus smiles genially, turns his back on her, and watches the numbers light up in descending order.

The women finger-jabs him in the shoulder, clearly looking for someone to commiserate with. "We just want to be where we're supposed to be," she says. "We just want to be with the people we want to be with. I don't think that's asking too much, ya know what I'm saying?"

The elevator arrives at the ground floor with a jolt.

"Yes," Marcus says. "I know just what you're saying."

twelve

Y*ou suck, suckity, suck suck suck.*

That's the thanks I get after how much I've worried about you?

You should be happy that the trauma to my brain didn't permanently change my personality. You should be relieved that I'm not mistaking you for a hat. And for the record, you missed your flight this morning because you overslept and didn't take your dad's ride or your mom's advice about the car service and got on the wrong security line.

You've made your point. Is that why I suck?

No. You suck because it's not even like you're making an effort in these dreams.

What dreams?

What dreams. See? This is what I'm talking about.

What you're talking about what?

The dreams like the one you're in right now.

What? This is a dream? Are you sure?

You just saw Barry Manilow turn into Marcus Flutie. How much more proof do you need?

Marcus is . . . Wait! He's gone! Where did he go?

[Long sigh.] Do I really have to say what you want me to say?

What is it that I want you to say?

That wherever he is, he won't be gone for long. That he's never really gone because he always comes back to you. Isn't that the whole BLATANTLY OBVIOUS AND NOT AT ALL SUBTLE takeaway message from all these—forgive my political incorrectness—retarded dreams?

And what's that supposed to mean?

It's like the caps-lock key is stuck. These dreams are SCREAMING WITH MEANING. Way too on-the-surface to be accurately called a product of the subconscious. If I were to turn in an essay with this kind of heavy-handed Psych 101 SYMBOLISM, you would tear it up and tell me to DO BETTER.

I don't know what you're talking about.

That's fine, Jessica. Deny, deny, deny. That's a surefire way to guarantee that you will totally fuck this up.

Fuck what up?

Sweet baby Jesus. You're even worse off than I thought. I mean, here I am, Sunny Dae, your alter ego, the Korean reincarnation of your younger self, Pineville High's current model of the cynical girl who has it all and yet has nothing at all telling you straight-out to STOP BULLSHITTING YOURSELF, and yet you STILL persist in doing everything you can to FUCK THIS UP. I beg of you, Jessica, DO NOT FUCK THIS UP WITH MARCUS.

Marcus? This is about Marcus? And watch your language. I am an authority figure, you know.

That's it. I'm going back under.

No! Wait! Don't!

You have the nerve to pretend that this isn't about Marcus?

I don't want this all to be about Marcus.

I know you don't. And you've been doing a fantastic job for the past three years not making everything about Marcus. And for the past six hours in particular, you have put forth a spectacular effort in not making everything about Marcus. But it's time to get real. These dreams—ARE ALL ABOUT FUCKING MARCUS. And I mean, like, fucking literally and not fucking as in a gratuitously obscene figure of speech. And don't get on my case about how I shouldn't abuse our close mentor/mentee relationship by crossing the boundaries of propriety by using foul language.

I am not going to have sex with Marcus.

So you've doth protested . . . and not without good reason.

You're actually agreeing with me?

Well, sorta. I mean, I understand why you wouldn't want to, you know, in light of what happened when you tried to have meaningless rebound sex with Len Levy after you broke it off with Marcus. You just don't have it in you to have a torrid one-night stand. It always has to mean something with you or you feel horribly guilty about it afterward.

So you're saying that I don't want to have sex with Marcus because it would mean too little?

No. I'm saying you do want to have sex with Marcus but are afraid it will mean too much.

Ack! What do you know?! Why should I listen to you? You're still in high school!

Right. I'm still in high school. Which means I know everything.

Wait. You said I'm using you as the means for having a sort of somatic Socratic dialogue, right? Like you're a representation of another part of my own psyche. Right?

Uh . . . I guess so.

So I'm really having this conversation with myself.

More or less. Yes. According to that theory.

Which means I'm the all-knowing one, not you.

So when you're having one of these conversations with yourself, you really should listen more closely to what you're saying.

Me as you or me as me?

I am me as you are me as you are we as we are the walrus, goo goo g'joob . . .

Har-dee-har-har. Are you sure this is a dream? My dreams aren't usually so talk-talk-talky.

You're right. Your dreams are usually more visual.

Like the business on the beach and in the park.

Right. That's your usual style. So maybe this isn't your dream. Maybe it's someone else's dream.

Someone else's dream? How would I end up in someone else's dream?

Come on. You dated that pot-smoking philosophy major in college. You're telling me you never smoked too much weed and got into one of those "what if we're all characters in someone else's dream?" meaning-of-life conversations?

That's irrelevant. Of course it's my dream. If it's not my dream, then whose dream is it? Yours? I'm just a character in your prolonged-coma dream?

You got it! Just like the surprise twist revealed in the final episode of a long-running dramedy!

Oh my God! I'm a figment of your imagination? How long has this been going on? Since I encountered the wedding party on the beach?

Maybe earlier than that.

This whole day with Marcus has been a dream?

Maybe earlier than that.

What? My whole life?! OH MY FUCKING GOD.

Now who gargled with the toilet water, Ms. Potty Mouth? Reeeeeelax. I'm just messing with you. This is totally your dream. Our brains dream for hours at a time, but we remember only a fraction of images upon waking. So you probably won't remember this whole conversation as being part of the dream. You'll be left with the memory of Marcus in the Barry Manilow suit and me sitting up in this bed with my bad hair, telling you that you suck.

That's all I'll remember?

No. You'll remember the earlier stuff on the beach and stripping down in Central Park. Those all-caps dream symbols are memorable by design.

Are you sure this is my dream?

I'm sure. Because if it were my dream, I would not waste time talking to the likes of you. My dream would not be suitable for viewers under the age of eighteen, because I would totally be doing the freaky deaky with Marcus Flutie.

Sunny! That's inappropriate!

What? I said "freaky deaky," not "fucky sucky."

What did you say? I can't hear you over Barry Flutie. Or is he Marcus Manilow?

You know I can't smile without you . . .
What?! It's too loud! I can't hear you!
Can't smile without you . . .
What?
Can't smile without you . . .
WHAT?!
Can't smile without you . . .

thirteen

The elevator doors *ding!* open, and Marcus marches out of the vestibule like a man on a mission. His harried pace is at odds with his leisurely attire, but he tries not to give a second thought to all the snickers and giggles as he hurries through the front lobby toward the hotel gift shop. As he approaches the all-glass entrance to the shop, he's relieved to see that it's still open but nearly emptied of customers because it's dinnertime. He grips the ends of his terry-cloth belt and gives them a firm tug, as if to shore himself up for the task at hand.

His hand is on the glass, ready to push open the door, when his phone buzzes inside his pocket. He removes his hand from the door, leaving behind a moist five-fingered print, and removes his cell from his pocket. He's hoping it's Jessica calling him from upstairs. He's disappointed but not surprised to discover that it's Natty yet again.

"What's up, Pampers?" Marcus says.

"Dude, where the hell are you?"

Marcus sighs as he watches his handprint evaporate. He puts his hand in the same spot, then pushes open the door to the store. "I'm at SHOP Here," he explains, making an effort to establish friendly eye contact with the store's only visible employee, a salesclerk whom Marcus guesses to be around his own age, but he looks clammy and unwell. Either this guy is suffering from a massive hangover or he hasn't seen daylight in months. Perhaps both. If the sight of Marcus in his bathrobe is at all alarming, the clerk isn't going to let his concerns interfere with whatever he's texting. His lips curl in on themselves in concentration.

"Shop *where?*" Natty asks, barely pausing for a reply. "Forget it. It doesn't matter. What are you doing right now?"

"Right now?" Marcus asks, making his way over to the stacks of T-shirts lining the far wall of the store. "Right now I'm wearing a bathrobe, talking to you on my cell phone, browsing through a collection of New Jersey–themed T-shirts so I can buy one and put it on so I don't have to wear this bathrobe anymore."

"Are you alone?"

"There's the salesclerk."

"Dude, you *know* that's not what I meant," Natty says with growing impatience.

Marcus passes over a T-shirt that brays FUGEDDABOUDIT, and another that asks WHAT'S YOUR EXIT? Finally, he picks up one that has the Here logo in modest type across on the chest.

Marcus nudges the cell phone between his shoulder and his ear, then holds the men's-size-large T-shirt up against his body. It fits his torso just fine, but there's enough excess material widthwise to fit another person. He switches it for a medium, which skims his skinny frame but would ride high above his navel like a hoochie crop top. As he tries to decide between forms of unflattery, Natty's voice jumps out at him by surprise, causing the phone to slip and clunk to the floor.

"Sorry, Nathanielsan," Marcus says upon retrieving his cell. "I forgot I was talking to you. What did you say?"

Somewhere in Princeton, NJ, a pint-size Rhodes Scholar slams his cell phone against the closest tiger-striped foosball table.

"Oh, right. Am I still with Jessica Darling?" Marcus asks in mock innocence. "Not at the moment. She's upstairs in our hotel room."

Marcus chooses the men's size L and then selects the same shirt in women's size small.

"You got a hotel room together?!"

"Yes," Marcus sighs, instantly regretting his candor. He doesn't want to talk about Jessica with Natty, who just wouldn't understand.

"Did you *hit that shit* already?"

"No," Marcus says wearily, loosening the tie to his bathrobe. "I didn't." He looks over at the salesclerk, who is giving him his full attention. "Do you mind if I put this on now?" Marcus asks.

The salesclerk looks him up and down skeptically.

"Put what on?" Natty asks. "Who are you talking to?"

"I just feel sort of, er, *awkward* here, half dressed."

"Who's with you?" Natty asks. "And why are you half dressed?"

"No one," Marcus says.

"No one my *balls*," Natty says, getting amped. "You've got another girl with you. No wonder you couldn't keep your mind on the conversation. Dude, you squander more ass than anyone I know. This is why you gotta man up and—"

Marcus shuts off his phone before his best friend can say another word. Until Natty allows himself to fall in love, he will never understand Marcus's unwavering devotion to Jessica Darling. Ten years after he first fell for her, Marcus still doesn't understand it himself. It is an alchemical attraction that transcends all reason, rationality, and—in the three years since she spurned him—reality.

"So the Hef look isn't working for you, eh?" the salesclerk asks, letting his thumbs rest for the time being. His voice is stuck in the back of his throat like a loogie that needs dislodging. He strains to smile for the first time since Marcus entered the store, revealing a too-wide mouth full of teeth that are all exactly the same shape and size. He reminds Marcus of a sinister porpoise up to no good.

Marcus shakes his head.

"I'd ask what happened to your clothes," the salesclerk continues tonelessly. "But the truth is, I don't really care." He barely glances around before thrusting his elbow toward the back of the store. "Go ahead."

"You sure?"

When the clerk nods in consent, Marcus scuttles behind a pyramid of Here travel coffee mugs. He quickly shrugs the bathrobe to the floor, then slips the T-shirt over his head. It's stiff and scratchy and has that "Made in China, Shipped to the U.S.A." plasticky smell that is especially disconcerting when the object isn't made of plastic. The shirt perfect fifths

reaches long enough to cover his torso but has so much excess material around the neck, chest, and gut that it would be a perfect choice for Marcus and his conjoined twin. He wishes he had stuck with the bathrobe. But now that it's off, he has no choice but to bend over and pick it up, along with the women's-size-S shirt that fell on the floor.

He steps out from behind the mugs to model the shirt for the salesclerk, but he's already returned his attention to his texting. Marcus neatly refolds the women's-size-S T-shirt over one arm and slings the bathrobe over the other. For the next few minutes, Marcus circuits the store, picking up a few items that hopefully won't push his already straining credit card past its limit:

- one (1) pair of women's-size-S boxer shorts with JERSEY GIRL embroidered on the ass
- one (1) pair of men's-size-L boxer shorts with JERSEY GUY embroidered on the crotch
- one (1) I ♥ NJ shot glass
- one twin-pack (two cupcakes) chocolate Hostess cupcakes
- one (1) dental hygiene travel kit, including a folding toothbrush, mini toothpaste, and floss
- one deck of playing cards

"Do you have any candles?" Marcus asks as he approaches the register.

The salesclerk snorts. "Nope. And no matches or lighters, either. They're considered dangerous." He grins in an unfriendly way. Marcus can't imagine that anyone would have his teeth sanded down to achieve this strange aquatic aesthetic, yet he can't imagine what confluence of genetic material would lead to such a malocclusious reversal in human evolution.

The salesclerk rings up the items, including the T-shirt already on Marcus's back. Marcus hands over his credit card, which the plane ticket has surely put within a decimal point of obsolescence. The card *does* clear, and Marcus sighs in relief as he signs the receipt. The clerk places the items in a SHOP Here bag, and as their transaction is about to come

215

to its logical conclusion, Marcus is compelled to ask a question: "Why did you trust me?"

The salesclerk snorts. "I didn't."

"You didn't?"

"Oh, no. No way. I still don't."

"Why not?"

"I know a tweaker when I see one."

"Tweaker? As in meth?! What?!"

"Oh, don't try to deny it. You're skin and bones and so strung out that you can't even get dressed."

Marcus barks out a retaliatory laugh. "I may look a little, er, unhinged, but I'm not a tweaker!"

"The first step is admitting you have a problem."

Marcus knows he could just grab his bag and go. But he needs to know one more thing. "If you thought I was a shoplifting drug addict, why did you let me put on the shirt before I paid for it?"

The salesclerk flexes and releases his fingers. "I was hoping you'd try to steal it."

"You were—what?" Marcus asks, slowly backing away from the register. "Why?"

The clerk's crazy eyes gleam as he reaches below the counter and pulls out a silver device that looks like a cross between an electric razor and a vibrator. "I wanted an excuse to Tase you."

Marcus reels backward. "W-w-why would you want to do that?"

He aims the Taser at Marcus, smiling wider than ever. "You look like the guy who screwed my ex-girlfriend."

For the first time, Marcus makes note of the name tag: NICK. Did he screw Nick's girlfriend? Maybe he did. But Marcus is certain he's never seen this Nick before. He would've remembered those teeth. *Those teeth.* Then again, maybe the teeth weren't always like that. Maybe Nick had a perfectly varied set of incisors, canines, and molars until he jawed them down to uniformity, as a teeth-grinding tweaker might do. And with this leery admission comes the follow-up realization: Maybe Marcus *did* screw this Taser-toting salesclerk's girlfriend. Maybe he met the girlfriend at a Pine Barrens bonfire, or at a beach party, or in a beer-skunked basement in the late nineties, wooed her with made-up poetry inspired by boy bands and misquoted Rimbaud, screwed her, and never called her again—the powers of the poet/addict manwhore used to their full effect. When he considers other coincidences of the strange-but-true variety, it's not at all far-fetched. He could find out for sure right now (*What was the name of the guy who screwed your girlfriend?*), and yet such validation or repudiation seems irrelevant. Maybe Marcus deserves to be Tased regardless of whether he was the guy who screwed Nick's ex. Even if Nick's ex wasn't one of the forty (and right now Marcus is going with the higher number because his guilty conscience demands it), she very easily (too easily) *could have been*. And if not him, then she was screwed by someone *just like him*. Maybe a good Tasing will be emotionally beneficial for both of them. For Nick: payback. For Marcus: punishment. In the moment, Marcus remembers a passage from one of the notebooks Jessica gave him the afternoon of their breakup: *I might never be able to forgive you for all the girls who came before me, nor myself for all the men who would come after you.*

He makes a decision. "Do it," he says, dropping his upheld palms. "I deserve it."

Marcus stands tall, ready to withstand twenty-five thousand volts of agony. Nick extends his trigger hand, winks in concentration . . . then falls onto the counter in laughter.

"Duuuuuude! I'm just playin'."

Marcus blinks once, twice, but otherwise doesn't move.

"I've never seen you before in my life," Nick says, his laughter slowing down.

"You sure?"

"You sound disappointed."

Marcus *is* disappointed by this anticlimactic surrendering of arms. Once he had accepted the idea of being Tased, he had embraced it as enthusiastically as he had other experiments in extremity, including a yearlong silence, a monthlong abstention from soap and water, a weeklong liquid (i.e., alcoholic) fast, a weekend-long priapic bender with a perimenopausal lover, and a daylong marathon of "My Song Will Never Mean as Much (As the One He Once Sang for You)" on MP3 repeat. He

217

already suspects the truth, however, that this seconds-long shock to his system would have been equally ineffective in making him feel any worthier of the woman who is still asleep in room 2010.

"That's the most fun I've had all week," Nick says, still wheezing with amusement. "I hate this job. I hope I get fired. My mom forced me to get this job because it works with *her* schedule at the airport. What about *my* schedule, huh? What about what's important to me? I hate my life."

Marcus isn't listening to Nick's rant. He stumbles backward and out of the gift shop, so dizzy and disoriented that it's as if he wasn't merely threatened but was actually Tased by the hungover saleclerk bored with life. If Marcus *had* been listening, he might have suggested that Nick try using the third-person-turning point of view to figure out where his life went so wrong.

fourteen

"WHAT?!" shouts Jessica as she is yanked out of sleep and into wide-awakeness.

I can't laugh and I can't sing . . .

It takes a few eye-rubbing, head-shaking moments for Jessica to realize that she isn't with Sunny in a bleach-bright hospital room being serenaded by Marcus Manilow (or Barry Flutie), but alone in a pitch-black hotel room being awakened by her cell phone. Jessica knocks over a small lamp in the scramble to grab it off the bedside table before Barry starts *finding it hard to do anything.* So sure of the caller, she answers it without even checking the ID.

"Sunny?!"

"Of course it's sunny," replies someone who is definitely not Sunny. "You're in the Virgin Islands, aren't you? But that's a strange way to answer the phone."

"Oh, hi, Bethany." Jessica tries her best not to sound crushed. "Thanks for calling. And I wasn't providing you with a spontaneous weather report. I thought you were someone else. And I'm not in the Virgin Islands. Yet."

"What happened? Where are you? Are you going to miss the wedding?"

Jessica replies to the questions in the order they were asked. "I missed my flight. I'm at the Here EWR until tomorrow. And yes, I'll probably arrive too late for the wedding."

"Oh, that's just awful!" Bethany tutt-tutt-tutts. "Horrendously, hideously awful."

Jessica judiciously refrains from explaining to Bethany that the sympathetic overtures are making her feel worse than she already does. "It's not that bad, really."

"Oh, to be alone in a hotel room, and on _today_ of all _days_."

Jessica rights the knocked-over lamp and switches it on. There is no long Marcus-shaped lump under the covers. The bathroom door is open, and the light is turned off. Unless he's meditating in the dark on the floor of the closet, he's not in the room. She appears to be alone _on today of all days_.

"Speaking of your day of days, there's someone here who has something she wants to wish you."

There's a slight pause before Bethany begins singing along to a thin string accompaniment.

> _Happy birthday to you!_
> _Happy birthday to you!_
> _Happy birthday, Aunt J.!_
> _Happy birthday to you!_
> _Annnnd maaannnnyyyy mooore!_

Today, the nineteenth of January, is Jessica Darling's birthday. However, this year the date has taken on new meaning: Today is three days after Sunny's accident. Today is one day before Bridget and Percy's wedding. Jessica knew it would be childish of her to insist on celebrating this nothing of a birthday when there were far more significant turning points clamoring for her attention on opposing sides of the emotional spectrum. Besides, after sweet sixteen and drunken twenty-one, the only landmark birthdays are those ending in zero or five, and this year doesn't qualify. And yet she has to admit that hearing the cheesy little ditty sung in her honor makes her feel grateful that there are at least two people (okay, plus her parents—that's four—oh, and Hope, who tried to wish her happy birthday before Jessica cut her off) who made note of her arrival into this world twenty-six winters ago. The emotions come at her all at once, tackling her like a too-tight hug.

"That was me on the violin and Mom on vocals," chirps Marin when she gets on the line.

"Thanks, Marin," Jessica says, trying to breathe normally. "It sounded awesome." She walks over to the minibar, opens it up to see that it is well stocked, and grabs a regular Coke and a Baby Ruth bar.

"Eh, I've heard better," Marin says dismissively. "So how old are you today, anyway?"

Jessica pops open the soda can and takes a long slug before answering. "Twenty-six."

Marin unleashes a loud, long whistle. "Wheeeeeeeeeeeeeeeeeew. That's getting up there, huh?"

Jessica can't help but laugh at Marin's candor. To her, any Disney Channel starlet who has aged out of her self-named sitcom qualifies as *old*. "I guess it is." Jessica tears into the candy bar, noting that if not for the vitamin-packed muffin purchased by Marcus, she'd be running on a nutritive deficit for the day.

"Wasn't my mom, like, married by twenty-six?"

Jessica can hear Bethany in the background, shushing loudly before correcting her. "I was twenty-*seven*, Marimba."

"Mooooom," Marin growls through her teeth. "Stop calling me that! I'm a *person*! Not a musical instrument!"

This combination comeback/takedown makes Jessica laugh but also reminds her of an earlier version of the same mother/daughter dynamic.

"Oh, Marin, tell your mom I saw a mother/daughter pair wearing matching BU! tracksuits."

"Ack," Marin gags. "Those tracksuits are fugly."

"Right. The ones made out of hemp? With the conflict-free rhinestones?"

"Hemp! That's right!" Marin repeats with an audible lip curl. "With conflict-free rhinestones!"

Jessica hears Bethany straining for information in the background. "What tracksuits? I hope you're not referring to the affordable and earth-friendly line of Be You merchandise."

"This is E-Car Jerry's influence, huh?"

"*Totally* E-Car Jerry."

Jessica can't quite make out what Bethany is saying in the background, but that's the point.

"Fine, Mom." Marin sighs. "Can you please leave the room so I can talk to Aunt J. in private?"

Bethany mumbles something else, and Marin whines, *"Okay! I got it!"*

"Is everything okay?" Jessica asks before trying to dislodge a chunk of caramel from her back molars with her tongue.

"She hates it when I call him E-Car Jerry," Marin says. "And when you say it, too. She says we should know better."

"We should."

"But it's funny."

"And you *like* E-Car Jerry, right?" Jessica discards the empty soda can and candy bar wrapper. Hands now free, she heads straight for the closet and flings open the doors. There's nothing inside but empty hangers, a dry-cleaning bag, a folding ironing board, and a safe. Jessica sheepishly closes the doors, feeling silly for thinking that Marcus could possibly be sitting there on the floor. Hadn't he told her that he doesn't do that anymore?

"Sure. He's nice. He makes Mom happy," Marin says.

Jessica walks toward his duffel bag, cinched tight, slouching against his unslept-in bed. Jessica furtively looks over her shoulder, as if Marcus could have stealthily reentered the room without her noticing.

"I like E-Car Jerry, but I hate those tracksuits. I refuse to wear mine," Marin says in a very prim and professional tone that cracks Jessica up. *"Why are you laughing?"* Marin is deeply offended.

"Nothing," Jessica replies before adding, "Just you. You're funny."

"I'm not being funny. I'm being serious. I hate those tracksuits. They are itchy aaaaaand fugly."

Jessica can't take her eyes off the duffel bag. "Those tracksuits put the FU in *fuuuuuuuuuugly.*"

Now Marin bursts into laughter.

"That's it!" Jessica cries out, egged on by her niece's enjoyment. "Tell your mom we just came up with the next conflict-free rhinestones-on-the-butt slogan. Not BU! FU!"

The joke isn't so funny, but that doesn't matter. It isn't really about the joke itself, but the idea of the joke and how Jessica can get away with joking—even lamely—about the fugly tracksuits, but Marin cannot because those fugly tracksuits could revive her mother's business and represent the first creative collaboration between her mother and her any-day-now fiancé. Jessica has always felt a special kinship with her niece. Marin looks exactly like Bethany ("a knockout," just how Marcus described her), but even the Darling grand-matriarch has noted that Marin comports herself far more like the younger and moodier of her two daughters, a comment that was delivered to the elder daughter with a resounding "Good luck."

Jessica grips both ends of the rope that ties (and unties) the mouth of the duffel. Why is she tempted to do this? What is she looking for inside? What hasn't Marcus already told her that she needs to know?

"Hey, Aunt J.?"

Jessica drops the ropes as if she's been caught. "Yes?!"

"I hope you didn't get mad before when I said that thing about not being married. Because I didn't say it because I'm still, you know, mad about not being a flower girl. I—"

Jessica doesn't wait to hear the rest. "Oh, no! I didn't get mad. In fact, it's kind of strange that you should bring it up, because . . ." She pauses, knowing that she probably shouldn't do this, and yet that grown-up appreciation of discretion can't quite overcome her childish impulse to tell all. All day she has kept this secret to herself, and now she really wants to share it with someone. And who better than Marin?

"Can you keep a secret?" Jessica is still looking at this duffel bag, which, upon closer inspection, appears to be coated in a thick layer of . . . nastiness. If this is what his bag looks like _before_ he spends a week in a tent pitched in outhouse mud, what will it look like afterward?

"Sometimes," Marin replies. "It depends on the situation. And the secret."

"I appreciate your honesty." Jessica hums in thought. She's feeling oddly unsettled by Marcus's luggage, and she's not sure why.

"What is it?! Aunt J.? What?! Don't leave me hanging here!"

Jessica is still trying to decide whether to tell Marin the real secret or to make one up when she spots Marcus's handwritten note on the desk. Jessica picks up the paper and is about to read the message when Marin breaks the silence.

"Did you see Marcus?" She says this as if she has just been tipped off via text: **c markiss?**

Jessica fumbles the note in shock. "What?!" The paper wafts gently to the floor.

"Woo! You did! You saw Marcus! That's the secret! Woo! Where did you see him? When? Does he look the same? Did he ask about me? Wooooo!" Marin has run out of breath and inhales long and loud before finishing up with the kicker. "Are you still in loooooooooooove?"

Usually, Marin's uncensored inquisitions are attributed to the guile-lessness of youth. But in this case, she's just asking the questions—_the_ question—that anyone who knows Jessica and Marcus would have asked, which is exactly why Jessica kept the news to herself all afternoon. Until now.

"Say something!!!" Marin begs.

Jessica replies to the questions in the order in which they were asked.

"Yes, I saw Marcus. I ran over him at the airport, then we spent the whole afternoon talking to each other over coffee. He looks the same but even better than the same. He did ask about you."

Jessica stops here, squats down, and looks for the dropped slip of paper.

"Aunt J.?! You haven't answered the most important question of all!!!"

"I haven't," Jessica says, crawling on her hands and knees. "Have I?"

"I'll answer it for you," Marin announces in the same all-business tone that declared she couldn't wear the fugly tracksuits.

"Oh, really?" Jessica spots the paper underneath the desk, reaches for it.

"And the answer is . . ." Marin takes a dramatic breath and delivers a speech that draws upon everything she has ever learned about love from watching too much reality television with her nanny. "YES! You and Marcus still LOVE LOVE LOVE each other because you and Marcus are TRUE SOUL MATES even though you haven't seen each other in, like, FOREVER, but it's just like MOM and E-CAR JERRY, who didn't see each other after, like, FOREVER, and it was, like, WHAMMO! BLAMMO! Cupid's ARROW with, like, MANY INTIMATE MOMENTS, and they knew it was FATE and DESTINY that had brought them back together . . ." Marin pauses just long enough to suck in a lungful of air.

"YES! You and Marcus are still in LOVE and you're totally going to get MARRIED and have ME as a FLOWER GIRL in the ceremony and MAYBE you'll even get married at twenty-seven like my mom did the first time which is ONLY A YEAR AWAY only YOU AND MARCUS won't ever ever ever split up because you are SOUL MATES with MANY INTIMATE MOMENTS you are DESTINED to live HAP-PLILY HAPPILY HAPPILY ever AFTER . . ."

Marin is hyperventilating. Jessica, too, is having trouble breathing. She shakily stands up, then backs herself onto Marcus's untouched bed.

"So?" Marin asks.

Jessica squints, trying to focus on the shaking paper.

> Gone for a while
> Hoping, always, to return
> If you will let me

"Aunt J.! Helllloooooooo? Are you there?"

Am I here? Jessica asks herself. *Am I really here? Is any of this really happening? Or is this really a long, vivid-coma dream?*

Jessica clears her throat. "I gotta go, Marin," she says, trying to steady her voice. "I'll talk to you soon."

"But you didn't answer the most important question of all!'

"I didn't need to," Jessica replies matter-of-factly. "You answered it for me."

She shuts off the phone. Sloppily folds the note and stores it in her back pocket. She calls out to him.

"Marcus Flutie."

fifteen

Marcus doesn't know how long he's been leaning against this wall with his eyes closed, recuperating from the strange encounter with the salesclerk. It's been long enough to get noticed.

"Aren't *you* a tall drink of water."

Marcus opens his eyes and looks down to see a woman whose complicated yellow feathered hat is half as tall as she is. From her vantage point, even Natty would qualify as a tall drink of water.

"My name is Lola."

"Er, hi, Lola."

"I am a showgirl."

"A *showgirl?*"

She flounces her wrists. "With painted feathers in my hair." Then risks another hip replacement surgery with a shimmy. "And a dress cut down to there . . ."

"Oh," Marcus says, slow on the uptake. "I get it. 'Copacabana.' "

"I knew you were good people!" She tries to punch him in the arm but doesn't come close enough to connect. "What are you up to?"

"Loitering," Marcus replies, smiling slightly, wishing Jessica were here to hear him say it.

"That's nice," says Lola, clearly not listening. "Listen, I've got sort of a wager going."

"A wager?"

"Yeah, a wager. And it involves you."

"Me?"

Lola has already taken him by the elbow and is leading him toward the sign at the entrance of a room that encourages guests to PLAY HERE. "Can ya sing?"

And before Marcus can answer, he is muted by the sight and sound of a blue-haired granny appropriately attired in a blue-sequined TRUE BLUE SPECTACLE T-shirt.

"Somewhere down the road . . . Our roads are gonna cross again . . ."

"We took over the place!" shouts Lola. "We turned Karaoke Tuesday into Barry-oke Tuesday!"

The stranded members of the Tristate Chapter of the Barry Manilow International Fan Club have indeed taken over the bar and the interactive gameplay arena. They have pooled their resources and have paid off the DJ, who for the under-the-table price of $250 was bribed into letting the BMIFC use their own backing tracks.

"What does this have to do with me?" Marcus asks.

"I bet Adele that I could turn anyone into a Can't Smile girl—or *boy*, in your case!"

"A what?"

"It's a Barry tradition dating back to the early eighties, when he would bring a girl up onstage to—"

"Shhhhhhhhhhhhhh!" hisses the crowd, eager to hear True Blue Spectacle bring her song to its dramatic close.

"Look," Lola says, sticking a knotty finger into Marcus's chest. "All ya gotta do is get up on that stage and sing a few bars of 'Can't Smile Without You,' and I win the bet."

This strikes Marcus as a fair request. At Princeton, always at Natty's prodding, usually as a diversion during stressful midterm or final exam weeks, Marcus has participated in wagers that were far more complicated and possibly injurious to one's health. The Fall of '08 Bet You Can't Drink a Blenderized Taco Bell Cheesy Double Beef Burrito, Caramel Apple Empanada, and Mango Strawberry Frutista Freeze While Arguing Why George W. Bush Is the Greatest American President in History comes to mind. (Marcus won . . . barely. And it wasn't the value-menu smoothie that posed the biggest challenge to his regurgitative reflexes.) Though he's anxious to return to Jessica, he knows this will be one hell of a story, one that would totally justify waking her up.

"Look, Lola . . ."

"SHHHHHHHHHHHHH!"

Marcus shuts up to give the song the reverence it deserves.

"You be-e-e-looooooong." True Blue stretches out the word, looking heavenward, before completing the line in a lilting, surprisingly plaintive alto. *"To-o meeeeeeeeeeeeeeeee."*

The crowd goes wild. Those who can leap to their feet, do. True Blue modestly averts her eyes, curtsies. When she looks up, she catches Lola's eye, claps excitedly, and motions for her and Marcus to join the rest of the Tristate Chapter of the Barry Manilow International Fan Club at the front-and-center table before the stage. This table is trashed. There are glasses decorated with half-sucked orange halves and spiky crescents of pineapple. Glasses foamy with machine-mixed coladas, daiquiris, and margaritas. Glasses swishing with pink and white but never red wine. Glasses thick with the Barrytini (vodka, maraschino cherry liqueur, chocolate liqueur), the official cocktail of the Barry Manilow International Fan Club.

The Tristate Chapter of the Barry Manilow International Fan Club is getting shitfaced tonight.

"Drink up," Lola says, handing Marcus a glass full of what looks like a chocolate milk shake. He takes a long pull. It tastes like a milk shake, too, but with a battery-acid afterburn.

"And now," the DJ is saying, "we've got Barbara singing 'Looks Like We Made It.' "

Barbara pushes herself up from the table, leaving a trail of FANILOW sweatshirt glitter in her slow-moving wake.

"This is a very sparkly crowd," Marcus observes out loud, already feeling the loosey-goosey effects of the Barrytini.

Hands are extended, names are offered, but Marcus forgets them all as soon as he hears them. They are all pleasant middle-aged women with beauty parlor hair who look like they've recently retired from various careers in elementary education—teacher, librarian, nurse, lunch lady. It is far easier to distinguish them through their homemade Barry Manilow–themed fashions than by their names he can't remember.

"That's today," Marcus says, pointing at a T-shirt with 1/19/2010 across the chest.

"Yes," says 1/19/2010. "That's the . . . It's his . . . I can't even say it!" She drops her head on the table.

"Get over it!" snaps Worldwide Symphony Tour '84. "The last show is tonight, and we're gonna miss it! Hmph!"

Barbara has finally lumbered up onstage.

"Maybe it *is* time for Barry to end it once and for all," says Lola.

The table gasps at this act of sedition. "Nononononono!"

The BMIFC respectfully settles down for the opening horns and the first line of Barbara's ballad. *"There you are, looking just the same as you did last time I touched you . . ."*

But a few members will not stand for this kind of talk.

"He's got another decade in him!" shouts True Blue with a raised fist.

"Maybe two!" chimes in Let It Shine, Let It Shine, Let It Shine.

"Sinatra kept it going into his eighties!" adds True Blue.

"I think we should just trust Barry to know what's right," Lola says. "Maybe he wants to go out while he's still on top."

"Hmph! If that were the case, he would've never sung another note after 1977. Hmph!"

More gasps.

"How can you say that?"

"I say trust Barry," says Lola. "He'd never intentionally let us down. Maybe he's got something even better up his sleeve. And even if he doesn't, shouldn't we be grateful for all the magic he's made for us already?"

They all concede agreement on this point.

"All I could taste was love the way we made it . . ."

"You're up next," Lola says, pointing at Marcus. "If you can get up there and sing the chorus, I win the bet!"

"I don't really sing," Marcus says, slurping up the last of his Barrytini.

"Neither does Barbara, but that doesn't stop her!"

The table earthquakes in laughter as Barbara painfully modulates between one chorus and the next.

"LOOKS LIKE WE MADE IT!"

"I haven't sung in public in a very long time." It's a halfhearted protest. Whether it's the Barrytini, or the strangeness of the situation, or rather, the strangeness of how this entire day has unfolded since he first heard Jessica Darling's name over the Clear Sky Airlines public address system, Marcus is ready to take the stage and win this bet not just for Lola but for Barry Manilow fans the world over.

"We MAY-ee-YAY-ee-YAY-ee-DIT . . ."

Another standing ovation! Marcus has just learned a key lesson of Barry-oke: A spectacularly delivered last line can make up for the previous three minutes and thirty seconds of caterwauling, especially if it is spectacularly awful, as Barbara's last line was, as opposed to just boring awful.

"And now, singing 'Can't Smile Without You,'" the DJ booms, "we've got . . . Who do we got?"

"What's your name?" asks Lola.

"Namesmarcus." Marcus is slurring. He is teetering on the borderline between tipsy and shitfaced.

"Nieman Marcus? Like the department store?"

Without a formal introduction to the crowd, Marcus shakily pushes himself into an upright position and wobbles toward the stage. Marcus has not been onstage like this since prom night 2002, when he sang his song for Jessica. He had hoped it would be like the depictions of such heartwarming novice-takes-the-stage scenes in movies, when the bright spotlight blinds the nervous singer and he can't see the audience so it's easier to pretend that he isn't onstage in front of a roomful of strangers, oh no, but that he's really alone in his own bedroom, singing into a hairbrush microphone as he has so many times before, and this little delusion tricks him into being the show-stealing rock star he has always been but until now has been too shy to show the world. However, in Marcus's case, (a) there is no difference between the lighting on the karaoke stage and the bar, so he can see the BMIFC's every wrinkle, mole, and flesh roll, and (b) he has never, ever sung into a hairbrush microphone, even in the privacy of his own bedroom.

The song begins with piano and a lackadaisical whistle. Marcus puckers his lips, but something (vodka) about this gesture (maraschino cherry liqueur) strikes him as funny (chocolate liqueur). He spit-laughs into the microphone.

"Sing it, don't spray it," grouses Worldwide Symphony Tour '84.

Marcus has just enough time to wipe his mouth with the back of his hand before singing. *"You . . . know . . . I . . . ."*

It's just like watching the wannabes on *American Idol* or any other talent competition. You can tell within the first few notes whether the performer has *It* or not. And while the standards that determine what *It* is and whether or not one has *It* vary greatly from show to show and judge to judge, the collective opinion of the stranded members of the Tristate Chapter of the Barry Manilow International Fan Club is unanimous: Neiman Marcus has *It*.

"Victory is mine!" boasts Lola.

The rest of the BMIFC shares her joy, always pleased for any opportunity to turn a neophyte Fanilow into an acolyte. They sway and snap their fingers along to the easy soft-shoe beat of the first chorus-verse-chorus. They whisper a digressive commentary about the performance.

"He's got a nice voice, this Neiman Marcus . . ."

"It's a bit deeper, more resonant, than the recording . . ."

"More of a baritone than a tenor . . ."

"Barry himself is more of a baritone than a tenor these days . . ."

"Hmph. He can't sing it in the original key anymore. Hmph."

"Hey! I like the way Neiman Marcus shakes his little butt!"

"He's got a nice butt!"

"Barry has a nice butt!"

"Hmph. Barry never had a butt like that!"

"You didn't see him back in seventy-seven!"

"Shhhhh . . . He's working himself up to something big . . ."

The song is approaching the bridge, the apotheosis of cheesetastic pop. Marcus is totally committed to bringing it home.

"I'm finding it hard leaving your love behiiiiiiiiind meeeeeeee!"

There might even be some jazz hands involved.

In this climactic modulation at the end of middle-eight, Marcus plants his feet wide, flings his mike-free arm in the air, throws back his head, and closes his eyes.

To the untrained eye, Marcus might appear to be just another hipster whose drunk logic convinces him that his ironic performance of this easy-listening easy target is waaaaaay funnier than it really is. Though such an observation would be accurate 99 percent of the time, his performance is the lonely 1 percent that is pure of heart. Marcus is wholly immersed in this music, this moment. He's right here, right now, reveling in the freedom to be an unapologetic nerd, celebrating his emancipation from the poet/addict manwhore so many still mistake him for. Marcus Flutie is letting his freak flag fly in the name of the Showman of Our Time! He's going balls-out for Barry Manilow! He's a true-blue spectacle, a worldwide symphony, letting it shine, shine, shine so bright that he can't see anything else, not the cheering ladies of the Barry Manilow International Fan Club, not the smirking DJ, not even the grinning fangirl groupie sneaking up onstage to turn his solo into a duet.

sixteen

Marcus Flutie is singing "Can't Smile Without You" as if it is his religion. Not just any religion but one of his own invention. If Marcus were in the mood to doctor up a fake church à la L. Ron and pass himself off as a prophet teaching the Gospel of Barry . . .

- He's been Alive Forever
- He wrote the very First Song
- He put the Words and Melody together

- He is Music
- He writes the Songs

. . . Jessica would renounce her vows made to the Universal Ministry of Secular Humanity and become his first converted congregant. His mesmerizing performance—so much like the one in the dream she didn't remember until she saw him onstage, frozen in the famous toilet seat cover pose—has brought Jessica to her knees.

How did she come to arrive at this sacred place? (She rushed out of Room 2010 and took the elevator down to the lobby.) When did she first hear the Call? (As she raced through the hotel's front hall, searching for Marcus, through the walls, a few steps away from the entrance of PLAY Here.) Why did she make this pilgrimage in the first place? (She needed to see Marcus, to touch him, to confirm that everything that had happened between them today had in fact actually happened. The line between her dreamstate and wakestate had never been so porous.)

None of this matters anymore. The spirit has moved her! She is reborn! She's the most repentant sinner at this revival meeting, and it's not enough for Jessica to be a passive spectator at the moment of her salvation. She is overcome by an evangelical desire to share her divine revelation (*Marcus Flutie!*). She raises up her cell phone to capture a few seconds of this holy vision. She says a silent prayer and sends proof of this miracle to Hope, Bridget, and Percy with a message: **I'll miss the wedding but will be there for everything after. I promise to tell all tomorrow. XOXO, J.**

There's one last way for her to testify her devotion. She must unite with Marcus Flutie on the altar and sing praises to the Showman of Our Time. Thus empowered by her epiphany, Jessica grabs the spare microphone dangling from the side of the DJ's booth and switches it on. She opens her mouth to join Marcus on the bridge.

"*I'm FinDInG iT HaRD lEaviNG yOur lOvE BeHinD meEeeEEeEeee!*"

The submusical sounds could be confused with Pentecostal tongues. The Tristate BMIFC is baffled by the appearance of this girl onstage until Lola points and shouts, "That's the mini-Maniloony from the customer service center!"

If Marcus is stunned by the sudden appearance of Jessica onstage, he doesn't let it show for long. His eyes startle, then quickly settle on the veins bulging in her forehead as she strains to hit even the easiest notes. He grins. He nods in encouragement. He even breaks into a chorus-style kick line in time with the clap-along-cymbals-crashing coda.

"I jUst caN't sMiLe WitHouT yOoooOoooOOOooOOooooOoOooooo OooOooooooooOooooooooOooooooU!"

Now Jessica and Marcus are smiling so broadly that they could be accused of overselling the song's message for the most literal-minded audience members. *Wait. You say you can't smile WITHOUT each other . . . So does that mean you CAN smile WITH each other? Holy cow! I never saw it that way before. I totally get it now . . .*

The moment the track ends, Jessica and Marcus nearly fall off the stage in incredulous laughter. *Did we just do that? Did we just sing "Can't Smile Without You" in front of a roomful of strangers? Are we really still here together? Did this strange-but-true story just get even stranger? Like, off-the-charts strange?*

Meanwhile, the BMIFC is whooping and whistling and banging cutlery against their emptied drink glasses. The sight of two young Fanilows in love makes up for missing the Final Show in Las Vegas. Well, almost.

When Jessica has finally caught her breath, she says pointedly, "You know, I *can* smile without you."

"I know that," Marcus replies, matching her tone. "I can smile without you, too."

"I can laugh . . ."

". . . but you sure as hell can't sing!" shouts Lola, which is when Jessica and Marcus realize they are still holding the microphones close to their mouths. They drop the mikes to their sides.

Marcus turns to Jessica, leans in close, and whispers over the din. "Jessica?"

She can't speak. She can only part her lips in anticipation. *Because Marcus Flutie is going to kiss me,* Jessica thinks. *Marcus Flutie is going to kiss me, and I am going to pass out right on this stage and hit my head and fall into my own coma dream.*

He gently squeezes her cheeks with his thumb and forefinger, pushing her lips into an exaggerated pucker. "You are the worst singer I have ever heard."

This is their second touch all day. Another shock passes between them, and this time there's no question that it isn't a case of static electricity caused by feet shuffling across the carpet.

seventeen

Jessica and Marcus have parted ways with the Tristate Chapter of the Barry Manilow International Fan Club. They head toward the elevators, his gait noticeably less sure-footed than hers.

"Was it my imagination, or did they recognize you?" Marcus asks.

Jessica slows her pace as she contemplates how to answer this question. "Strange but true," she begins. "A woman crashes into her ex-boyfriend at an airport. She hasn't seen him in three years. This woman once received a decoupage Barry Manilow toilet seat cover from this ex-boyfriend right before their last attempt at reconciliation. Soon after the crash, the woman gets on line at an airport's customer service center. In front of her are twenty furious members of the Tristate Chapter of the Barry Manilow International Fan Club who have missed their flight to Las Vegas to see the one and only Barry Manilow, the Showman of Our Time, in his final performance of his Final Farewell Tour . . ."

"Aha." It dawns on Marcus that he saw them, too, from afar.

"*Aha.* And wait, there's more. As she is waiting, she receives a phone call. Her ring tone? 'I Can't Smile Without You,' by the one and only Barry Manilow, the Showman of Our Time. The twenty members of the Barry Manilow International Fan Club immediately embrace her as one of their own."

Jessica doesn't even bother telling Marcus about the Barry Flutie dream because this story is already strange enough, true enough without it.

"Do you believe me?" she asks.

"Of course I believe you," Marcus says. "Why wouldn't I believe you?"

Jessica doesn't answer. Without saying it, each knows what the other is thinking:

If Marcus hadn't chosen His *Greatest Hits* eight-track to play in the Caddie as he drove Jessica to their first "nondate" at Helga's Diner ten years ago, would He have served as the cheesy leitmotif throughout their relationship, starting with the eight-track, peaking with the toilet seat cover, and culminating with tonight's performance of one of His songs in front of an audience consisting solely of rabid members of His fan club? If Marcus had chosen another eight-track in the stack left behind by the Caddie's octogenarian pre-owner, say, Dolly Parton's *Greatest Hits*, would Jessica and Marcus have found themselves—through predestined fate disguised as random happenstance—duetting on "Here You Come Again" in front of an audience of crazed Dollywoodies?

Jessica and Marcus simultaneously slide uneasy smiles in each other's direction because there is no way of answering any of these questions.

The empty elevator opens up to receive them, and Jessica breaks the silence by asking a question Marcus can answer. "So what's in the bag?"

"If I tell you, it won't be a surprise."

"Like there haven't been enough surprises today already?"

"Oh, you can handle a few more."

Jessica honestly doesn't know if this is true. The doors close, cutting them off from the outside world.

Marcus is humming to himself. It's a familiar tune, yet Jessica can't quite place it. She's about to ask Marcus about it when he stops humming.

"You really are a terrible singer."

"Oh, *that* again?"

"But there's a certain magic to your tone deafness," Marcus explains. "You were singing an imperfect fifth."

The elevator stops on the tenth floor. Jessica and Marcus take a step backward in anticipation of a crowd. When the doors open, no one is waiting to get inside.

"Clearly, I know nothing about music," she replies, jabbing the close-door button. "What's an imperfect fifth?" She presses it again and again until the doors finally shut. The elevator resumes its ascent.

"A *perfect* fifth is an interval between a note and seven semitones above it." Jessica nods, her eyes on the up arrow because she's too nervous to look him in the eye. "The first two notes in the theme to *Star Wars* are a perfect fifth." He clears his throat, then sings, "*Staaaaar Waaaars . . .*"

"Oh my God," she honks. "When did you become such a nerd?"

Marcus sighs. "I was always a nerd, Jessica," he says. "I just hid it better than most nerds."

"Too well?"

Marcus purses his lips, nods. Jessica is only now beginning to understand just how much of Marcus's cock-first confidence is subterfuge for deep-seated . . . nerdiness.

"There's another example I could give you, but I'm not sure if I should."

Jessica gives him a measured look. "It's already out there. You might as well."

Marcus takes a deep breath, clasps a clenched fist to his heart, and in a spot-on imitation of a certain geeksta performer they both know well, sings two words from the chorus of the eighty-seventh most popular song on iTunes.

"*My . . . SONG . . .*"

Jessica gasps in instant recognition. "So you *do* know about Len's song!"

"*Of course* I know about Len's song!" Marcus clears his throat, then launches into the chorus.

"*You have stopped the arrow of time . . . There's no meaning to this rhyme . . . Because my SONG will never mean as much as the one . . . He once sang . . . For you, yes, you . . .*"

Marcus had known about Len's song all along, just as Jessica suspected. Therefore, he also knows about how she fucked Len after refusing Marcus's marriage proposal, knows as much as there is to know on the subject of Jessica and Len. He knows, he knows, he knows, *and he doesn't care*. He doesn't care in the same way that Jessica suddenly real-izes that *she* no longer cares about the ex-lover who gave him the gor-geous cashmere sweater, or any of the girls who came before her, for that matter. She doesn't care, and he doesn't care, because none of those other people are in this elevator right now. It's just Jessica and Marcus, oxymoronically alone together.

Jessica applauds, and Marcus takes an operatic bow. She wants to tell him that Len was right about his song never meaning as much, that is, until Marcus just sang it for her in the elevator. But she can't. Not yet.

They take another anticipatory step backward as the elevator stops on the fifteenth floor. But, as before, no one gets on. There are still just the two of them in this elevator, and Jessica is both aching for and aching from this realization.

"When you started singing with me," Marcus continues, "I was singing the note as it should have been sung. You were singing an imperfect—or, if you want to be technical, bare, open, or empty—fifth above it. Together, we created a vocal spark that *sounded* like a perfect fifth, the most stable of all harmonies."

A vocal spark? Is that the explanation behind the evangelical fer-vor she felt onstage? Jessica can tell that Marcus is being totally sincere about this, but she can't allow herself to agree to it, nor follow up in the obvious way. *In other words, Marcus, we were perfect in our imperfection.*

Instead, Jessica blurts, "You once called me sloppy firsts."

"*What?!*" He snaps to attention, quickly sobered by this statement.

"You did."

"That's offensive," he says with a frown. "And it doesn't even make sense. I mean, I've heard of sloppy seconds, but sloppy firsts? I guess I didn't know what to say to you, so I just said something stupid to fill the void. Something like *Blame Byron!*"

They both laugh at this very recent memory.

"Sloppy firsts," Marcus says, rubbing his temples. "What does that even mean?"

"I don't know, either," Jessica says, "and I've been spending the last ten years trying to figure it out."

Jessica can hear motors grinding as the elevator continues its climb.

Then, over that whirring sound, Jessica hears the sound of skin sliding against skin as Marcus rubs his palms together.

"Strange but true," he says. "A man pays one hundred dollars to have his fortune read by a New Orleans voodoo Queen. She takes his money, then takes his hands. She tells him he's going to get run over. Two days later, he is run over in the Newark Liberty International Airport by the only woman who has ever mattered to him."

"Wait," Jessica says sharply. *"When* did this happen?"

"Two days ago."

Her eyes narrow. "You were in New Orleans two days ago? But I thought . . ."

"I was coming from New Orleans when you ran over me, not going."

The gears turn, turn, turn. "So you're not flying out anywhere tomorrow?" Her voice is pinched.

Marcus can't let his over-the-top impulsiveness, his need to prove that he still cares, be the very thing that drives her away yet again. He won't join her on her flight to St. Thomas. The ticket will go unused. He'd rather lose $895 (he doesn't have) than lose her again. He briefly considers the possibility that his name might be called over the Clear Sky public address system, as Jessica's was this morning. *This is a final boarding call for passenger Marcus Flutie . . .*

"Marcus?"

"No," he answers. "I'm not flying anywhere tomorrow."

"Then," she ventures hesitantly, "why are you still here?"

The words are still fresh from her mouth as he offers himself as an answer, reaching across the bare, open, and empty space between them, collecting her hands in his. All these hours together spent talking, she has strenuously avoided touching him, smelling him, tasting him, afraid of how her body would respond. She flinches. He tightens his grip. He won't let go that easily. He pulls her toward him.

"Birthday presents," Marcus says, close enough that the top of her head is warmed by his every breath.

"What?"

"This bag is filled with birthday presents."

Jessica points to herself in dumb disbelief. "For *me?*"

He nods. *This is the difference between bittersweet reunion and restraining order,* he thinks.

Words fail her. Her mouth glug-glug-glugs like that of a fish. *How did you know it was my birthday?* she wants to ask. *When did you know?*

"Last week," he replies, answering her unasked question.

Last week, thinks Jessica. *Of course he realized it last week.* Marcus had never forgotten that January 19 was her birthday, just as she had never forgotten that July 19 was his, just as there would be parts of their shared past that they would never be able to forget. She slowly lifts her eyes to look up at Marcus. The tenderness in his unwavering gaze makes her want to laugh and cry at the same time. She giggles—the middle ground.

"You're giggling," Marcus says.

"I am."

"And you're chewing on your lip," Marcus says.

"I *am?*"

"You are. Or were, until I called you on it."

"I didn't think I did that anymore."

"Well," Marcus says. "Apparently, you do." He lifts their still-interlocked hands and gingerly brushes a knuckle against her lips. Jessica's mouth parts, wanting more. Ten years earlier, Jessica had conjured a birthday celebration not unlike this, a sweet-sixteen variation on what she referred to in her journal as her "standard stuck-in-an-enclosed-space-and-the-trauma-bonds-us-sexually-and-otherwise daydream." Despite her best efforts to act her age, Jessica is tempted to punch the open-door button between floors to fulfill this long-ago fantasy.

The elevator *dings* open on the twentieth floor. A middle-aged couple is taken aback.

"Oh!" exclaims the woman.

"Erg," grumbles the man.

Jessica and Marcus, standing inches apart, separated only by a quartet of clumsily clutched hands. Jessica and Marcus, alone together in that elevator, are a far more intimate sight than any less innocent act could be. This anonymous middle-aged husband and wife are embarrassed to have found themselves as accidental interlopers.

"Sorry," calls out the wife as Jessica and Marcus silently push past them and head for their room.

eighteen

As instructed, Jessica is waiting on Marcus's bed. He has turned off all the lights and is now walking toward her with two Hostess cupcakes balanced in one hand and a cell phone in the other.

"*Happy birthday to you,*" he's singing. "*Happy birthday, dear Jessica . . . Happy birthday to you.*"

He kneels down on the floor next to the bed and holds up the cell phone, on which she can see he has uploaded the photo of a lit candle. "Er, I couldn't buy any candles, so this will have to do." He hands over one cupcake and keeps the other for himself.

Jessica shyly shrugs an okay.

"So close your eyes and make a wish on the count of three."

Jessica does as she's told.

"One . . ."

I wish . . .

"Two . . ."

. . . our love was right now and . . .

"Three!

Jessica opens her lids, and Marcus snaps the cell phone shut. He's right beside her in the darkness, but it isn't close enough. She reaches out to take Marcus's hand, to pull his body on top of hers on the bed. She grasps empty air instead of his warm skin. He has already gotten up off the floor and is halfway across the room to switch the lights back on.

Jessica is relieved and frustrated in equal measure. She is feeling more earthbound than she did when she saw him onstage, even a little ashamed that she so eagerly testified her love. But as she watches him move across the room, she cannot deny her powerful physical attraction to this man, nor how half of her is begging to renege on her chaste promises and fuck Marcus Flutie straight through the night until tomorrow morning. But no! The other half knows intellectually that fucking Marcus all night long will not only lead to regret, as it did with Len. It will also prove Marcus right about her inability to make good on such celibate claims.

Jessica counts the loop-de-loops on the cupcake—*one two three four five six seven*—then stuffs the whole damn thing in her mouth. Her cheeks balloon with synthetic chocolate and artificial cream.

"We've never celebrated a birthday together before," Marcus says, coming toward her with the bag of gifts.

Jessica chokes down a spit-thickened wad of synthetic chocolate and artificial cream. "Uhhuunnhh?"

He perches himself cross-legged beside her on the bed, then very deliberately places the shopping bag between them. "We were never together for our birthdays."

The mattress is quivering. At first Jessica thinks her pent-up sexual energy is manifesting itself as a geotectonic phenomenon. After a moment, however, she realizes that she's not the one responsible for this involuntary bedquake.

nineteen

Marcus is flapping his knees in and out and up and down faster-faster-faster than the suicidal moths on The Queen's dilapidated doorstep. He wonders if he might have to excuse himself to the bathroom and rub another one out.

I will prove to her that I've only got the best intentions, he promises himself. *I will prove to her that this is not just about sex. That this is not just about tonight.*

Jessica dances her chocolate-covered fingertips along his bicep. He blanches.

"What did I do?" Jessica asks innocently.

"Nothing," Marcus says, composing himself. "I just zoned out there for a moment . . ." He trails off.

"Can I have my present now?" Jessica asks, eyes aflutter. If he didn't know any better, he would swear that she was sort of . . . maybe . . . perhaps . . . coming on to him? *No, this is another test. She's just hopped up on sugar. This isn't sexual.* He squirms and pulls his T-shirt down over his crotch. *Ohhhhhh, maaaaan.* He hasn't been this torqued up since he was a twelve-year-old virgin popping boners whichever way the wind blew.

"Pleeeeeeeeease?" Jessica whines.

Marcus opens the bag just slightly, takes a peek, removes the boxer shorts he bought for himself.

"These are mine," he says. "But the rest . . ."

"Gimme! Gimme! Gimme!" Jessica lunges, grabbing more of Marcus than the bag. To defend himself, Marcus releases the bag into her arms, rolls off the bed, and stands militarily (ahem) erect.

"Er," he says, his hands jangling around inside his front pockets. "So there's a T-shirt and boxers in there because I thought you might need them to sleep in. And a toothbrush because I assumed you packed yours and it arrived in the Virgin Islands without you. And a shot glass for, er, well . . . doing shots. Not that I'm suggesting we get drunk or anything, but . . ." He's filibustering madly. "And there's a deck of cards in there because I thought I could maybe, I don't know, teach you how to play hearts. Remember? That was the game your grandmother Gladdie always played . . . It was weird, but I thought of her when I was with The Queen. It was a memory I hadn't thought of in a long time. She was such a great woman, your grandmother. Oh, man. Oh, shit. I just realized that you need four players for hearts. Maybe we can play rummy or something instead. I don't know. That Barrytini really scrambled my brain and . . . I . . . uh . . . gotta excuse myself to use the bathroom, okay? So you might want to turn on the TV or something, because I might be in there a while and . . ."

Midramble, he backs himself into the bathroom, shuts the door, and locks it behind him. He collapses against the door like the sole horror-movie survivor of the scythe-slashing psycho killer's rampage.

twenty

Something just happened. And Jessica is not sure what. She can hear the sound of running water in the bathroom. The sound of Marcus taking a shower.

Marcus is naked in the shower, she thinks. *Goddamn him for making me think about him naked in the shower right now!*

To distract herself from thoughts of Marcus naked in the shower *(STOP THINKING ABOUT MARCUS NAKED IN THE SHOWER)*, Jessica teethes on the deck of cards, bites off a piece of plastic, spits it across the duvet. She unsheathes the cards from their wrapping, shuffles the deck. The cards make a fluttering sound that brings her straight back to the Silver Meadows retirement home, waiting patiently while her grandmother shot the moon, beating Marcus, her late-in-life partner, Moe, and a perpetual crank in sweatpants whose name Jessica can't remember. Three out of four of those players are dead. Death. Gladdie's funeral . . . Jessica and Marcus furtively kissing behind closed doors . . . their first kiss . . . in a bathroom . . .

This is not helping her get her mind off of Marcus naked in the shower.

The phone lights up. Barry Manilow sings. Jessica sees the Pineville area code followed by an unfamiliar number. She picks up, expecting to be disappointed. "Hello?"

"I'm *totally* breaking the rules right now."

Jessica nearly drops the phone. "Sunny?"

"Anyway, I had to wait until everyone left before I could call you. I'm supposed to be resting, but I'm, like, hello?! I was *comatose* for three days, I think I've rested enough."

"Y-y-y-you're awake?" Jessica stammers.

"Well, *duh*," Sunny says. "How could I talk if I were still unconscious?"

"B-b-but you suffered a traumatic brain injury. You can't just wake up and go right back to normal! I read all about it on the Internet. It only happens in the movies."

"It's not like I just woke up a minute ago. I was kind of in and out all through last night and the early morning, then more awake than not as the day went on. I still look like hell. I mean, I look like I've been run over." Sunny pauses dramatically before adding, "*Which I was.* And now I've got an even worse haircut to grow out. But other than that, the doctors say I should make a full recovery."

Jessica's throat is closing. "Did you know I was with you last night?" she croaks.

"I have a memory of you talking to me," Sunny replies, "but I honestly don't know how much of what was going on in my head was really happening or a figment of my imagination."

Jessica nods in commiseration even though Sunny can't see her. Her phone *beep-beep-beeps* to warn her that the battery's almost dead.

"My parents told me that you were so worried about me. I told them the only reason you like me is because I'm your alter ego, the Korean reincarnation of your younger self, Pineville High's current model of the cynical girl who has it all yet has nothing at all . . ."

A spider army skitters up Jessica's spine. *What did she just say?*

The phone *beep-beep-beeps* again.

"It's almost too bad I got into Columbia early decision, or this would have made one hell of a get-into-college essay, huh? Oh, and think about that supa-dupa bonus layer of depth and profundity you could have added to my letter of recommendation—oof!" Sunny gasps. "Shit, I gotta go, I hear the nurse coming. I'll talk to you later."

The call ends without good-byes. And to belabor the point, Jessica's phone *beep-beep-beeps* one last time before shutting down completely.

Jessica cradles her darkened phone, stunned by how quickly tragedy turns to comedy and back again. She crashes onto the bed, shaking seismically from the inside out, laughing and sobbing ferocious tears of relief.

twenty-one

Marcus isn't proud of cranking it twice in six hours, but desperate times call for desperate measures. If he unloads (again), he's fairly confident he can make it through the next few hours with monklike reserve. He fills his palm with liquid soap and is about to commence another round of jerk-and-pull when he hears a terrifying noise over the sound of the water rushing out of the shower head, the guttural wail of a wounded mammal. He slows the flow of water just to confirm that he's actually hearing what he's hearing. He is. And it's coming from right outside the bathroom door.

He cries out, "Jessica!"

Without hesitation, Marcus scrambles out of the shower stall, his sopping feet slip-sliding across the slick tiles. He bursts through the bathroom door and sees Jessica thrashing around on the bed, choking on agonizing sobs.

He rushes over to her, envelops her entire body in a wet embrace. "What is it?" he pleads. "Tell me!"

Jessica gasps for air. She takes a ragged, gurgly breath. She's shocked by her body's response to this good news. She had no idea just how much emotion she'd bottled inside until it all came gushing out. "She's okay!"

"Who's okay?"

"Sunny . . . hit by a car . . . in the hospital . . . coma . . ."

Her half-sentences are horrifying enough. "Why didn't you say something sooner?"

She squirms. "I didn't know how deep you wanted to get."

"Deep," Marcus says without hesitation. "Always deep." He cradles her in his still-wet arms, strokes her hair. "Tell me more."

Jessica obliges. She tells Marcus about Sunny, the only Girl she worked with over the past two years who had become more than just a character in a story, but a complicated person who defied all narrative conventions. This process—from one of many to the One—began, ironically, with the give-and-take exchange of—what else?—stories. Jessica had once told Sunny the story of the decoupage Barry Manilow toilet seat cover. Sunny had loved that story, had become slightly obsessed with that story, a story so beautiful and bizarre, unlike anything that she—ever-boyfriendless at sixteen, for whom the delayed loss of virginity was, in her opinion, well-nigh inevitable to go to whatever frat boy was first to get her sufficiently but not prohibitively passed-out drunk during college orientation week—had come close to experiencing herself. To Sunny, this story begged to celebrated and commemorated through—yes!—a ring tone. A ring tone! Ha! What could be a better example of the inane ways that people chose to express themselves through mass consumerism?

"She's why I'm getting my master's in education," Jessica explains. "I liked many of my mentees, but it was Sunny who made me realize that I could be good at this. That I could inspire young women the way Mac or even Haviland inspired me . . . Oh, fuck, I sound so goddamn pageant. I better snark on someone quick!"

Marcus laughs without any sound. It's a distracted laugh. He releases Jessica just enough so he can look her in the face. "There's something I should tell you."

twenty-two

Jessica nods to encourage this confession. For a split second, she prepares to hear him confirm the worst of the rumors blitzing her brain:

He wants to be just friends.

He doesn't want to be friends or anything else.

He loves another woman.

He doesn't love me.

"I won an Inter-Ivy Fellowship."

She says nothing, anticipating that there's more to it than that.

"It provides tuition for any graduate school program in the Ivy League."

Jessica nods slowly, almost afraid to acknowledge what this might mean for her.

"That's why I was in New York City a few weeks ago. I was touring Columbia's School of International and Public Affairs."

What it might mean for *them*.

There is a thoughtful pause. Jessica's eyes spring wide-open, but her lips shut tight.

"What?" Marcus asks. "You look like you want to say something."

Jessica makes a show of looking away. "You're naked."

Marcus looks down as if he himself is just discovering this fact.

The rest is unnecessary.

Jessica wriggles herself from Marcus's embrace and sits up on the bed. He remains kneeling on the floor beside her, then drops face-first into the duvet cover. Jessica cannot tell if this is a gesture of supplication or defeat, neither of which sits well with her. She grazes the top of his scalp with her fingernails. He moans into the Egyptian cotton.

"I think I've changed my mind," she says simply.

He lifts his head. And when their eyes lock, there is no question what Jessica is referring to. She skims his right bicep with her fingertips, lingering just long enough to acknowledge what mistake was once there but isn't anymore.

She continues, "Strange but true: A woman finds herself on line with the Tristate Chapter of the Barry Manilow International Fan Club . . ."

He brushes his mouth against her closed eyelids. "Strange but true: A man receives a prophecy from The Queen . . ."

She breathes into his ear. "Marcus Flutie."

He whispers back. "Jessica Darling."

Lips slide across cheeks rough and smooth.

Mouths meet and . . .

"Ow!" yelps Jessica. "You bit me! You nipped my lip!"

Marcus smiles knowingly. Jessica slides lengthwise across the bed, saying nothing. Marcus waits . . . one second . . . five seconds . . . ten seconds . . . a lifetime . . . until he can't wait anymore.

"Are you quiet because you're surprised or because you're repulsed?" Marcus asks.

"Neither," Jessica replies. "I'm quiet because we've done enough talking."

twenty-three

marred kiss

markissmarkissmarkiss

marcusmarcusmarcusmarcus

origami mouth opening and closing

taunted and tempted

together again

the mouth he used to bite mine

sweet and smooth

telltale throb

below-the-belt thumping

scrambled soft porn

waves of sensation

need not want need

this weird whatever relationship

i want to, oh god, do i want to

the five wonders

what you miss when you don't look hard enough

a game i used to play

spinning out of control

how far i could push you

kismet or synchronicity or even mere coincidence

orchestration manipulation

the one who changed my life

made him forget all the other girls who came before

maelstrom of love lust

laughing hard loud crazy

crazy-good crazy-bad

blindsided

shock me

here finally here

MARCUS FLUTIE MARCUS FLUTIE MARCUS FLUTIE

christ that feels good

MARCUS FLUTIE

again

andagainandagainandagainandagainandagain

cock-a-doodle-dooooooooooooooooooooooooo

magic! enchantment!

i began to levitate

rosy-cheeked bright-eyed bliss

happiness chose me

still holding on for dear life

is this making any sense

present or past tense now or then

past imperfect

and i need you

falling falling falling

i like it here

all i ever knew only you

shoot the moon

cominghome

chaos called creation

it happens it happens

it's all connected last year this year

connected we're connected

samadhi

the universe as an interconnected whole

samadhi samadhi samadhi

hurdling through the air crashing out of the sky smashing

into stars

ready to take a chance again

breathe in deep to take him in

his scent burning leaves in late fall

pulled me tighter, closer than we'd ever been

Marcus

Jessica

moist and messy and perfect

returning somewhere safe

like coming home

soft succulent sweet

please, please, please

keep going, going, going

fast far and long

you yes you

without speaking and barely breathing

slowly nervously tenderly

like i had imagined

all this time

worth the wait

holy shit was it worth it

fade into slumber

his mouth still on my neck

bodies fit together like a living breathing yin-yang

perfect in our imperfection

we are the way we're supposed to be

lying there naked and laughing

together

the entire universe as an interconnected whole

seconds minutes hours weeks months and years to come

deliriously deliciously happy

me yes me

furious flutter awakened hummingbird heart hello hello love

oh thank god

we're in love so

we're always making love

even when we're fucking

writhing roaring

no simple beginning middle or end

love has the longest arms

transcendentally intertwined

i wish our right was love

love i wish was our right

i love our wish was right

right our love was i wish

the only thing that matters is
the everlasting present
my thoughts create my world
we love each other because of our flaws
they make us who we are
the silent heart giving life to those connections
not the end not even the beginning of the end
perhaps the end of the beginning
tasted his sighs tickled by salt in his sweat
every microscopic cell in our one united body expanding and
contracting in pleasure
now
friends become lovers become strangers become friends once
more
and over and over
and
we're still here aren't we
wherever you go here you are
your teeth nipping my lower lip
your fingertip tracing the curve of my hip
your tongue teasing the underside of my breast
tickling nerve endings
cognition overcome by sensation
i wish i wish i wish
i wish our love
was right now
and
(you yes you)
forever

twenty-four

Room 2010 is cast in penumbral early-morning light. Jessica's flight leaves in three hours. Marcus can return to campus anytime.

Jessica leans over the bathroom sink, wiping suds out of her eyes with a washcloth. The stubby end of a travel toothbrush juts out of her foamy mouth. Marcus comes up from behind, wraps his arms around her and nuzzles the nape of her neck.

"You never finished telling me about the happy stories." His voice resonates against her skin like a finely tuned bass string.

She blinks open her eyes, takes out the toothbrush, spits. "Happy stories?"

"The significance of happy stories told from a third-person point of view."

She taps the brush three times on the edge of the sink. "Most happy stories are fantasies that never happened. A form of wish fulfillment."

"Surely there are some happy stories that have actually happened."

She rests the toothbrush on the countertop. "Telling happy stories that actually happened lends a sort of fairy-tale quality to real life. They remind the teller and the listener of the magic that can be found in the mundane if you pay close attention."

"Mission statement?" Marcus asks.

Jessica smiles at him in the mirror. "Mission statement." She turns around and presses her lips into that patch of skin at the base of his collarbone that had been untouchable, uncontemplatable, only eighteen hours ago.

"Well, this will make a good happy story," Marcus says. "Whenever you decide to tell it."

At first Jessica nods in agreement, the top of her ponytail striking his chin with every head bob. But then she corrects herself with a decisive head shake. "We," she says.

"We?"

"Whenever we tell it," she says. "Because it's *our* story."

Jessica slips through his arms and out of the bathroom. She pulls back the blackout shades one side at a time, filling the room with an orangey-pink glow, the stunning kind of sunrise that can be seen only in a chemical skyline. She gazes out the window and down below to the hotel parking lot, which is obstructed by a barely navigable maze of plywood and scaffolding, concrete and construction cones. A patriotic red-white-and-blue banner that extends a whole city block, from one end of a temporary wall to another, reads:

EXCUSE OUR APPEARANCES
WE ARE TAKING APART YESTERDAY
TO MAKE WAY FOR TOMORROW

Jessica casts a backward glance toward the bathroom. Marcus is hunched over the sink, removing her toothbrush from his mouth. She's thinking about the toothbrush and how some couples who have been married for decades—like the middle-aged couple who gasped at them in the elevator, or her own parents—might choose to share their lives but not a toothbrush. And that's okay. She's thinking about Bridget and Percy and how happy she is that they are committing themselves to a lifetime of toothbrush sharing. She's thinking about telling Sunny about the toothbrush the next time she talks to her, if only to hear the eighteen-year-old lecture—in the way that only naive know-it-alls can—on how sharing a toothbrush, even with someone you've slept with, even with someone who is your *soul mate*, crosses the line between intimacy and ickiness.

Marcus spits, then wipes his mouth with the back of his hand. Jessica is overpowered by love, not just for him but for the life she's living right now. She can't wait to tell Sunny how lucky she is to be awake and alive, how much she has to look forward to in life, that there's nothing more beautiful than choosing to spend that life with someone, sharing everything that is intimate and icky and in between. She can't wait to tell Hope in person about everything that has happened over the last eighteen hours, certain her best friend will understand why she didn't blurt it out over the phone, as best friends understand these things. She can't wait to tell Marin that maybe, just maybe, the breathless answer to her own question will turn out to be true.

I can't wait! I can't wait! I can't wait! When she looks at Marcus, she feels just like a child bursting with big news, desperate to shout it loud enough for the whole world to hear. He turns his head and returns her goofy grin, a simple gesture that instantly tames the incorrigible mantra bouncing around her brain. *I can wait,* Jessica thinks. *I have waited. I don't have to wait anymore.*

And it's all at once—between thoughts of dental hygiene, devo-.tion, friendship, life, and death—that Jessica becomes convinced that everything that has happened to her and Marcus for the last ten years—whether through strange-but-true coincidence or cosmic design, she doesn't really care—has led them right here.

"That banner is just like us," he says.

"I was thinking the same thing," she says.

And these two—Jessica Darling and Marcus Flutie—nod in wordless affinity, both knowing that this is the perfect ending for the story they'll tell time and again, year after year, decade after decade, whenever anyone asks, "How did you know?"

And so it is.

Acknowledgments

Many thanks go out to:

Everyone I've ever acknowledged before. You were there when I needed you then.

Heather Schroder at International Creative Management and Tina Constable, Suzanne O'Neill, Sarah Breivogel, Annsley Rosner, Mary Choteborsky, Patty Berg, and Heather Proulx at Crown, for being here now.

Rachel Cohn, Patty McCormick, and Carolyn Mackler, who wanted more for me.

Puthea Chea at UCLA, Samantha Keefe and Zeta Gamma at Wellesley College, Kelli Plasket and everyone from ED2010 at the College of New Jersey for letting me entertain you. Callie Freitag, Maggie R. Borders, Rachel Simon, Kathryn Gaglione, Ariel Reinish, Casey Freedman, Georgia Wei, Rhoda Feng, Colleen Conedy, Vania Xu, Stella Deng, Samantha Wildfong, Allyson Townsend, Megan Wible, Tara Turley-Dean, Camille Hamilton, Maniza Ahmed, Tanya Seal, Sophie Sumrall, Hannah Tennant, Rachel Lamar, Tatiana Christian, Heather Taylor, Brittany Lewis, Rochella Villamil, Caroline Donnelly, Mallory Tuckey, Whitney Moon, Rebecca Prowler, Justine Anne DeAngelis, Jessica McKeever, Anna Ssemuyaba, Tiana Sidawi, Jordan "Butch" Sondler, Elaine Chau, Madeleine Douglass, Aimy Tien, Mallory Carra, Amy Bydlon, Sara DiSalvo, Jenna Zenk, Annie Shields, Cassandra Leveille, Brianne Kennedy, Errin Mitchell, Tara Powers, Anna Najduch, Stephanie Thomson, Sandy Cox, Audrey Barlow, Jessica Tackett, Sara Blaney, Elissa Shortridge, Zoe Vrabel, Kailey Bennett, Samar Khan, Erica Michelle Vona, Sara Wegman, Jaclyn Rapadas, Sara Blaney, Kelsey Light, Natalie Reed, Leigh Purtill, Caitlin Yates, Katherine Blaney, Megan Mihans, Lynn Rickert, Christi Cook, Andrea Sanow, Zhenzhen Gong, Sharon Hoffman, Alexa Laudenslager, Alisa McQuaid,

Tiffany Medeck, Connie Bisesi, Sarah Nishanian, Jessie Schuster, Lauren Brignone, Britni Puccio, Cecilia Rahme, Jodi Lehman, and Madeline Jones, for sharing your stories.

Yaz, W. Somerset Maugham, and Sir Winston Churchill, for providing quotes embedded in chapter twenty-three.

Alastair Gordon, author of *Naked Airport*, for providing the inspiration for the "EXCUSE OUR APPEARANCES . . ." quotation.

Barry Manilow, because he is the Showman of Our Time.

And last—but never least—my two favorite nerds. I love you always. And forever. And whatever.

MEGAN McCAFFERTY is the author of the hit novels *Sloppy Firsts*, *Second Helpings*, and the *New York Times* bestsellers *Charmed Thirds* and *Fourth Comings*. She lives in New Jersey with her husband and son. To find out more about Megan and the Jessica Darling series, visit www.MeganMcCafferty.com.